AN IRRESISTIBLE KISS

"Cat?" Garrett breathed against the shell of her ear. "Do you want me?"

Nothing could have prevented the honesty of her response. "Yes," she answered in a soft breath of acquiescence. "But—"

He drew her tighter into his embrace. He feathered another soft kiss across her lips. The words of protest trailed off into a soft sigh of pleasure.

In truth, she found it harder and harder to form any words that made sense. She really should stop him. He shouldn't be doing this. Another sigh escaped her lips. She should stop him.

As if of their own accord, and with a mind all their own, her hands smoothed over his shoulders, and her arms looped around his neck. Nothing on this earth could have stopped her from loving him.

She curled her fingers into the thick hair at the back of his neck. Soft, so tempting. She gave in to the temptation and ran her fingers higher through the dark waves of hair. It would be so easy to lose herself in the feel of his hair against her fingers. To lose herself in him.

Surrendering to him, Cat leaned closer into his tender embrace. He trailed a fiery line of kisses along her ear, to her jaw, and across her cheek. Eac_____ _____ demanded more than the last. His lips met hers _____ _____ her speechless with its urgency . . .

Books by Joyce Adams

REBEL MINE
GAMBLER'S LADY
MOONLIGHT MASQUERADE
LOVING KATE
TEMPTING TESS
DARLING CAT

Published by Zebra Books

DARLING CAT

Joyce Adams

Zebra Books
Kensington Publishing Corp.
http://www.zebrabooks.com

ZEBRA BOOKS are published by

Kensington Publishing Corp.
850 Third Avenue
New York, NY 10022

Copyright © 1998 by Joyce Adams

Zebra and the Z logo Reg. U.S. Pat. & TM Off.

First Printing: May, 1998
10 9 8 7 6 5 4 3 2 1

Printed in the United States of America

*To Mary Adams—thanks for being my "Mom" and
for your constant encouragement.*

*To Sueann Snow—the best friend and critique partner ever.
Thanks for everything.*

*To Mary Laveta and Ronald McCravy for making
this one possible.*

Prologue

"If that preposterous saying about only the good dying young were true—then Jake Garrett would live forever," St. Peter stormed.

"Tamera!"

St. Peter's booming voice shook the air around her silver-white curls, and she cringed at being caught eavesdropping. She scrambled to appear before the supervisor of all angels, tripping over the hem of her gown and knocking her golden halo askew in her haste.

"Yes, sir?" Her voice held a betraying tremor. As she tried to straighten the golden ring dipping over one eye, her white gown slipped off one plump shoulder.

"Oh, feathers," she muttered under her breath, then smiled up at her superior.

St. Peter sighed and looked upward as if seeking divine assistance. "Oh, Tamera, I can't believe you're still having trouble with landing and materializing after all these years."

Her rosy cheeks darkened with embarrassment. She really should have been practicing instead of reading the book tucked away in the cloud's depths. "I can manage fine, except when I'm startled," she declared in her own defense.

"Well, you're about to get plenty of practice."

Angel Tamera gulped down her nervousness. "I am? Why?" she asked, her voice rising slightly on the last word.

The great angel glanced upward again and sighed. "As it is, only divine intervention saved that gunslinger's life this time."

Tamera blanched as pale as her white gown. The problem of Jake Garrett had been discussed up here in great detail over the past week, before one of the senior guardian angels had been chosen and dispensed to earth.

"But I thought Clarence was guarding—"

"Clarence took a bullet in the wing at noon. One meant for Jake Garrett."

"Oh, dear me," she gasped. Wringing her hands together in the concealing folds of her gown, she mouthed the words, "A bullet."

She took an involuntary step backward, catching her heel in the hem of her gown, and almost tumbled off the edge of the cloud. Only St. Peter's quick action saved her, pulling her back and setting her solidly on both her feet.

Sighing, he reached out and resettled her gold halo on the center of her head. Then he stepped back and studied her.

As if reaching a decision, he finally spoke. "An immediate replacement is needed." He paused. "And you're the only angel available on this short notice. With it being spring and so many children out playing, we are frightfully short-handed."

"Me?" She squeaked out the question, unable to believe what she was hearing. She was truly going to be sent on an assignment.

She'd dreamed of this day for more years than she cared to count. She wrapped her arms around her grandmotherly shape. A smile lit up her beatific features.

She fluttered a few inches above the cloud, then at St. Peter's frown, settled her toes back onto the fluffy surface. She could scarcely contain her excitement. Being chosen as a guardian angel was heaven's highest honor.

"You're going to have your wings full with this one," he warned her, gentle caring in his normally stern voice.

Her hands trembled, and she clenched them together, hiding them in the folds of her gown. The white cloth slipped off her shoulder again.

Tamera pulled it back up and met St. Peter's frown. "When do I leave?"

He sighed deeply. "Immediately."

With this he waved his hand, and she disappeared. A single shimmery feather floated down after her to land in his hand.

He closed his fingers around the feather. Her enthusiasm never ceased to amaze him. While he'd never admit it aloud, Tamera was one of his favorites. She cared so much, but her caring was bound to get her into trouble.

"Heaven help us," he whispered, closing his eyes.

Chapter One

Texas, 1880

Caitlan Parker felt a shiver skitter across her shoulders and creep down the back of her shirt. She tossed her braid over her shoulder and tried to pretend nothing was wrong, but she knew full well otherwise.

Someone was hot on her trail. Again.

Cat threw a glance behind her and caught the barest glimpse of a man before he ducked back out of sight into the shelter of the mercantile doorway.

Him again.

She'd seen that same skinny Easterner on three separate occasions during the past two days. Coincidence? Not likely.

In fact, she'd bet her last gold piece he was tailing her. But why? Sure, she'd made a few enemies—try a lot—she told herself. In her line of work that was a given. However, the reason behind her persistent shadow remained a mystery no matter how hard she pondered it. She caught her carpetbag close against her chest.

She'd better lose him and fast. Or she stood to lose everything she'd been working toward for three long, hard years. She'd rather die first.

Ducking into the closest alley, she sprinted for the end building. She heard the pounding of rapid footsteps behind her. It spurred her on, giving her more speed. Thankfully, she had on her breeches and could move faster. Reaching the building, she scurried around the corner and crawled beneath the stairs. She ignored the crawling critters skittering away from her.

Not even daring to draw in a breath, she waited. Closing her eyes tight, she sent up a prayer. She heard a man's curse from the alley. Sounded like her pursuer in the bowler hat was plumb confused. Good.

The minutes ticked by, eating up precious time. She could almost imagine the train departing the station for north central Texas without her, carrying the camelback trunk she'd seen to loading ahead of time. As the skinny man stomped around searching the alley for her, she forced herself to remain still.

At last, with a final oath, he returned the way he'd come. Cat counted to ten, then crawled out from her hideaway. Not even taking time to dust off her breeches, she grabbed up her bag and raced around the corner and up another alley.

She dashed onto the boardwalk, then ran across the street and skidded onto the train platform. The welcome sound of the train whistle relieved her more than she was willing to admit.

"All aboard," the conductor called out before he swung up the steps to the second rail car.

Cat waited until he stepped out of sight. Throwing one last glance over her shoulder, she bounded up the steps of the baggage car seconds before the train pulled out of the station.

She'd made it. Quickly she stepped back out of sight and hid behind a large brown trunk. Her breath came in short pants. She'd rest a minute, no more than that, she vowed.

Sure to her word, minutes later she slipped farther back between the assortment of trunks and bags, secreting herself from any prying eyes. She didn't mean to steal passage. She'd planned on buying a ticket, but now she couldn't reveal her presence until farther down the line. Not when someone was after her and her plan hung in the balance.

Not yet. Soon. She set her precious carpetbag down on the floor, then opened it and carefully withdrew a bundle. She'd saved the fancy new dress for the last leg of her trip.

By the time the train rolled into the next town, Cat's transformation was complete. In the place of the dust-covered breeches and man's shirt, she now wore an elegant traveling suit of deep russet fit for any lady. Even one supposedly from New York. Her braid had been painstakingly turned into a cluster of golden curls.

Daring a peek out from her hiding place, she deemed it safe to proceed. Cautiously she slipped out of the baggage car and descended from the train. Within minutes she was standing in line at the station waiting to purchase her ticket. No one looking at her now would ever connect her with the woman of her not so pristine past.

Now she was Miss Caitlan Parker from New York, who had scarcely even heard tell of Illinois.

The miles rolled past outside the train window, and her destiny drew nearer. Cat wiped a damp palm down her skirt and smoothed her fingers over the pair of new gloves in her lap.

Could she do it?

She raised her chin as if meeting an enemy, then shoved an errant curl back into the carefully arranged curls atop her head. She stared out the window of the train. The scenery passed in a blur much the same as the memories that persisted in chasing each other through her mind.

Her Jesse lying dead in the street, while *he* turned and walked away. Out of her life.

Pain, humiliation, and anger followed in rapid succession. They gave her the resolve to raise her head and face the reflection of the stranger in the glass. Herself.

Was that elegantly clothed woman truly her?

Cat tentatively lifted her hand and touched a carefully coiffed curl. It felt as strange to her touch as it looked. She started to shake her head, but stopped herself. It had taken her the better part of an hour to put her hair up properly; she didn't want to chance mussing it before she arrived at her destination.

It was imperative she look every inch the fine Eastern lady when she stepped off the train. A golden tendril slipped free to lie temptingly against her nape as if trying to prove it couldn't be forced into a mold any easier than its owner.

Cat tucked the wayward curl up, then ran her fingertips across the sweetheart neckline of the russet-colored gown. The fine material was silky smooth beneath her fingers. It was the prettiest thing she'd ever seen, next to her pearl-handled Colt. 45s.

Not a gown, a traveling suit, she corrected herself, brushing a speck of dust from her skirt. The proprietor who had sold her the fancy piece had assured her it was the height of fashion for travel.

"Briscoe!" the kindly conductor called out. "Next stop Briscoe."

Cat jumped, nearly upsetting her reticule from her lap. She grabbed the small bag by the drawstrings. It felt so foreign to her. Her usual attire of breeches and boots left no room for such feminine frippery.

Neither had her life on the farm in Illinois where she and Pa had barely scratched out a meager existence together. Now all that was in the past. Pa had been in his grave for nearing three years, the farm sold, and her plan begun. Her eyes burned with painful memories, and she smoothed her hands over her skirt, feeling the unfamiliar petticoat rustle against her legs. She wished her ma were here to tell her about those lady things, but she'd died of a fever when Cat had been only a child.

Would she ever get used to the feel of fine material against her skin?

Yet, get used to the fancy ladylike trappings she must. And fast. Or she didn't have a chance in hell of carrying off her deception. She clapped a hand over her mouth; she'd have to remember not to swear. Not ever. One slip could give it all away.

Cat sat forward, absently nibbling on the tip of one fingernail. She pondered her current problem of how to stop herself from swearing when it came so natural like. Then inspiration struck her. It would work.

She nibbled on her fingernail again and sought through her most used swear words. She'd simply combine a couple of them and make her own word—one she could use with no one being the wiser.

A smile grew, and she tested the new word aloud, "Shams."

Yes, it felt good—almost as good as the words it came from.

Weariness tugged at her, teasing with the offer of a nap. She rejected it. She dared not doze off.

Not even for a moment could she relax, set aside the practiced pretense, and be herself. Instead she rested her head against the seat, letting the repetitive *clack-clack-clack* of the train soothe her tense nerves.

The haunting question rose up again like a specter. Could she do it? Going over her plan, she focused on her upcoming performance.

She'd do it. She had to.

"Millwood," the conductor announced, then paused beside her. "Ma'am, this here is your stop coming up."

She smiled as prettily as she could and thanked him. He had been quite kind to her, even agreeing to have her trunk unloaded and delivered to the hotel. Although she certainly would have received a different welcome from him had he known who she truly was.

It was nice for a change to be able to smile back at someone and not have to wonder what they were planning. Odd feeling, she admitted, but still nice.

As the train slowed for its upcoming stop, Cat slipped on fancy gloves the same color as her skirt. Lifting a dainty Belgian straw bonnet trimmed with russet faille, ivory ribbons, and colored feathers from beside her, she settled it atop her curls.

As ready as she would ever be, Cat caught her velvet reticule tightly for a moment, wishing she could withdraw the small derringer tucked at the bottom of the bag. For courage, she told herself. Instead she practiced smiling like the demure Eastern lady she pretended to be.

A giggle of laughter bubbled up in her throat, and she tapped it down with a force of sheer effort. Lady? Her? Green eyes flashed back at her with a determined glint from the glass window a mere instant before she schooled her features into a mask of innocence any child would envy.

When the train drew to a halt, Cat Parker was every inch the fashionable lady. She had to be—her life depended on people believing that fact.

She gathered up her carpetbag in one hand, and her reticule and the skirt of her traveling suit in the other. Stepping from the rail car, she came face-to-face with her greatest challenge.

Jake Garrett stood not ten feet from her.

Even from the side she recognized him instantly, unable to ever forget. He stood as tall and disturbingly handsome as she'd remembered. In fact, he'd become even more handsome with the passing of years. The skin on his arms and face was a sun-darkened tan. A knot formed deep in her stomach, and she had to resist the compelling urge to rub at the spot with her hand. Instead she tightened her grip on her bag, drawing strength from deep inside herself.

She stared at him, taking in everything about him at once. Impressions swarmed over her. She could no more tear her gaze away from him than she could readily abandon her plan.

Dark, almost black hair brushed the bottom of his collar and skimmed his forehead from beneath the black Stetson he always wore at an angle that couldn't be called anything but rakish. It made her want to reach out and smooth his hair back into place, just as before when she'd run her fingers through the soft strands. She clenched her fists tighter.

While his white shirt set off his dark hair, the rest of his clothing added to the aura of danger that had always surrounded him, setting him apart from other men. Black pants snugly molded his long, muscular legs like a lover's touch, then ended at black boots. Without those boots he stood at just over six feet. She knew that well.

A gun belt hugged his hips, and a pair of matching Colt revolvers sat in the holsters. He was nothing but a hired gun, she reminded herself. Don't ever forget that.

Memories, then a single thought sparked in her, racing through her, wiping out everything in its path. Her thoughts fled as surely as if they had been burned up.

He was waiting for her.

She'd been uncovered. Her carpetbag slipped from her grasp and landed on the dusty boardwalk.

No, he couldn't know she was coming, she realized. *No one* knew she was coming to Millwood.

Her heartbeat slowed, nearer its normal pace. Assured that her secret was safe, Cat released her grip on her skirts and smoothed out the wrinkles with her hand. She noticed it trembled slightly, and anger rose in her. She wouldn't let him do this to her.

A long, deep breath calmed the betraying shake of her hands, but did little for the state her mind was in. She blamed her anxiety on his heart-stopping appearance, but admitted that her nerves had been worn ragged this past week.

Could she do it?

The recurring question rose up to taunt her, daring her to say no.

Cat stiffened her spine as straight as a fence post and raised her chin. Not only could she do it, she damned well would.

Then *he* turned around.

All coherent thought fled Cat's mind. It left her shaken on the inside. She called up every bit of resolve to hold her straight and proud.

She was supposed to be a fine, well-bred lady, she told herself. And she'd better start acting the part—fast.

Lowering her gaze, she took in the lean, strong planes of his face sculpted in strength, and her heart took pause for a moment. She was certain of that. His mouth held the barest curve of a smile, and her heart started up again, only racing this time.

He knew. The words screamed in her mind.

His gaze traveled in a leisurely perusal down her body, and Cat felt her skin heat in response.

It was positively shocking.

Improper.

And it felt wonderful.

She dropped her gaze in a gesture of demure gentility that she'd worked hard to master. It gave her the time she needed to collect her thoughts. However, the image of Jake Garrett stayed in her mind like a tintype.

Her resolve wavered for a moment; nothing about him was wavering. She reminded herself that Jake Garrett—gunslinger—was a man who could and would survive anything that was thrown at him.

"Well, Garrett, what do you think?" a man beside him asked.

The sudden question startled Cat. Until this moment she hadn't even noticed the man standing beside Garrett. Her eyes had been on him only.

Turning her attention to the stranger, she scarcely halted her gasp of amazement. The man was approaching his late forties; silver edged his temples. But what held her full attention was the sheriff's badge pinned on his shirt.

The law.

She hadn't needed the tin star to tell her what he was. She recognized the authority he wore like a pair of broken-in boots. It wasn't his looks that gave him away, but rather the very way he stood.

Over the past three years since she'd set on this course, she'd had enough run-ins with lawmen to recognize one on the spot. Settling her hand on her stomach, she tried to do the same with her agitated senses.

Who could have ever dreamed that Garrett would be friendly with a lawman? She hadn't planned on this. Would the lawman's keen insight see through her disguise? Was her true identity about to be unmasked?

As Garrett looked over the departing passengers before he

answered, she was certain he could hear the overloud pounding of her heart. What was he waiting for?

"Looks like an innocent enough group of passengers today, don't you think?" the sheriff pressed.

"Seems so," Garrett answered at last, turning back to face the other man.

Cat tensed even more at the rich sound of his voice. It hadn't changed—it still had the same effect on her today as three years ago, causing her breath to catch with his first words. He spoke in a low drawl that was purely Texas. And his voice— velvet with a hint of steel beneath.

Memories teased her. With an effort that took nearly all the strength she possessed, she shut and locked the door on the recollections pounding through her. She had to.

Lost in the past, Cat missed the next words between the two men. She brought herself up with a snap. Studying the lawman beside Garrett, she took one step closer to the men. She had to hear what they were talking about so earnestly in tones too low to overhear. Her conscience mollified, she tilted her head and eavesdropped shamelessly.

"Word of your decision has spread like a wildfire driven by a fierce wind," the sheriff warned, his tone low and tense.

"Sorry, Ty. The last thing I wanted was to bring trouble to Millwood."

A short bark of laughter came from the lawman, startling Cat.

"Trouble? I'd say it's more like a hornet's nest," he added. "And about as hard to get rid of peaceably."

She noticed that Garrett's face tensed with the lawman's words. He nudged his black hat farther back with his thumb, and another dark strand of hair tumbled across his forehead.

"That's the way I plan on handling it."

"Garrett, you're likely to get yourself killed your way."

Cat's mouth dried to the texture of kindling. If he . . .

"It's my way, or no way." Garrett's tone brooked no argument.

What in the devil were they talking about? Unable to stop

herself, Cat inched another step closer, her slipper scuffing the wood boardwalk. It drew the men's attention to her as if she'd shouted at them. In unison, both men turned to face her.

"Damn," she mumbled beneath her breath before she caught herself. She was going to have to work harder on her swearing.

Garrett tipped his hat to her and started walking toward her. Cat's knees turned to jelly, and she was certain her tongue had stuck to the roof of her parched mouth.

Something the sheriff muttered made Garrett pause for a moment. Unable to stop herself, Cat covertly watched him.

"Will do," he called out to the sheriff, and gave a slightly mocking salute.

"Just see that you be careful." The sheriff gave a snort of disgust and strode away.

Garrett turned back to her. Until now she had avoided meeting his gaze directly, but she couldn't put it off any longer without arousing suspicions. She dared not do that. This would be the true test of her disguise. Raising her chin, she forced her eyes to meet his.

She was unprepared for her first encounter.

He had the kind of eyes that enticed, teased, tempted. Dark, so dark that she found herself drowning in their velvety depths. How could she have forgotten their power?

Would he recognize her? She held her breath in anticipation. Waiting. Wondering. Half hoping.

His smile widened, and her heart pounded. Her well-rehearsed plan became forgotten. Then the impossible happened.

She dropped her reticule, the material slipping right through her fingers. Strangely, it felt as if the bag had been *yanked* from her hand. She was certain she'd been holding it tightly. It landed almost a foot away with a *thud* directly at his feet. She stared at it in disbelief.

Garrett bent to scoop up the small bag. Returning it to her, he let his fingertips brush the palm of her hand.

"Ma'am."

He couldn't help the widening of his smile when he felt her

hand tremble beneath his touch. Her ploy of dropping her bag had been so obvious that even a schoolboy would realize it as an attempt to get his attention. Something this lady didn't need to try to do.

Hell, she had the full attention of every man under eighty years of age within shouting distance. All she had to do was stand there.

She was all proper-bred lady on the outside, but her hair the color of rich, ripe apricots more than hinted at a passionate nature simmering below the fine lady's surface. He took in the delicate, heart-shaped face with its soft, creamy skin, and about the most tempting lips he'd ever seen. He ran his gaze all the way down to her dainty slippers. Just looking at her made a hunger start up in his stomach and spread lower.

He forced his gaze to her face, then settled on her lush lips. Dangerous territory, he told himself. He pulled his attention away and up to her eyes. They were as green as a dew-sparkled meadow.

He almost shook his head at the errant thought. Give him much longer and he'd be reciting poetry to her beauty. Beauty that was almost marred by a too-pert nose. Poetry, he silently scoffed at himself. His thoughts usually had more in keeping with staying alive than with quoting verses. Especially lately.

The woman lowered her startled gaze from him, timidity obvious in her every movement. For a moment he thought she swayed.

"Ma'am? Are you all right?" Garrett drew a step closer, unable to stop himself. She looked confused or lost. He noted that the top of her head missed reaching his chin by a good two inches.

"I . . ." She cleared her throat. "I seem to be a bit turned around. I'm looking for a hotel."

"The town's only hotel is that way." He pointed down the street to the right. "I'd be happy to walk you there."

She stared at him as if searching for something. It made him decidedly uneasy.

"Ma'am?"

She started as if caught off guard.

"I'd like that very much ..." she paused delicately, "... Mister ... ?"

"Jake Garrett, ma'am." He sent her a smile that had enticed more than one woman in the past.

"Caitlan Parker." She hesitated and lowered her eyes shyly. "From New York."

"Long ways to come here."

"I have my reasons." Her lashes fluttered up, and she smiled at him, then quickly glanced back at the dust-covered boardwalk.

"How long will you be staying?"

Garrett took her arm, and she jerked away as if he'd scalded her.

"My ... my bag," she said breathlessly. As if unable to say more, she pointed to where a large carpetbag sat on the wooden platform.

Garrett scooped the bag up with one hand, then extended his arm to her. Perhaps a lady like this preferred a more gentlemanly approach, he thought. He shifted the bag beneath his elbow, noticing it was surprisingly heavy for such a little bit of a lady to be carrying.

After a moment's hesitation she placed her hand on his forearm. "I'm not sure."

He felt her touch all the way to his soul. "What?"

She looked up at him and stepped closer. "You asked how long I'd be staying, and I said I'm not sure." Her voice was scarcely above a whisper and held a certain huskiness that hadn't been there before when she'd spoken.

At the husky quality in her soft voice, an inkling of memory sprang up. It battled with his intellect and lost. The memory seeped back to the recesses of his mind.

"The hotel?" she reminded him gently but firmly.

A faint smile tipped her tempting lips, and damned if he wasn't inclined to give in to the temptation they offered. But he was certain the lady wouldn't welcome so bold a move. He had to be content with placing his hand over hers and anchoring her touch on his arm. For now.

All too quickly they reached the hotel. Caitlan seemed to be almost relieved when he released her, for she slipped her hand from his forearm in a quick-silver movement.

"Thank you for your kindness."

"My pleasure." He stepped back from her before he added, "I'll be seeing you, Caitlan."

Utter silence greeted him for a moment, and he wasn't certain that she even breathed. At last she answered.

"Yes, you will."

"Garrett. The name is Garrett."

"Thank you," she hesitated, "Garrett."

He nodded to her, then turned away. Pausing, he glanced back, and his gaze met hers again and held it for the space of a slow heartbeat; then he tipped his hat and turned away. Cat's knees weakened, and she barely kept herself standing in place. What she wanted to do was sit down.

Instead, she stood in front of the hotel and watched his firm stride. She swore the man was enough to steal any woman's breath away. Especially hers. Why, he'd left her practically speechless several times in the last few minutes.

Then it hit her. The remembering. The feeling . . .

She hardened her heart, knowing full well its usual softness often got her in trouble. She'd thought those feelings were dead. Buried with—

Cat stiffened her spine and cut off the thoughts. Not here. Not now.

Unable to stop herself, she continued to watch Garrett walk away. Pain lashed at her. While she'd deny it to the hilt, a tiny part of her had longed for him to remember her. Needed for him to remember.

A flash of memory jolted through her, and she worried her lower lip. Her emotions fought a desperate battle within herself.

How in the hell was she supposed to kill him if he continued to look at her that way?

Chapter Two

Garrett dried his freshly shaven chin with the hand towel beside the bowl and pitcher. Tossing down the towel, he looked around the town jail. Ty had been called away shortly before dawn, and as usual Garrett had agreed to fill in during his absence.

Today looked to be a quiet one. The three spartan cells stood empty. It had been a quiet night, too. Not even a shout of trouble from Ruth and Judy's place either. Yup, the early morning had all the earmarkings of a peaceful day.

If it would just stay that way.

He fingered the deputy badge lying beside the towel, then picked it up. Crossing to the worn wooden desk, he pulled the center drawer open and dropped the badge inside. He didn't deserve to wear it yet. No matter how much Ty insisted otherwise.

Garrett shook his head in denial. There was too much past to take care of first.

And that past seemed determined to come to him here in Millwood. He was still surprised at how many young, would-be killers had passed through town in the month since his decision to stop living by the gun. And the young guns kept coming, determined to make a name for themselves with his death.

All those years ago, he hadn't started out trying to make a name for himself. But it had happened just the same. He'd been content serving in the cavalry—until that fateful day when he hadn't been given a choice in the change his life took.

The army didn't look fondly on a lieutenant who shot his commanding officer. Not even if he'd done so to save lives. Especially not when those lives had been Indian. However, he hadn't been able to stand by and allow the callous commander to lead the attack on the innocent women and children left in the village.

Like he couldn't stand by now and let the young guns coming into town destroy Millwood. One decision had led him into the life of a man who lived by his gun. Would his latest decision lead him out of that life or leave him dead?

He had too much to live for to give up and go back to his old life. He'd *make* a way. He wanted to put down roots. It had been so long ago he'd forgotten what it even felt like to lead a respectable life and have a home. Until he came to Millwood. The growing town needed him, and he needed the town.

At least yesterday's train hadn't brought any gunmen. No, it had delivered the prettiest thing he'd laid his eyes on in a long time. Caitlan Parker.

He'd surreptitiously watched her from the moment her dainty feet had touched the platform. Before that he'd enjoyed the glimpse of a pretty turn of ankle he'd been treated to as she climbed from the train. And he'd felt her watching him.

He smiled at the recollection. A mental picture of her sprang to mind, recalling a different kind of need. A man's need. As if in response, another part of his body came to life, and an ache formed in his gut.

He couldn't let himself respond to the lure she held for him. Danger dogged him like a persistent hound on a scent. Caring for someone—especially a demure beauty like Caitlan Parker—could well cost her life. He wasn't willing to risk that. Not even if his body ached for her.

Although she was one heck of a tempting distraction.

The image of her all prim and proper had plagued his sleep all night long. And it had been a long night.

Perhaps he'd acquaint himself with the lady again, after all. Real soon.

Angel Tamera found Garrett sitting at the sheriff's desk, deep in thought. She watched her charge from her perch on the windowsill. He was smiling. What she wouldn't give to know what he was thinking.

She'd bet it had something to do with Caitlan Parker from the train. For some unknown reason their meeting disturbed her. What she'd felt sizzling between Garrett and Caitlan might burn hot enough to scorch them all if they weren't careful.

The lady bothered her, and she couldn't put her finger on why. And that bothered her even more. She fluttered, then resettled her wings.

In truth, she was quite put out over the situation. She crossed her arms, tapped her heel against the wall, and stared at Garrett in consternation. The lady was not what she appeared. She knew that for an absolute fact.

Tamera had felt the weight of a derringer in the city lady's reticule. Why, she'd been so shocked that her toe had caught the hem of her gown, and she'd practically fallen. Right into Jake Garrett's arms. A quite unsuitable place for a grandmotherly guardian angel such as she to find herself!

After that shock, she'd nearly materialized in amazement. She'd had her wings full fighting off the sensation in time.

She'd only meant to appease her curiosity and see what was in the bag that the lady held on to so tightly. She hadn't meant to actually pull it from her hands and drop it. However, she hadn't been able to prevent releasing the bag in shock the moment her fingers felt the cold metal of the little gun's barrel. It had been loaded.

What was a fine Eastern beauty from New York doing carrying a derringer in her bag? There was more to this lady than met the eye. Much more.

And she intended to find out precisely what that was.

Tamera gazed at her charge with all the protective instincts of a mother hen over her chick. Miss Caitlan Parker presented a threat to her charge, and no one was going to harm a hair on Jake Garrett's head while she was on guardian duty!

Tamera blew out her breath in agitation and looked away from Garrett. She could feel the pristine white feathers of her wings ruffling in distress. Oh, dear. She really *must* calm herself.

She closed her eyes, imagining a pretty, fluffy cloud. Within moments she felt the calm sweeping over her. Ah, much better. A glance back over her shoulder assured her that her feathers lay smoothly in place. All of them.

Near disaster had been averted. She hadn't lost a single feather—quite a wondrous feat for the only angel in heaven who molted when upset or excited.

"Tamera!" the voice of St. Peter boomed from above, nearly toppling her from her perch on the windowsill across from the desk.

She quickly turned her attention upward and stood to her feet, all the while straightening her gown and brushing away a speck of dust.

"Yes, sir?"

"Garrett." St. Peter stated the single word as if giving an order.

"Sir?" Tamera tilted her head back to look up at the ceiling, almost expecting St. Peter to appear. Her halo slipped, and she barely caught it before it rolled down her back to the floor.

"Where is Garrett?" St. Peter asked with exaggerated patience.

"Why, he's right—" Tamera took another look at the empty desk chair.

She whirled around and stared. Garrett had left the office. Vanished. Disappeared.

While she'd been woolgathering in imaginary clouds, the gunslinger had slipped away from her.

"Oh, feathers."

Forgetting all about St. Peter, she flew through the open door of the office and chased after her charge.

Later, she'd set to learning more about the mystery lady.

Cat straightened each item in the armoire for the third time, almost changing her mind and her gown. She was sorely tempted to pack everything back into the camelback trunk sitting in the corner. Why was it so difficult to decide on which of the new dresses to wear? Could it be because she'd never in her life dressed for a man before?

Her cheeks heated at the thought. She reached out and brushed at a dust spot on the hem of her gown, pushing away the unwelcome reminder of the past. Maybe she should have worn the blue—

She dropped the skirt as if it had burned her. No, she wouldn't change her gown yet again. It had taken her two tries to decide on the green silk gown with emerald trim. The rows of pearl buttons on the front had been the very devil to fasten.

The two fancy gathered flounces at her ankles felt so foreign to her, and she resisted the impulse to kick them out of her way. She twisted around and glanced in the mirror, checking that the bustle was still in place. Satisfied, she forced herself to quit fiddling with it.

The clothes hanging in the armoire gleamed with crisp newness. The fancy lady's wardrobe had cost her a shocking amount. More than the sum total of the winnings she'd earned from three poker games.

Turning away from the stranger in the mirror and the new clothing, she made up her mind. She couldn't stand the close confines of her hotel room another minute. Not when she was so close to . . .

To Garrett, a little voice whispered in the recesses of her mind.

Why couldn't he have changed for the worse—looked different, sounded different? Why couldn't he have taken to drinking too much? But, no, he was as . . . as . . . *everything* as before.

Attempting to shut him out of her thoughts, she grabbed up the matching green bonnet. It was a tiny thing, really not much more than a bit of straw and lace and pretty-colored feathers. And she had the devil's own time getting it placed right on her head. In fact, she managed to stick herself with the hat pin twice before anchoring the hat at long last.

Cat wondered that the air about her hadn't turned blue with the words that had slipped out before she could stop them. She must work harder on that if her plan was to succeed.

Now it was about time to go on to the next step in her plan. To attract the attention of Garrett.

She took a moment to smooth on the pair of green-colored gloves. A fine lady always wore gloves, she reminded herself. Patting the little bonnet for courage and a bit of luck, she scooped up her reticule and left her room. She'd start off by surveying the town and its buildings. Then she'd find Garrett.

She absolutely refused to admit she might be stalling.

Ten minutes later found her in the town mercantile, looking for what she didn't know. However, it had sounded the best of the three buildings she had passed on her stroll: A sheriff's office—that one had sent a chill down her backbone. A saloon bearing a brightly painted wooden sign with the name the Long and Short Saloon—later, she promised herself. And a bank— she preferred to keep her money to herself.

So, here she stood, in the dusty mercantile store. She walked down an aisle past lanterns and candles. Looking at wares she didn't need, at practically anything, was better than sitting alone in her hotel room with her thoughts for company. Or worse, rushing into her plan before the time was right.

At least, that's what she thought until the bell jangled, interrupting her reverie. She turned and spotted the gunman immediately. She'd know the dark brown, curly hair, blue eyes, and slightly bowlegged man anywhere. In spite of his even temper, he had a tense alertness about him that was hard not to notice.

As Cat recognized Bill Thomas, she quickly stepped back behind a row of men's boots and out of sight. Things in Millwood were not turning out the way she'd planned. She had to leave the store before he spotted her. He'd give everything away without meaning to.

She sneaked down the aisle and around the next one. She'd almost made it to the door when the sound of Bill's deep voice brought her up short.

"Hey, what are you doing in town?" he hollered, his booming voice sure to draw attention.

The hair at her nape prickled, and she closed her eyes to the warning and casually took another step toward the door.

"And, hooey," he whistled. "Look at the fancy duds on you, girl."

Ignore him, she told herself. Concentrate on escaping with your disguise intact.

She heard the slap of a hand against a thigh, followed by laughter. Oh . . . oh, shams, she substituted the word at the last moment. Bill was not going to be content unless she faced him.

Chin high, she tried her best to ignore him and took another step.

"Trying to sneak out like a coward, are you?" he accused.

That did it. Her body stiffened straight as a fence post at the taunt. Papa had once told her that her temper could strip the bark right off a tree at twenty paces. And Bill Thomas stood closer than that.

Cat whirled on him without giving a thought to her disguise. "You—"

"Well, if it isn't the female—" He never finished the sentence.

Desperate to stop him before he could say more, Cat pretended to stumble. Lurching forward, she brought her right foot solidly down atop his, cutting off the damning words he'd been about to say.

Bill let out a howl of pain.

As he straightened up and made a grab for her, Cat gave a

very feminine scream as if fearing for her virtue. It had far more than the desired effect.

The bell tinkled above the door, and Garrett rushed into the store.

Could things get worse? she wondered.

The instant Bill and Garrett faced off on either side of her, she knew the answer to her question. Not only *could* things get worse—they just had.

Bill raised his chin and flashed a wide smile "Well, lookee here," he drew the words out. "If it isn't the gunslinger who's set everybody's tongues to wagging."

Before Cat had time to question what he meant, Bill pushed her to the side out of his way.

"Are you all right, Caitlan?" Garrett asked her, his eyes never leaving Bill's.

She felt strangely like a little kitten standing between two tomcats. Two large, angry tomcats, aching for a fight.

At her nod of assurance, Garrett turned his full attention to the new arrival in town. "Why don't you finish your business here and ride out of town."

"I might want to stay around awhile. Renew old acquaintances." Bill threw a glance Cat's way. "Have me a good ole time."

"Not in Millwood," Garrett informed him.

"You planning on stopping me?"

"If need be." Garrett's soft voice carried a blatant threat.

Bill snorted at him.

"You owe the lady an apology."

"Why, she's no lady, she's a—"

Garrett's fist connected solidly with Bill's chin. The blow cut off the remainder of his words.

Bill shook his head, then rubbed his jaw with one hand. "After I wash the dust out of my mouth, we'll settle this in the street." He rested his other hand on the butt of the gun in his holster.

"No." Garrett said the single word low and serious.

Bill ignored the warning. "In an hour." He shoved past Cat and strode out the door.

Garrett caught Cat by the shoulders, his strong hands drawing her close. "Are you all right?"

The sudden movement caught her unaware. She told herself that was the reason for her near breathlessness. It had nothing to do with being held in Garrett's arms. He drew her against his chest, his arms close around her, longer than was necessary to steady her. Strangely enough, she was loathe to rush him into letting go of her.

"He didn't harm you, did he?" he asked softly.

Garrett's breath warmed the skin at her temple.

"No." Right now, it was the only word she could push past her tongue.

As he lowered his head and gazed down at her, Cat's chest tightened, surely squeezing her heart. At least that's what it felt like.

"Are you sure?" he said, his voice scarcely above a whisper.

"Don't fight him," she pleaded, hardly realizing that she had been the one to utter the words.

Garrett smiled down at her. "Worried about me?"

The memory of that tender smile tugged at her heart; then followed the pain of betrayal. He had destroyed her life, she reminded herself, her future.

Reason returned to her with a jolt. Yes, she was worried about him. Worried that perhaps Bill Thomas would kill him and cheat her out of doing it herself.

Liar, a little voice accused in the back of her mind.

As Garrett lowered his head toward her, the voice fell silent. Unable to move away, she watched him draw closer. And closer.

He was going to kiss her.

And she was going to . . . to . . .

The moment his lips touched hers, all chance of regaining any sensible thinking left her. She could only feel.

She felt the warmth from his hands flowing through the fine

material of her gown. The firm pressure of his fingertips against her back.

And the gentle tenderness of his lips pressed against hers. His lips had never been this tender before. This wonderful.

Chapter Three

Garrett resisted the urge to deepen the kiss and slip his tongue between Cat's barely parted lips. It took all the resolve he had not to do so. She felt so good in his arms. So right.

He forced himself to keep the kiss simple, but tightened his hold on her, the pads of his fingers kneading the soft skin of her back. Something told him that holding on to Caitlan Parker might be like trying to hold on to quicksilver.

Reality nagged at his mind, threatening to destroy the moment.

When she learned of his background, learned *what* he was, learned what he'd done, she'd want nothing more to do with him. She'd back away from him, fear in her eyes. Or worse, disdain written across her pretty face, she'd whirl away. The same thing had happened to him numerous times in the past with what people called good women. He'd gotten used to it, he told himself.

He clenched his gun hand into a fist. Slanting his lips over hers, he surrendered to temptation and let nature have its way, and did what he swore he wouldn't do. He deepened the kiss, giving himself over to the pleasure of her soft lips beneath his.

Holding and kissing a woman like Caitlan Parker caused a man to think of a house he could call home, a warm woman who would be waiting for him at the end of a long day, and children. Unexpectedly, while he'd avoided any chance of that in the past, now the thought wasn't so unpleasant anymore.

A vague warning rose up in the back of his mind, telling him to watch out, he was getting into unknown territory. Dangerous territory.

Garrett ignored it

Instead he concentrated on the feel of Caitlan in his arms. She was soft, fitting against his body just right, but with lush curves for such a tiny bit of a woman. Once again he noted that the top of her head didn't even meet his chin. But he didn't mind the fact one bit.

It made him feel protective, and strong, and eager for her. All at once.

A shudder racked his body, and he schooled himself to restrain his desire. He wanted her more than he'd wanted any woman in a long time. He eased his hold on her tiny waist, but refused to release his hold on her completely. Not yet.

Not that the lady was offering any objection, he noted. The hint of a smile teased his lips, and he slanted his mouth more fully over hers, taking her next breath in his, melding them together until he wasn't certain where he ended and she began.

None of that mattered, only the feel of her body leaning against his chest, her hands clutching his shoulders.

Garrett could have gone on kissing her until—

Ty cleared his throat from the doorway. Garrett jerked himself up and felt Caitlan stiffen in his arms. The spell woven about them was broken, shattered into a hundred pieces of glittering, unfulfilled yearnings.

He steadied Cat and took a step back from the enticement she offered. He could see it in her slumberous eyes, a gaze that told him she had been thoroughly kissed. And liked it.

Garrett took another step away, putting more distance between himself and temptation. No temptation came without a price. The act of losing himself in her could extract the ultimate cost of his life.

He knew better than to allow anything to distract him. Especially now.

Damn, anyone could have sneaked up on him and put a bullet in his back while he'd been so distracted with no thought to anything but the woman held close in his arms. Damn.

"Heard there was some trouble brewing." Ty interrupted his thoughts.

Garrett glanced at his friend to see a wide grin splitting his face.

"Seems I heard wrong," Ty added. "Looks like you've got everything in hand."

Cat's gasp of dismay gave a second's warning to the men before her temper erupted. Before either man could anticipate it, she landed a resounding slap across Garrett's cheek.

"Good day, *gentlemen,*" she said in a voice dripping with sarcasm and scorn.

"Caitlan," Garrett called out.

She stepped back. "The name's Cat."

With a hand on her skirt, she whirled about and practically ran out of the mercantile store.

Horrified, she felt the sharp sting of tears. But by the time she reached the other side of the street, she had them fully under control. She wasn't about to cry for the likes of Jake Garrett. Or for the humiliation she'd undergone at his hands.

Head high with pride, she stepped up onto the boardwalk. A pride she was far from feeling, she chided herself. Not when her emotions and dignity were both in tatters. She reached up and straightened the tiny bonnet atop her curls.

She glanced back over her shoulder, then hated herself for her weakness. Garrett stood in the doorway of the mercantile watching her and rubbing his cheek. She whirled away from the sight of him.

What in blazes had she been thinking letting him kiss her like that?

Letting him? her conscience prodded sharply. She winced at

the reminder. Not only had she let him, she'd kissed him back.
Thoroughly. Her face heated with the recollection of how wonderful his firm lips had felt against hers.

Why, she hadn't offered even a whit of resistance. Truth be
told, it had never crossed her mind. She'd been too caught up
in . . .

And right out in public, in view of heaven knew how many
people. This was not the way to carry out her charade as a
fine-bred Eastern lady. While she'd never met a lady from New
York, she was certain they didn't behave the way she had only
minutes before.

Horrified then angered at what she'd done, she gathered up
her senses and stomped down the wooden planks. She kicked
her skirt out of the way with her feet. How could she have
done such a thing? Allowing Garrett to kiss her like that—
kissing him back.

Just like the night—

She stumbled on an uneven board in the plank boardwalk
and barely caught herself from falling. Landing in a heap would
be the final humiliation now. She straightened her bonnet again
as it slid to one side, but couldn't restore her thoughts so easily.

What of her disguise? Was it wearing a bit thin?

How was she to repair the damage she'd done to her well-
rehearsed masquerade? Hopefully the slap she'd given Jake
Garrett would help. If nothing else, it had made her feel better.

Suddenly realizing what she'd done, Cat groaned. The second
step in her plan had been to attract Garrett's attention. Well,
she'd most assuredly accomplished that feat, and without any
difficulty at all.

But what had she done by slapping Garrett? She'd risked
the success of her entire plan.

Could she even hope to attract Garrett's interest now? After
what she'd done, she doubted it. If Bill Thomas killed him,
she wouldn't need to worry about Garrett's interest in her.
Unexpectedly it felt as if a hand closed around her throat.

A barrage of emotions warred in her—dismay at Garrett's
interference, guilt at being the cause of the upcoming gunfight,

and mixed feelings over the outcome. She tried to tell herself she should be happy that Garrett was facing a gun, even if it wasn't hers. However, a tiny part of her knew differently.

Cat drew to a halt in front of her hotel. She nibbled on her lower lip.

In truth she wasn't so certain she wanted to see Garrett die now that she'd seen him again. And been held in his arms.

Feathers ruffled, Tamera settled her feet on the wooden boardwalk outside the only hotel in town. Cat's hotel.

Tapping her toe in vexation, Tamera didn't take her eyes off Cat. She wasn't about to let her near Garrett again anytime soon. She tapped her toe faster.

She'd barely stopped herself from grabbing hold of Cat at the mercantile. The slap had come too fast for even an angel to anticipate.

Cautious now, she watched Cat stand before the hotel as if in deep thought, then dash through the open doors of the hotel. Tamera humphed at her departing back.

Things were not going the correct way at all, Tamera thought. She hadn't been able to prevent Garrett from being slapped. Although, she did question if perhaps he hadn't deserved it. If she couldn't prevent so small an act, how was she to stop him from getting himself killed?

"Oh, feathers."

Then a more serious repercussion of the second meeting struck her, chasing out all other thoughts.

Because of Cat, Garrett had been issued a challenge to a gunfight!

Dear, dear, dear. Now how was she supposed to keep him from harm? She'd been assigned to keep him safe, not see him *killed* in a gunfight, and she wasn't about to fail that task. She shuddered at the thought of taking a bullet for her charge. Of course, she'd do it if need be, but nothing said she *had* to do so—not if she could think of something else.

What she needed was a plan. The countdown to the upcoming

gunfight was ticking down even as she concentrated on any possible way to prevent its occurrence.

Maybe she could stop the gun battle before it began. At her wit's end, Tamera fluttered her wings, then set to thinking.

She acted on the first idea that came to mind.

Taking a moment to straighten the neckline of her gown and steady her tilted halo, she focused all her energies on her upcoming task. A twinge of conscience troubled her, but she shushed it. This called for drastic measures if she was to save Garrett. Surely St. Peter would see the reason in her plan.

It was a brilliant plan. She'd simply materialize as a human and talk this Mr. Bill Thomas out of following through on his threat.

Tamera closed her eyes, and seconds later the feat was accomplished. She opened her eyes to find herself standing outside the Long and Short Saloon. A less than angelic smile touched her proud lips. As she noticed a strange prickly itch on her chin, she raised her hand and scratched a crusty furry beard!

Next, she looked down to see herself wearing dirt-stained breeches held up with a length of rope, very large boots on her feet—and a whiskey bottle clutched in one hand. She gasped and smelled the distasteful scent of potent liquor; then realization struck her.

She was a male . . . and a very drunk one. She'd become the town drunk! Why, she nearly fainted dead away, except angels couldn't faint.

Muttering, she smoothed down her now scraggly white hair, straightened her shoulders, and pushed her way through the saloon's batwing doors. That same swinging door caught her in the backside, and she nearly fell as her legs insisted on staggering like they belonged to some drunken lout.

She knew all eyes had turned to her. Ignoring their curiosity and censure, she sought out and found the young challenger. Carefully, she weaved her way across to where he sat at a table. Plopping the whiskey bottle in front of his face, she sat down across from him.

"Care for a drink, my friend?" Tamera offered with a cherubic smile.

Never one to turn down a friendly drink or two, Bill accepted the offer and the company. Tamera smiled again, scratching her beard.

Forty minutes later, with the bottle emptied and Bill sleeping soundly with his head propped on his arms atop the wobbly table, Tamera stood up and dusted her hands off. She hadn't touched a drop of the strong alcohol, instead encouraging Bill to drink her share, too.

By now—nearly the appointed hour of the gunfight—Bill was far too drunk to walk, much less shoot straight. In fact, he couldn't even lift his gun if he had to.

Poor man. She scratched at her beard again.

Now that Garrett's safety was assured, Tamera heard a booming voice no one else in the saloon could hear—St. Peter!

She suddenly recalled that taking human form was expressly forbidden. Now anxious, she flinched and instantly disappeared, heading straight away for heaven and a sure-to-be stern lecture. One white feather fluttered to the floor in her wake.

Garrett snapped his head up and stared out the window of Ty's office. He'd had the oddest feeling of trouble for a moment. Then it dissipated. He rubbed a hand over the back of his neck.

"Losing your touch with the ladies, Garrett?" Ty asked, his face wreathed in smiles.

"Shut up."

Ty's lips twitched in spite of the warning.

"Not another word," Garrett threatened.

His friend ignored the words.

"Left her mark, did she?" Ty jerked a thumb to Garrett's cheek.

"Ty . . ." His voice was deceptively low.

"Care to wash away the taste of the lady with some of my aged bourbon hidden away in my desk?"

Garrett sighed in disgust and muttered, "Sounds like the best offer I'm likely to get today."

His friend slapped him on the back.

Garrett sipped the fine bourbon, savoring the taste. He rarely indulged in drink, and when he did so, he kept it to a limit of one glass. Drunkenness ensured a man's death in a gunfight, a fact he'd witnessed years ago.

Long minutes passed with neither man speaking. At last the silence was broken by Ty capping the bottle and shutting it away in the squeaky desk drawer.

Garrett watched his friend and waited. He knew the man couldn't hold his tongue much longer.

Straightening away from the desk, Ty pulled out his watch and glanced at it, then slipped it back into his pocket and faced Garrett. "Well, it's nearly time."

"Yup."

"What are you going to do?" Ty's voice held a tense edge to it.

"I'm going to put an end to it," Garrett told him in low, even tones.

"How do you plan on doing that? Without getting yourself shot?"

Garrett reached down and unbuckled his gun belt. He leaned forward and laid it on the top of the scarred wooden desk. "There can't be any shoot-out if I'm not wearing my guns."

"Have you thought about this?"

"Yup. Plenty."

"Garrett, you're crazy to do this."

Silence.

"You're going to get yourself killed." Ty reached for the discarded weapon.

Garrett laid a hand on his arm to stop him.

"Bill Thomas isn't some young kid to be scared off," his friend warned.

"I know."

"This one won't back down."

"We'll see," Garrett responded, confidence edging his low voice.

Ty grabbed his hat from a peg by the door. "I'm coming with you."

"Ty—"

"And don't try and stop me."

"Then don't interfere," Garrett ordered.

Ty held up his hands in mock surrender.

Throwing him a look of warning, Garrett turned away and strode out the door. He heard it slam behind his friend with a loud thud of disgust.

It took only minutes to walk the distance to the saloon. Without pausing, Garrett pushed his way through the batwing doors.

"Thomas, I'm here to tell you there isn't going to be any fight," he announced.

Garrett's declaration was met by utter silence. He spotted the other gunman immediately, then stopped so suddenly that Ty almost ran into his back.

"Bill Thomas?"

Garrett stared in disbelief at the sight of the gunman, his head atop his arms, fast asleep.

"Thomas?"

A loud snore was his only answer.

With a caution bred from years of living by his wits and his gun, Garrett approached the other man slowly. Reaching out, he shook him by the shoulder.

"Wake up. It's time for you to move on. There isn't going to be a fight," he informed the gunman.

Another snore was the only response.

Ty leaned forward and prodded Bill Thomas's shoulder. "He's out cold."

"I can see that for myself," Garrett answered.

"Well, I'll be danged," Ty straightened and muttered from behind him.

Garrett shook his head and stepped away. He'd never seen the likes of a trained gunman up and getting too drunk to shoot.

"I'll see he's gotten out of town. Doubt if he'll want to challenge you again after this," Ty said, then scratched his head in obvious puzzlement.

"Yup. It looks like he's going to be out for some time." Garrett threw another look at the sleeping man, then turned away.

He stopped suddenly when he spotted something lying on the wooden floor. At his feet, he noticed a single, white feather. Glancing at it, he stooped down and picked it up. The feather was pure white and seemed to almost shimmer. He shrugged off the thought.

"Hey, Ruth?" Garrett called out to one of the two saloon proprietors. "You or Judy losing the fancy feathers off your dresses?"

Chuckling, he laid the feather on the table and strode to the batwing doors. Shoving the swinging doors outward, he stepped into the bright sunlight.

And right into Cat Parker.

The impact nearly sent them both off the boardwalk. He caught her by the shoulders to keep her from tumbling off the wooden planks. Then he found himself tightening his hold on her.

As she stared up at him, the strangest sensation of déjà vu swept over him. It took him several moments to shake it off.

Cat continued to stare up at him, her lips parted in surprise.

"Ah, hell," he muttered under his breath.

Chapter Four

The brief flare of hurt he saw in Cat's eyes reprimanded him in a way no words could have done. Garrett felt something within him soften. It never crossed his mind to fight it.

Instead, he rubbed the pad of his thumb across her shoulder in an almost caress. Cat simply stared back up at him. He knew he had to say the words.

"Sorry, ma'am," he murmured, the low apology meant for her ears alone.

A soft smile touched Cat's lips, and he felt as if the sun had burst free from behind a cloud. Damn, there he was spouting off poetry again. What was it about this woman . . . ?

He knew he was too rough, too old—too world weary—for the likes of her, but for right now he didn't care.

Some unexplainable force drove him to step closer. He closed his hands around her shoulders, drawing her nearer. Then nearer again. She felt so right in his arms.

Garrett liked the feel of her finely boned shoulders under his hands. He liked the feel of her smooth skin beneath the material of her gown.

He liked the feel of her too damn much for his own good.

Remember, a little voice chided.

Once again that vague sensation eased over him.

Ignoring the warning that was whispering in the far recesses of his mind, he rubbed the pad of his thumb against her shoulder and up the curve of her neck. He threaded his fingers through the curls lying against her nape. They swirled about his hand, trapping him.

As he stared down into her upturned face, the faint whisper of warning grew louder. He took a step closer, silencing it and closing the distance between them until it didn't exist anymore.

Drawing Cat to him until her skirts brushed his legs, he sent the warning back into oblivion.

Cat stared up into the velvety darkness of his gaze, and memories swept through her with the force of a windstorm. They buffeted her. Powerful, weakening to her, devastating.

The warmth of his hands penetrated the silken material covering her shoulders. It rippled through her, silencing the memories, robbing them of their power. Until only one thought remained.

It was so like the one time. . . . He had been so tender, so loving, so . . .

"Cat, have supper with me. Tonight?" Garrett asked suddenly.

His words startled her, catching her with her guard lowered and her defenses down. She knew she should refuse, simply tell him no. She needed time. Time to rebuild her defenses against his charm.

That was exactly what she would do. She opened her mouth to speak, but before she could stop the words, they escaped.

"Yes, I'd like that."

She snapped her mouth closed. Too late. She wished she could bite her tongue, or at the least call back the unintentional words of acceptance. What had she just gone and done?

Anger rose in her. She hated feeling defenseless. Hated not being in control of herself and her life. Jake Garrett had always been able to reduce her to this state. Once she'd been too young, too naive, too in love with him. But not now.

Not now.

Now she was three years older, and wiser.

Cat drew on every bit of strength she possessed to fight the tempting memory of being in Garrett's arms. Drawing in a breath that was tinged with the very scent of him, she pulled her wayward emotions back where they belonged.

Remember, she ordered her mind.

Remember what he did.

Once again the memories returned, only this time the pain came, too, giving her the strength she needed to raise her chin in renewed determination.

She would do what she'd come here to do.

Releasing the silly grip her hands insisted on retaining on his broad shoulders, she pushed herself away from Garrett.

He maintained his own hold on her for a moment, and Cat feared that he might draw her closer. He *might* lower his head to hers.

He might kiss her again.

She held her breath.

Waiting for . . .

Garrett released her at last, and Cat nearly tumbled off the boardwalk. So much for thinking he might be going to kiss her, she chided herself. As if that had been what she wanted. Not likely.

She refused to believe that his careful restraint had actually hurt her. But darned if it didn't. In truth, it felt like he'd reached out and slapped her.

Cat clenched her teeth to hold her forced smile in place. It worked—barely.

She smiled until her jaw ached, hoping it would be long enough to get her temper under control. Swearing at Jake Garrett would do absolutely nothing to help maintain her masquerade. Although it would make her feel a lot better. A whole lot better.

She was a fine Eastern lady, she reminded herself. At least she was supposed to be acting like one. Angry with herself, she tossed her head in a burst of indignation. One curl fell free to land against her cheek. She shoved it away in a rush of irritation.

What was it about wearing a skirt that gave men such ridiculous ideas of how they could treat a body? No man had ever dared treat her this way when she was wearing her breeches and her six-shooters.

Jake Garrett was definitely not going to get away with treating her this way either.

Reaching into her reticule, she whipped out her fan. Before Garrett could even see it coming, she smacked the ruffled fan soundly across his right wrist.

"For your forwardness, sir." Her words carried the perfect amount of censure.

She raised her chin and faced him straight on. Her very stance dared him to react.

Garrett smiled and took it all in stride, feeding her temper with his every action. Raising his brows, he tipped his hat to her.

"My apologies, ma'am."

His wide smile told her he meant the words about as much as a black snake regretted eating a field mouse. Not the tiniest bit.

She wished she dared reach up and strike the smile from his face. But she knew better. It would ruin everything. First of all, a *lady* didn't behave that way. Everyone knew that fact. Especially a well-traveled man like Garrett.

Cat slipped the cord of the fan about her wrist, pretending it was something she did every day of the week. It had taken her untold days of practicing to perform the feat without dropping the fancy fan. Why, she'd broken at least half a dozen of the blasted things learning how to open and flutter one just so.

Remembering this, she carefully flicked the fan open with a great pretense of nonchalance, secretly praying she hadn't broken the fancy thing. She hadn't. Holding on to her sigh of relief, she fluttered the fan back and forth in front of her face a few times for effect. In truth, the cooling air across her heated cheeks felt good, but she'd never admit it.

Snapping the fan closed, she let it fall to swing back and forth from her wrist. With a delicate sniff, she caught up the front of her skirt in her best ladylike imitation. Then came the hardest part. She turned and walked away from Garrett.

"Good day, sir," she called over her shoulder, never taking her eyes off the boardwalk in front of her slippers.

"The name's Garrett," he returned in a low, soft drawl.

The silken sound sent a shiver up her back. Why, she'd swear she could feel his gaze centered on her backside. And she'd be willing to bet it was a very ungentlemanly look, too.

She swallowed down a response and forced her feet to keep walking at a perfectly paced, dainty walk.

"Cat."

She jumped when she realized his voice had come from just above her ear. How on earth had he gotten so close to her so fast? And so quietly.

He's a gunslinger, she reminded herself. As if she needed reminding of that particular fact. Not a day had gone by that she didn't recall it. And how his gun had destroyed her life— taken away her future.

She forced herself to raise her chin a notch in a show of determination, and then she ignored him. She could practically *feel* Garrett stiffen in reaction. She bit back the smile that tempted her lips.

"Cat."

His voice was lower than before, more determined, and held even more of a drawl. It stroked her like a lover's caress. She fought its lure, but lost bit by bit. She stopped dead in her tracks, unable to move a breath even if her life had depended on it.

"I'll be by for you at six."

He made the words sound like a feather-soft promise. She swallowed the growing knot in her throat.

Without looking at him she knew he was smiling again. When he spoke she was proven right.

"Don't make me come looking for you," he said in a tone

that carried an aura of authority, making it a promise and not a threat.

At the words, she jerked back and looked up into his face. The smile was there just waiting for her to see. It merely fed Cat's anger.

She wanted to shout and damn him to hell, but Jake Garrett would likely as not go straight to the place, shake hands with the devil himself, and return with the same smile on his face.

Darn him and his charming ways!

She blamed that charm for her earlier acceptance of his supper invitation. However, she feared that just perhaps there was a little bit more behind the ease with which she agreed to his request.

And for the life of her, she couldn't tell him no even now.

Resisting the impulse to fan her overheated face, she turned on her heel and walked down the boardwalk. Away from Garrett.

He watched her depart, enjoying the gentle sway of her bustle. Cat Parker was one sweet, hot-tempered lady. The smile on his face widened to a full grin of pleasure. He'd bet she had no idea.

He was drawn to her like he'd never been attracted to a woman before. Her ladylike airs were guaranteed to stir a man's blood, and more. However, this feeling passed well beyond simple attraction.

Her blend of fine lady and earthy temptress rocked him all the way to his boots. Sometimes the smallest hint of something other than a lady peeked out at him, teased him. And made him ache.

If Cat had known the path Garrett's thoughts had taken, she would have run all the way to her hotel room. Instead she walked the distance, never once allowing herself to give into the temptation to look back over her shoulder at him.

Once she reached the sanctuary of her room, she leaned against the door, sagging weakly. She drew in several bracing breaths. Her plan was getting more complicated by the minute.

She was succeeding in attracting his attention, but it scared the daylights out of her.

Now what was she supposed to do?

She removed her bonnet, tossing it on the bed in frustration. A moment later she dropped down on the mattress beside the little hat. So much for the piece of fluff bringing her luck.

And if her luck didn't change soon, she was in danger of losing this hand, as well as the entire game. She knew for a fact she couldn't go through loving and losing again. The pain had nearly crippled her spirit once. She couldn't face it a second time.

While she trusted in lady luck to an extent in a poker game, she also believed one made their own luck. That was exactly what she would set to doing.

Oh, she'd meet Jake Garrett for supper. At six like he said. Only this time, she would be the one in charge. She would lure him, so that he would be the one caught off guard.

Not her. Not again.

She couldn't afford to get careless. Her left could depend on that.

Getting to her feet, she crossed to where her carpetbag sat on a chair. Opening the bag, she reached down into the dark recesses until her fingers brushed across the small packet.

As she withdrew the bundle of letters tied with a pink hair ribbon, a flash of pain rippled through her. Maybe Jesse hadn't been the best man in Shelbyville, but he'd loved her in his own way and promised to take her far away from the farm. Gently she ran her fingertips over the two lone envelopes. She didn't need to open them again to know the words. She'd committed them to memory years ago.

Blinking away the sheen of tears from her eyes, she raised the letters to her lips and placed a single kiss against the coarse paper.

"I promise," she whispered, the words loud in the quiet of the room. "Vengeance."

With tender care, she replaced the packet of letters in the

carpetbag and snapped it closed. Then she gently smoothed her fingers across the clasp of the bag.

Taking a deep breath, she turned away with renewed determination.

Cat glanced at the ornate, feminine watch fob and frowned. It read a mere two minutes since the last time she'd looked at it. A quarter hour before six.

She sighed in frustration and paced the expanse of her hotel room. This was ridiculous. She wasn't nervous. No, not the tiniest whit.

She was merely ready this early for her supper with Garrett because she believed in being prepared. Her promptness had nothing to do with eagerness or any anticipation about the evening ahead.

Her conscience told her she was lying.

Cat strode across the room, reached the fall wall, and turned around, then paced back to the opposite side of the room. Smoothing down the nonexistent creases in her skirt, she wrinkled her nose in disgust. She had been ready over ten minutes ago.

No, she wasn't eager to see Garrett, she told herself. She was only interested in putting the next step of her plan into action. That's all it was. Simply that and nothing more.

She stopped in her pacing to stare at herself in the mirror. Critically she surveyed the blue gown. The sapphire skirt of faille was trimmed with a deep gathered flounce. Tiny, darker sapphire blue buttons fastened down the length of the bodice.

The fancy new gown set off her figure. In fact, it seemed to be hugging her body a tiny bit too much for her way of thinking.

Even though she knew the gown was the latest style and most assuredly proper for an Eastern lady, the sweetheart bodice dipped low enough to cause her concern. She was accustomed to wearing her men's shirts buttoned all the way up. She tugged at the low neckline but to no avail. It didn't raise even the tiniest bit.

Trying to ignore her bosom, she again ran her gaze over the reflection of herself in the mirror. Then she turned this way and that way for a better look. She'd never looked like this in breeches for certain.

She reached behind her and adjusted the bustle for the tenth time in less than that many minutes and turned away in frustration.

Whatever was wrong with her tonight?

Her gaze settled on the rumpled bed covers, and she felt her cheeks heat. She'd attempted to take a nap earlier to calm her nerves. The act had had the opposite effect on her, as she now recalled the dream she'd had of Garrett. It had been shameful.

Embarrassed, she whirled away from the bed. The movement left her facing the mirror again. Only this time she could see the foot of the bed with a sheet trailing over it reflected therein.

Turning away in sudden determination, she grabbed up the long matching gloves and tugged them on, then scooped up her reticule. She would wait for Garrett downstairs in the lobby. Far better to appear eager, or frightened of his warning not to make him come looking for her, than to allow him entry to her room when she was in this state.

In fact, she had no intention of allowing him within spitting distance of her bedroom.

Not yet, an impish part of her prompted.

Not ever, a little voice in the back of her mind argued.

She slammed her hotel room door behind her on the disturbing thought. The restrictive skirt tangled about her feet, and she paused to kick the material out of her way. She'd only taken a couple more steps when her foot caught in the skirt again.

"Shams," she muttered.

Catching up her skirt in both hands, she headed down the hallway. As she felt the rush of air against her ankles, she released her skirt. It fell softly about her legs covering her to her slippers.

Shams. She had most assuredly been showing much too much ankle for a lady to show. Would she ever become accustomed to walking about in the fancy long skirts and lace-edged petticoats? She missed the freedom of movement offered by her old breeches.

Not that it would matter much longer. She wouldn't be keeping up to the masquerade of an Eastern lady after she did what she come here to do.

She smoothed down the wrinkles in her skirt. Then taking more care, she caught up the front of her skirt in one hand, so she could walk without tripping over her own feet, then adjusted its height. Satisfied she was indeed showing nothing improper this time, she started down the stairs to the lobby.

She'd reached the stairway landing when she paused out of habit to take stock of her surroundings. She knew better than to dash headlong into a room without checking it over first. The wrong end of a gun could be waiting for her. However this time, she'd been so caught up in thinking about Garrett and the evening ahead that she'd nearly waltzed down the stairs without looking first.

What had come over her recently?

She was becoming absolutely addle-brained. She placed the blame right where it belonged—on Jake Garrett.

Resting her hand on the sleek wooden handrail, she drew in a deep, calming breath. As she glanced about the lobby below, her gaze settled on one skinny man wearing a bowler hat.

Her breath rushed out in a gasp of fear and disbelief.

Chapter Five

No, it couldn't be.

Cat couldn't move for the space of a heartbeat.

"No," she whispered, her hand to her mouth. "It can't be."

But it was. The skinny Easterner stood not fifteen feet away from her, talking to the desk clerk. Fear, so real she could taste its bitter sting, rose up in her throat. It nearly choked her.

How had he trailed her here? She'd been so careful, so certain she'd covered her tracks.

Without even taking time to draw in a breath, she whirled around and raced back up the stairs, nearly catching her toe in the hem of her gown in her haste. Grabbing the banister to steady herself, she hiked up her skirts. Not caring a whit about appearing ladylike, she resumed her dash up the remaining steps, not stopping until she was safely locked inside her room.

Leaning against the door, as if her action could keep someone out, she sucked in several deep breaths and tried to slow her racing heart. She remained there for countless minutes. Waiting.

Finally, when no one knocked on her door, she dared to breath normally. The man who had been tracking her so diligently wasn't coming up to pound on her door, or break it down.

Maybe she'd been mistaken. Maybe it hadn't been the same man as before. She attempted to reason away her fears, but to no avail. She *knew* who she'd seen downstairs, and it had most certainly been the same man who had been dogging her trail for nearly a week.

Where had he gone to now?

Unable to wait any longer, she crept to the window. Inching up bit by bit, she peered out, making certain that she kept herself well hidden from anyone below.

The skinny Easterner was standing right in the street for all to see. It was definitely the same man. She didn't retain the slightest doubt.

And he was talking to Garrett.

She clenched her fingers into a fist, suddenly noticing that her palms were sweaty. She wiped them on her skirt, not paying any attention to her action.

Garrett's strong build towered over the skinny man, making him seem even shorter. The contrast also added unnecessary emphasis to Garrett's broad shoulders and lean hips. Even from here she could see the way his gun belt hugged those hips. He was a powerful figure of a man, and she knew his hands were lightning fast with a gun. Or surprisingly gentle with a woman. Her stomach lurched, then resettled.

Quickly, she brought her wandering attention back to the scene below. How she wished she could listen to what they were saying.

She'd give almost anything to know what the little man and Garrett were talking about. However, there was no possible way she could eavesdrop from the second floor of the hotel.

Cat worried her lower lip and tried to find a way to get the information she so desperately needed. Perhaps over supper tonight . . .

Suddenly Garrett turned away from the other man and strode toward the hotel. She could almost hear his boots hitting the hard-packed dirt with each step he took. Cat's breath stopped on the way to her lungs. Had he seen her spying out the hotel window?

She ducked back farther behind the curtain and continued to watch him. He moved with a natural confidence. She'd seen it in other gunslingers before, but none had possessed it so naturally as Garrett.

Confidence was a part of him. He was well aware of his abilities.

She swallowed down the nervousness that observation caused in her. As she followed his progress, she noted how he avoided the narrow alley he passed on his right, instead keeping a careful eye out for any dangerous shadows it could hold.

The only chance she stood with him and his fast gun hand would be to see that he dropped his guard. Her stomach fluttered with nerves, and she laid her hand against the spot. Jake Garrett was better than good—he was reputed to be the best.

Well, she would have to be better. Cat tossed back her head with determination. There was more than one way to be the best. She was about to try one of those other ways. Tonight.

To begin with, she'd simply charm Garrett over supper, ask a few carefully worded questions, and keep her fingers crossed that she didn't run into the skinny Easterner.

It sounded simple enough. And that was what worried her.

For the life of her she could not think of how to ask him about the stranger. While she was certain that the man was trailing her, was Garrett aware of it now too? She would have to carefully word her questions. And guard her answers to him.

When she'd started out on this venture, it had seemed like such an easy plan. One any simpleton could carry out without a hitch. However, she'd managed to encounter enough hitches for a whole team of horses.

Now what? She nibbled her lower lip, wondering what could possibly go wrong next.

At a sharp rap on her door, Cat nearly jumped out of her skin. She laid her hand against her stomach again and took a deep breath. If she didn't steady her nerves she'd never survive the evening. Determined, she swore she would make it through tonight if it killed her.

Poor choice of words, she thought with a shiver.

Forcing a smile to her lips, she caught up her wrap and crossed to the door. The sight of Garrett freshly shaven and dressed in black with his gun belt riding low on his hips stole her smile clean away. And darn near took her heart as well.

Careful, she told herself. He was a dangerous man in more ways than just his reputation with a gun.

However, she was not susceptible to his many charms nowadays. Absolutely not one whit, she assured herself proudly. Yet, that assurance held a distinct ring of falseness to her ears.

Then he smiled. And she knew without a doubt that her assurance was an absolute lie.

Shams, she amended the swear word before it could slip out.

"Evening, Cat." He raised a finger to his dark hat and tipped it in greeting. A dark curl dipped low over his forehead.

Her heart skipped a beat, and she swallowed her sudden nervousness. "Good evening," she answered in a prim and proper voice.

At least she hoped it sounded that way.

"You look beautiful," Garrett murmured, the soft drawl coloring his voice.

Cat could only stare back at him. She didn't have the slightest idea of how to answer him, or if she was supposed to do so. This was the first time anyone had ever told her such a thing.

"But, of course, you already knew that," he added, his lips curling up at one corner in a brief instant of derision.

Before she could think of what she was doing, Cat shook her head in denial. "No, I didn't." She nibbled on her fingertip, trying to think of what she should or shouldn't say next.

Garrett caught her hand in his and smiled down at her. This time his smile was genuine.

The air in the room seemed to fly right out the window past the curtain. Not only that, it left behind an uncomfortable heat. Cat resisted the impulse to fan herself with her other hand.

"You constantly amaze me," Garrett told her.

This time she was wise enough to keep her response to herself.

"Ready?" he asked.

Somehow the single word coming from him seemed to hold a newfound warning for her. It almost sounded ominous to her ears. Or was that anticipation she felt? She truly couldn't tell.

As he draped the wrap about her shoulders, she figured she'd better watch her back when she was near this gunslinger.

When Garrett held out his arm for her, she decided that maybe she'd better keep an eye on every part of her body whenever he was within arm's reach.

She didn't trust herself right now, much less him. She'd learned the hard way just how much she could trust Jake Garrett. And her foolishness had cost her everything.

Cat gathered up all her courage and placed her hand on his arm and let him lead her from the room. A slight sigh escaped her lips when she heard the reassuring sound of the door clicking shut behind them. At least she'd kept him out of her bedroom.

For now.

But what was she supposed to do about the warmth of his forearm seeping through her fingertips? Ignore it, she ordered her senses.

They paid her about as much mind as a cow in the middle of a stampede.

The pleasant warmth spread through her palm and proceeded up to her wrist. She started to snatch her hand away, but Garrett must have read her mind, for he laid his other hand over hers, trapping it as surely as if he'd set a snare.

His palm heated her hand like a ray of sunshine on a summer day. It made her feel all cozy warm inside, and she had the strangest impulse to snuggle up against him. Or worse yet, to rub her cheek against the strength of his shoulder that was by far too close for comfort.

What a foolish thought! Garrett was the last man she'd ever want to snuggle up against—it would be akin to snuggling up with a big, dangerous rattlesnake.

She raised her chin, tried to ignore his nearness, and stiffened her spine in resolution. She would not let him tempt her. She was here for a purpose. However, her body resisted those sensible thoughts. A strange tension coiled inside her.

Garrett felt Cat tense beside him and resisted the urge to sweep her into his arms and reassure her that he would act the part of gentleman. Tonight. Though if he dared take her in his arms, a gentleman was the last thing he'd end up being.

He'd never been much of a gentleman to begin with, and he had nothing to offer a woman like Cat Parker. She had home and hearth written all over her. He knew to avoid that kind, and he usually did. Nothing could prove more dangerous to him. He'd long ago faced the truth that he'd done away with his right to love when he'd shot that cavalry officer dead.

What he should do was set her away from him, turn his back, and walk away. But he didn't. He settled for rubbing the pad of his thumb over her soft knuckles. It was poor comfort when what he wanted to do was haul her up into his arms and carry her back to her room. And to bed.

He cleared his throat. It felt as if something had lodged in it. He knew something had lodged a whole lot lower in his gut.

In his time living by the gun he'd met more than his share of women. But he had yet to meet one like Caitlan Parker. What was it about her that set her apart from other women?

She possessed a rare innocence blended with the strongest temptation he'd ever faced in his life. It was hard keeping his hands off her. However, he vowed that tonight he'd treat her like the lady she was, and deserved to be treated.

What he needed was a stiff drink. A long one.

However, Dena's Restaurant didn't serve spirits. And since they had reached the restaurant, he'd have to settle for coffee. The wooden sign hanging above the door swung in the faint breeze. Dena's was spelled out in bold black letters, and a red apple sat crookedly painted at the corner of the placard.

Cat tilted her head back and studied the sign. "Why the apple?" She held up a hand to forestall him from answering. "Let me guess. She serves the best apple pie in town?"

Garrett grinned back at her. "Nope. Folks in town say it's

for her years spent teaching in Dallas before she moved here to Millwood and opened up the best eatery around.''

Cat looked up at the sign with renewed respect. Since she'd taught herself to read and write and do sums, she figured teachers should most assuredly be looked up to. Maybe she'd enjoy the evening after all.

As Garrett reached around her and opened the door for her, she felt like a real lady for the first time in her life. Farming in Shelbyville didn't give one many chances to be ladylike. Yes, she just might enjoy tonight.

She swept up her skirts in one hand and sashayed through the open door into the restaurant. Pretty rose-colored tablecloths covered the dozen or so tables scattered about the room. In the center of each table sat a glowing lamp.

Cat barely held back her ''ooh'' of appreciation. She'd never been in a place this pretty before. Tantalizing aromas teased her nose. She rested a hand over her stomach and realized she was indeed hungry.

Garrett led her to a table, his hand gently settled on a spot near the end of her spine. She could practically feel her bustle tingle in response to the nearness of his hand. Goodness, what had come over her? Goodness has nothing to do with it, a little voice in her mind whispered in warning. She chose to ignore it.

As Garrett pulled out the chair and waited for her to be seated, Cat reveled in the gentlemanly attention. One fact was certain, no man had ever pulled out a chair for her when she'd been wearing breeches and her six-shooters. Maybe there was more to this lady thing than she'd first thought. It most assuredly had its benefits.

She watched him circle the table to the chair opposite hers. He removed his hat, placed it brim up on the empty chair next to him, and seated himself across from her. As he crossed his arms on the table and leaned toward her, the muscles of his shoulders rippled beneath his shirt. She knew from memory that whorls of dark hair covered his chest.

All plans of questioning Garrett fled for the moment. She

had to force her gaze away and hastily looked down at the menu in front of her. However, she didn't see a single word written there.

In her mind's eye all she could see was the gunslinger seated across from her. Irritated with herself, she shoved back a stray curl.

Garrett watched the play of light across Cat's features. Looking at her in the soft lamp light was a new experience for him. The flickering light's glow set her eyes to sparkling, and her hair practically shimmered. He sighed; there he was thinking in poetry again. He cleared the sudden dryness from his throat.

He knew better than to be entertaining those kinds of thoughts. Perhaps he shouldn't have asked her to supper in the first place. It was madness, but one he'd been unable to resist giving in to. What he should do was see the evening through, escort Cat back to her hotel room, and not lay a hand on her tempting body.

Tonight should be the last he'd see of her, but he knew he wouldn't listen to the voice of reason.

"Would you like me to order for you?" he asked in an unsteady voice.

His long silence had grated on her nerves. To Cat it seemed as if he were regretting his decision to ask her here. Well, he wasn't the only one with regrets.

She opened her mouth to retort that she was quite capable of telling somebody what she wanted to eat. Then she remembered that she was supposed to be an Eastern lady. She meekly smiled her acceptance, nearly biting her tongue in the process.

The moment the food arrived, Cat regretted her decision. She most assuredly should have ordered for herself. She watched the pretty dark-haired woman set the food on the table in growing disbelief.

At last Cat looked from the plate to the restaurant's proprietress, then back to the plate.

What was going on? Where was her meal?

The meager amount of food on her plate wasn't enough to feed a—

She cut the remainder of the thought off, reminding herself that she was a lady and this was a lady's supper. A very small one, too, from the looks of it.

She stared down at the ladylike portion on her plate, then eyed the oversized steak hanging partways off Garrett's plate, and barely stopped herself from licking her lips. What was he trying to do—save money?

Who had determined that a *lady* should only eat tiny portions of food that surely wouldn't fill up a nice-sized bird? Likely, it had been a man.

She eyed Garrett's steaming steak one more time with barely disguised envy and held back her sigh. Instead she picked up her fork and stabbed a ladylike bite from her own meal. Her stomach emitted a low rumble. Somebody would pay for this injustice. She was hungry.

Forcing herself to merely nibble at the delicious food, she pretended to be enjoying herself. She toyed with her fork the way she'd seen ladies do in restaurants before. She'd wondered back then why they did such a thing, and she was no closer to an answer now.

Perhaps they did it to make the food last through the meal.

However, she wasn't here to enjoy the meal or the evening. She needed answers. And she'd better set to getting them. Soon.

Her life could well depend on who the skinny Easterner was and what he was up to trailing her. A knot formed deep in her stomach. She had a bad feeling about the snooping stranger. Her appetite fled right out the restaurant door.

As Cat smiled and responded properly to Garrett's question about the quality of her meal, she mentally tried out and tossed aside at least a dozen questions to ask him. Not a one of them would do. One was too obvious, another too vague. And a third question revealed entirely too much.

She wanted to just up and ask him outright, but knew better. In her masquerade nothing could be that plain and simple.

"What do you think of our town?" Garrett asked. He stretched out his legs, accidently bumping the chair beside him.

His hat balanced precariously for a moment, then resettled safely.

Finally, the opportunity she needed. Cat barely held back her grin.

"It seems very nice. Does everyone wear those hats?" She pointed toward his Stetson, sitting brim up on the chair beside them.

His deep chuckle was almost her undoing. She forced herself to continue.

"You can laugh all you want to, but we don't see many of those hats back in New York." At least she assumed she wouldn't see them if she ever made it to New York.

"I guess you wouldn't."

"I swear I've only seen one bowler hat on a gentleman since I arrived in Texas." She batted her eyelashes at him the way she'd seen saloon girls do at men. The men had always seemed to appreciate it.

"Cat, are you all right?" Garrett asked, leaning forward in concern.

She jerked back. "Yes. Why?"

"Did you get something in your eye?"

"What?"

"I wondered . . . you keep blinking like you've got a speck in your eye." He reached into his pocket. "Would you like to use my handkerchief?"

Cat sputtered her refusal. Embarrassment heated her cheeks. The first time she tried cozying up to a man and he offered her his kerchief. Why, she was too insulted to swear.

"I'm fine. Just fine." She forced the words past the smile she'd pasted to her lips. "But thank you for your offer," she lied.

"Any time."

Somehow the words took the sting out of his earlier insult. Maybe she'd better stick to acting closer to her real self.

"I'm sorry I interrupted you, Cat. You were talking about the Pinkerton?"

"Pinkerton?" she whispered past nearly frozen lips.

The man dogging her steps was a hired detective? She couldn't believe it.

"Yup, if you're talking about the new stranger wearing the tenderfoot's hat. Louis Winston came in today on the afternoon train."

"What . . . what is a Pinkerton doing here?" She hoped the question sounded innocent.

Garrett shrugged. "Can't figure why they'd send a tenderfoot out here hunting somebody. And it's his first case to boot." He wiped his mouth and tossed his napkin down in disgust.

Cat wasn't sure how to respond, but he continued on, giving her a reprieve.

"Fella won't last thirty days out here the way he's going about things."

"Oh? What is he doing?" Cat tried to appear interested, yet not too much so.

"Following the rail line where he last lost the person he's after—"

Cat's breath stopped on the way to her mouth.

"He's asking questions. Too many questions for a man's own good. And he's being mighty pushy about doing it."

"What's he asking about?" Cat dabbed at her lips with her napkin, then dropped her hands in her lap to hide their slight tremor from him.

"Claims a man hired him to find his sister." Garrett leaned back in the chair.

Cat forced herself to meet his steady gaze. "His sister?"

"Yup. But it doesn't sound right to me."

"It doesn't," she echoed his words.

"Nope."

She waited for him to add more. When he didn't, she gathered up her courage and asked, "Do you think I'm that woman?"

Garrett laughed, his grin lingering afterward. "Nope. You are clearly not what he described."

Cat made herself smile back at him and cock her head the way she'd seen a saloon girl do once. "Oh?"

"Not by a long shot. He was looking for a breeches-clad, gun-toting female who's skinny as a rail."

For an instant Cat was insulted. She was not "skinny as a rail." She hadn't been in years.

She joined in Garrett's rich laughter. Her identity was safe.

"He claims her brother is willing to pay dearly to find her."

Cat held up her palms in pretended resignation and sighed. "And here I am all alone in the world."

"You are?" Garrett asked in concern.

She steadied her voice before she answered, "Yes."

He turned his hand over and caught her hand in his. She glanced down at her lap, unable to meet his eyes, afraid he'd see too much.

She was alone. That was true.

For an instant, tears stung her eyes. Then bitterness rose up in her, shutting off all other senses.

She had no one.

Thanks to Jake Garrett's gun.

Chapter Six

Sunlight streamed through the window and across the bed, right into Cat's eyes. Blinking several times at the bright intrusion, she turned her head away.

She wasn't ready to face the day. Last night she'd had scant few hours of sleep after her supper with Garrett had ended in disaster.

Leaning up, she plumped her pillow, then dropped back down onto the soft, feather mattress. With her remark about being alone in the world, she'd nearly ruined everything. If that didn't raise Garrett's suspicions, nothing likely would do so.

Angry with herself, she thumped the pillow again. She had to keep the past at bay or she'd never keep a steady enough hand to go through with her plan to kill him and fulfill her promised vengeance.

Cat shut her eyes, hoping to block out the painful memories of Shelbyville. The time for mourning was past.

Now it was time for action.

Tossing back the covers, she scrambled out of bed. She scarcely remembered how she'd gotten through the remainder of supper last night. It had ended with her pleading a headache. Her excuse later became reality in the loneliness of her hotel room. This morning, the remnants of a real headache still remained.

A hot bath sounded like the perfect cure. It took several smiles and a little fluttering of her eyelashes for the young desk clerk to accomplish the feat, but within half an hour her bath awaited her. Way ahead of any other patrons.

Perhaps she'd learned how to bat her eyes right after all, she thought, eyeing the enameled tub filled with fragrant steaming water that sat in the middle of her room. She sniffed appreciatively at the edge of the tub, then stepped into it.

As she leaned her head back against the smooth surface, she thought on how this provided the consummate place to think on her new plan. The heated water relaxed her aching muscles. She swore wearing those fancy slippers made the ache in her feet extend all the way up her body. What she wouldn't give for her own boots.

She let her thoughts drift like the steam rising from the tub. She was in no hurry to dress and leave the sanctity of her room. The single accusation stung her that she was dodging a confrontation. She refused to admit that she was stalling—avoiding any chance of meeting either Garrett or the Pinkerton.

After another fifteen minutes the water had cooled, and her mind had begun to nag her. She'd never avoided a confrontation in her life. And she wasn't about to start to now.

Standing to her feet suddenly, the water rose in a wave and sloshed over one edge of the tub. Meanwhile a chilly draught of air cooled her skin. Grabbing up a towel, she dried both herself and the damp floor. She couldn't put the day off any longer.

If she didn't put in an appearance soon, she had a disturbing feeling that Garrett would likely as not come up to check on her. And her headache. She couldn't allow that. Her emotions were still too raw from last night. Too close to the surface. She needed time to bury them again.

Like she'd buried—

Cat cut the thought off. Striding away from the tub in a rush, she slipped on a puddle of water and barely caught herself from falling right on her backside. She dropped the towel over the spilled water.

"Shams."

Served her right for not paying a whit's attention to what she was doing, she told herself in irritation. She knew better than to allow herself to be so distracted. Frustrated, she mopped up the spill and tossed the towel over the edge of the tub.

Pulling on her wrapper, she set to righting the room. Then she withdrew each of her Colt revolvers, cleaned and oiled them. Afterward she carefully replaced them in the bottom of her carpetbag.

After nearly an hour of puttering about the room, Cat stomped her foot. She'd had enough. She absolutely refused to hide out in her room another moment.

She'd practically worn a path in the thin floral carpet anyway what with her pacing between the window and the chair and the door. All the fretting she'd done had accomplished nothing but to give her sore feet. Whirling away from the window yet again, she walked to the armoire.

She'd put on one of her prettiest dresses and face Garrett. And maybe the snoopy Easterner, too, and pray he didn't recognize her.

What she needed was to take charge of the situation. First off, she would go hunting Garrett before he came looking for her. That would effectively switch the tables and put her in control of her own fate.

She hoped.

Thirty minutes later, she was ready and dressed in a gown of yellow sprigged muslin the color of sunlight. On impulse she caught up a fawn-colored silk parasol trimmed with lace. She felt like she needed all the armament she could muster today.

Who knew how long the Pinkerton might remain in town? She couldn't hide out in her room without food or fresh air forever. She had to chance seeing how good her disguise would hold out. If Garrett hadn't seen through her masquerade, then chances were the skinny Pinkerton man wouldn't either. Then again, she might not encounter him at all.

As her stomach rumbled, she recalled the meager supper she'd eaten last night. What she needed to start the day proper was a healthy breakfast, and hang the ladylike portions. She caught up her reticule and slammed the door behind her in a mixture of irritation and defiance.

The sound echoed her feelings perfectly.

She faced the fact that a meeting with Jake Garrett was long overdue. Avoiding him would accomplish nothing, and might even put her plan at risk.

Cat stepped out into the bright warm day. She recalled last night Garrett had mentioned that he was living in a boarding-house. How difficult could it be to find the place in a town the size of Millwood?

She'd go and thank him for supper, that's what she'd do. Turning to her right, she set off at a leisurely lady's pace down the boardwalk, ensuring she wouldn't trip over the ruffle edging the hem of her skirt. Once she found Garrett, she'd flutter her eyelashes at him the same way that had worked so well on the hotel desk clerk this morning, smile prettily at him, and then she would . . .

She wasn't sure what she'd do, but she'd figure something out.

"Psst!"

Cat reacted instinctively to the hiss of noise. She dropped her parasol and automatically reached for the six-shooter on her hip, but it wasn't there. Her guns were back in her hotel room at the bottom of her carpetbag.

Shams, she thought.

She whirled about and faced the alley where the sound had come from.

"Psst!"

There it was again. Only this time it was a lower sound than before. Remembering her alternate weapon, she inched her hand down into her reticule, reaching for her loaded derringer.

While it wasn't much use at a long distance, up close it could be deadly.

"Don't even think about drawing that pea shooter of yours, Cat."

She recognized the friendly voice. Bill Thomas. However, she wasn't feeling any too friendly right now herself.

She was still downright mad at him for making fun of her fancy dress in the mercantile. Furthermore, she had no intention of being seen talking to another gunfighter.

Did things have to keep going from bad to worse? She'd run through more than her share of bad luck since she'd arrived in Millwood. That was for certain.

Unwilling to face anybody without having the edge, she eased her right hand farther into her bag.

"Hold it right there," Bill ordered. "I've got my own hogleg pointed straight at you. And it ain't no pea shooter like that one."

Cat swallowed the lump of anger that persisted in rising in her throat, threatening to choke her. She couldn't accept the fact that he'd gotten the drop on her. If she'd been paying attention to her surroundings instead of thinking on Garrett, it never would have happened.

"Now step on back here with me." Bill gestured to her. "And do it real easy like."

"No," Cat answered him plain and simple.

"What do you mean no?"

"Just that. No."

"Now listen here, lady gunfighter, I'm the one with the gun."

She motioned him to hush.

"Are you going to shoot me right here?" she asked in defiance. "In view of how many people here in the town? I don't think you will. They'd hang you for shooting an unarmed *lady*."

"You know I wouldn't shoot an unarmed anybody," Bill protested.

He sounded plumb affronted to her.

"And that's why I'm not taking one step into that alley with you," she answered. "I don't have to."

"Aw, come on, Cat. All I want to do is talk to you without that gunslinger Garrett around to interfere. Or having him take it the wrong way."

"Then, why the gun?" she asked pointedly.

"So that you wouldn't start a'screaming again and bring him down on me. That's why."

"Oh."

A sharp memory of their earlier meeting in the mercantile returned full force. He was bound to be mad about it. Part of her admitted he had a right to be upset with her.

"I'm sorry about that, Bill."

"Darn it all, Cat. You didn't have to go stomping on my foot that way. I've been limping ever since."

A smile tugged at her, but she held it back. She glanced over her shoulder to make certain they weren't being observed.

"I'm sorry, Bill, but I couldn't let you go telling everybody who I was—" She lowered her voice.

"Speaking of that, who are you supposed to be? And why?"

Cat shook her head. "Never mind. It doesn't concern you."

Bill refused to accept that. "Cat? We're old friends. What's going on here?"

"Oh, all right. I'm *supposed* to be a lady from New York—"

Bill's hoot of laughter interrupted her. "You?" He laughed harder. "You never even seen New York."

She reached into her bag again.

Bill held up his hand. "Okay. You're a lady." He leaned forward and peered out the alley a moment. "Now will you get in here so we can talk."

She crossed her arms and stood her ground.

"For old times sake?" he asked.

Cat opened her mouth to refuse, then changed her mind. He sure seemed all fired eager to talk to her about something. What would it hurt to talk to him? "For old times sake."

Glancing over her shoulder one more time, she scooped up

her silk and lace parasol and slipped into the alley out of sight of the boardwalk. And any nosy townspeople.

"All right, Bill. I'm here. What do you want to talk about?"

As he looked around nervously, she plopped her hands on her hips. "I've already apologized about—"

"That ain't it, Cat. Although I was a mite put out over you acting that way to an old friend."

Cat smiled back at him. They had been friends for a couple of years, ever since she'd come upon a group of men all set to have a lynching party with Bill as the guest of honor. His crime had been being on the wrong side of a range war. She'd sort of ended their party early.

"But later I got to thinking that knowing you, you probably had your reasons for hushing me that way. Anyway—"

"Is that what you came back to tell me?"

"Heck no. Wanted to tell you I shared a camp fire with some drifters. 'Cept they weren't."

"Weren't what?" she asked, confused.

"Drifters." Bill wiped away the sweat from his forehead with his shirt sleeve. "They were part of an outlaw band. And they were mighty interested in Millwood."

Cat swallowed down the nervousness that began to close off her throat. She didn't like the sound of this at all.

"And you," Bill added.

She gasped. "Me?"

"That's what I thought, too." He eyed the toes of his dusty boots. "Sorry to say this, Cat, but your gun reputation ain't that good." He peeked back up at her obviously waiting for a reaction.

While she'd wounded a few men, she'd never killed one. And she'd only seen one man die—Zeke Baker, who had taught her to handle a gun and draw—except he'd died from consumption.

"I never set out on this to get a reputation."

He shrugged. "Like I said, I couldn't figure out why they was so all fired interested in you. So I figured I ought to at least let you know about them. Word is they plan to rob and shoot up Millwood.''

''When?''

Bill shrugged. ''Don't know that. Their leader's a bad one from what I heard. They call him Lazarus. But that's not his real name.''

''And?''

''That's all. I didn't stick my neck out too far nosing around. I'd like to keep it just like it is. Not stretched.''

''Why are you warning me of this?'' Cat asked, caution in her voice.

''Ah, hooey.'' He paused to slap the dust off his thigh. ''You and me been through a bit together.''

She met his look, refusing to be the first to look away.

''Bill? Quit prancing around it. Why?'' she demanded an honest answer.

''All right. I owe you. And I always pay my debts.'' He rubbed his sleeve across his chin.

''We're square, Bill. You saved me that time in Dodge City from a bullet in the back,'' she reminded him. ''You didn't own me more. Why this?''

He didn't answer, and silence echoed loud in the alley. Cat remained silent, waiting. Patience had its virtues, or so she'd been told.

At last he spoke. ''You saved me from getting killed by Jake Garrett.''

''I what?''

''Sending that old white-whiskered man to get me drunk. Scraggly-looking he was, too. I always knew you was a smart one, but—''

''Wait, Bill, I didn't have anything to do with that. I haven't even seen anyone like that around town.''

''No sense in you lying about it, Cat. I owed you. Leave it at that.'' He wiped a trickle of sweat from his cheek with his shirt.

''Bill—''

''I've warned you. Now we're even,'' he declared.

Cat nodded in agreement. He wasn't about to take no for an answer. "Thanks."

"No thanks needed. I pay my debts." He took a step back away from her, then stopped. "You take care of yourself, you hear?"

"I'll try."

"Cat?"

"Yeah?"

"I don't know what you're after here, but I hope you get it."

A flash of doubt flared up in her, but she snuffed it out.

"Thanks. I plan to."

Bill turned away and strode down the alley and out of sight. Cat remained there for a minute staring after him, deep in thought.

What would an outlaw gang want with her?

Another question struck her. What was she going to do with the information Bill had given her?

And how could she do anything without revealing her true identity?

Cat wasn't the only one troubled by the meeting. Angel Tamera stood up on the boardwalk behind Cat, tapping her foot in agitation. She'd arrived too late to hear more than the last few words. Their talk of a "plan" worried her. She needed to know what Cat was here after and what her plan entailed.

She scowled at Cat. What in the name of heaven was that city woman up to now?

Tamera stepped off the boardwalk into the alley, nearly tripping over the hem of her gown. As she stepped closer, she could feel Cat's indecision. And her fear.

Cocking her head, Tamera crossed her arms and fluttered off the ground in uneasiness. Something strange was going on with the pretty woman from New York. Something was also very wrong.

Tamera could sense it. In fact, her feathers were all standing on end, and she tingled from head to toes. Quite a discomforting feeling for an angel to experience.

The woman was up to no good. She knew it as sure as she could fly.

All was definitely not as it appeared on the surface of the finely dressed Eastern lady.

Just what was Cat Parker hiding? How would it affect Garrett? Well, she intended to find out.

She would peek into the corners of Miss Parker's life— starting with all four corners of her hotel room.

Tamera whirled away from Cat and flew off for the hotel, leaving behind a sudden flurry of dust. She flew straight through the open doorway, right past a skinny man in a bowler hat, and up the stairs.

Without pausing to consider the rightness of what she was doing, Tamera landed smack in the middle of Cat's room. She frowned at the damp spot on the floor.

Turning straight away to the camelback trunk, she lifted the lid. It held nothing of interest. She crossed to the bureau, eased open the first drawer, shifted through pretty underthings, and closed the drawer. Neither of the other drawers yielded anything of concern.

She headed next to the armoire and threw open the door. Making short work of her search, she carefully yet quickly examined each article of Cat's wardrobe, then frowned.

She recognized the russet traveling outfit, as well as both the green and the blue gowns she'd seen Cat wear. Tapping her chin, she rechecked the other clothing in the armoire.

Odd, every gown and wrap looked new, almost as if they had never been worn before. Now, why would a lady come to a town like Millwood with only brand-new clothes?

A vague tingle of angel sense nagged at her. Giving in to the impulse, she turned away and ran her gaze over the room, searching for what it was that called to her.

A worn carpetbag sat atop a chair, and Tamera could swear it called out her name. She flew across to it, settled to her feet, and flicked the bag's clasp open.

Peering inside, she jerked back at the sight of a pair of breeches. Men's breeches!

Her halo slipped to one side, and she resettled it before bending to peek inside the bag again. She wrinkled her nose and pushed the breeches aside. They revealed a pair of boots.

These weren't a lady's riding apparel either. She gingerly set them aside on the floor and reached down into the recesses of the bag. What she found this time nearly sent her halo toppling from her head.

A pearl-handled revolver gleamed up at her.

"Oh, dear heavens," she gasped.

Pushing the gun aside distastefully with the tip of her finger, she lowered her head to look into the bottom of the carpetbag. She snapped her head back, slipped, and landed on her backside on the floor.

Why, the lady in question possessed two guns. Two. A matching set of pearl-handled Colt .45s.

Tamera levered herself to her feet with some degree of difficulty. She was really too cushiony to do so gracefully. On her feet at last, she dusted off the back of her white gown.

"Feathers. Why would a woman carry guns?" she asked aloud.

She looked closer at the weapons. Why, they looked remarkably like the ones Garrett carried. Oh, dear, was Cat a gunslinger, too?

Gathering up her scattered senses, Tamera approached the bag again. She sucked in a big breath and plunged her hands into the darkness therein. Only one item remained. This time she withdrew a ribbon-tied packet.

Tamera didn't hesitate to slip the ribbon aside and read the first letter, then the second brief note.

The moment she finished, she pushed the bag aside and sank onto the chair. Love letters. She held in her hands creased and obviously well read love letters to Cat from some man named Jesse.

Who in feathers was Jesse?

The brief note troubled her more than the first letter. It spoke of the possibility of him not surviving the gunfight and relayed strange instructions for Cat after his death. A shiver skittered down her spine, ruffling her feathers in its wake.

Realization struck her with enough force that if she hadn't been sitting in the chair, it would have knocked her down. As it was her halo tilted to one side and teetered. She ignored it. One thought consumed her.

Cat Parker planned to kill Garrett.

"Oh, feathers," she whispered in horror, one hand over her lips.

Blinking her eyes, she reached up and resettled her halo, then stood and straightened her gown. Cat Parker would fail— she'd see to that.

Stomping in barely veiled anger, Tamera replaced the items in the carpetbag and set it on the chair. Vengeance would not have its way. She'd been sent here to protect Jake Garrett, and that was precisely what she would do.

She fluttered several inches off the floor, deep in thought. There had to be a way to stop . . .

A serene smile lit her face, and a warm glow filled the room. Of course, why hadn't she thought of it sooner? Love was much stronger than either hate or the need for revenge.

If Cat loved Garrett, she couldn't kill him.

She'd reached the perfect solution. She'd simply help her fall in love with him. Tamera's smile widened into a proud grin.

With a little heavenly assistance from her, Cat Parker would be in love with Garrett in no time at all.

After all, what could go wrong with a plan like that?

Out of patience, Cat stomped her foot on the boardwalk. Where could Garrett be? The hard wooden plank stung the bottom of her slipper-clad foot, and she resisted the urge to hop on one foot.

What else could go wrong today?

She'd tried the mercantile first. After all, a shop like that always contained the town's gossip. Not today. Her carefully worded questions about Garrett had been met with near silence.

"Shams," she grumbled.

Her next attempt at the restaurant hadn't fared any better. She'd departed Dena's Restaurant with a frown. While her meal had been delicious and quite filling this time—thanks to her ordering for herself—success had eluded her.

She hadn't located either Garrett or his boardinghouse. Although she'd asked several pointed questions of the pretty, dark-haired proprietress, she'd received few answers in return. The citizens actually seemed protective of Garrett.

"Shams," Cat muttered.

"Tsk, tsk, such a word from a lady," a deep voice came from behind her.

She'd recognize that voice even in her sleep. *Jake Garrett.*

Cat stifled her groan and fixed a smile on her face before she turned about to face him.

"I hear you're looking for me," he announced.

His words took the breath clean out of her lungs. She stared up at him and swallowed. Twice.

"Why are you in Millwood?" he asked, his eyes never leaving her startled gaze.

"And I want the truth," he ordered.

Cat's heart skittered straight to her toes.

Chapter Seven

The truth was the one thing Cat couldn't give to Garrett.

She raised her chin in defiance without even realizing she'd done so. The sign above her head proclaiming Dena's Restaurant in bold black lettering with its red apple in the corner gave her the needed inspiration.

"I came for a teaching position."

"In Millwood?" Garrett's eyes narrowed in disbelief. "Not likely. Miss Simms has no plans of leaving that I've heard about."

Cat forced a laugh past her frozen lips. "Not here, silly."

She laid her hand over his forearm, then ignored the feel of his tensed muscles with only a great deal of effort. "In Madison."

"Madison is a ways from Millwood."

Cat's smile faded. She pretended to blink away approaching tears. "When I got there, the job was taken. I was so upset that I just got back on the train and didn't get off until it stopped here." She threw out her hands and added a sniffle for extra effect.

"What—"

"I know it was foolish of me, but I couldn't go back home a . . . ," she paused and sniffed delicately, then added in a near whisper, "a failure."

She rummaged in her reticule for a kerchief, carefully keeping the derringer concealed from his sight. She started when Garrett pressed his own handkerchief into her other hand.

Keeping her eyes averted, she spoke in a purposely low voice, "Thank you."

She raised the handkerchief to her eyes and dabbed delicately at the nonexistent tears. She felt like such a fraud. For the first time since she'd started this masquerade, her conscience rebelled at her act.

What was happening to her? And to her plan?

Cat stiffened her back and her resolve in the same moment. Just because he'd been nice and lent her his handkerchief was no reason to abandon her plan. No, not the slightest reason.

"Cat, I'm sorry," Garrett stated. His voice held a tinge of uncertainty.

She waved his apology aside. "Never mind. I'm fine." She dabbed at her eyes again.

She had to get away from him. She'd panicked when he'd caught her off guard. Not only that, she'd made up the story about a teaching job on impulse. What had happened to the planned out speech she'd set up months back? It had fled right out of her mind with Garrett's demand for the truth.

She needed time to gather her scattered thoughts and marshal her senses. He wouldn't catch her up a second time.

"Cat?" His voice held concern.

"I think I'd like to return to my hotel room." She faked another sniffle and raised her chin. "I'd like to be alone."

Turning on her heel before he could see that there wasn't a single tear stain on her cheeks, she left him standing on the boardwalk.

Garrett nudged his hat back on his head and watched her walk away. Walk, hell, the lady sashayed down the wood planks of the boardwalk, her bustle swaying with each step. Tempting. Daring him to come after her.

Not today, he responded silently.

He swore he'd never understand women. Particularly that woman. He'd caught her in a lie, and she'd had the audacity to be affronted. Figure that out.

He was beginning to believe that Caitlan Parker was a bundle of contradictions. But darned if he didn't want to unravel those tempting contradictions one by one and see what lay beneath.

When he had a chance he'd ride over to Madison and check out her story about the teaching job. One couldn't be too careful. Especially not now.

As Cat's shapely figure disappeared around a corner from his sight, he turned away and traveled back the way he'd come. A glass of Ty's private stock sounded pretty good about now.

Garrett stared out the window at the unrestricted view of the town's main street and sighed deeply. He'd taken refuge in Ty's empty office to think. And drink. What he wanted to do was drown away his thoughts of Caitlan Parker. However, he knew better.

Turning away from the window, he crossed to the desk and dropped into the chair. The sheriff wouldn't be back from his rounds for another half an hour. He nudged his hat farther back on his head, leaned the old wooden chair backward on two legs, and contemplated his glass of fine liquor.

Deep in concentration, he nursed his one self-allotted drink, sipping absently at the glass of Ty's best bourbon. A picture of Cat Parker filled his mind and absorbed his thoughts.

The yellow dress had set off her creamy skin and golden hair to perfection. It had hugged her body the way he ached to do. He tossed back the remainder of the liquor in one swallow.

Slamming the front legs of the chair to the floor, he jerked forward. His throat burned as if it had been set on fire. Tears filled his eyes, and he gasped for breath. Coughing, he could almost hear Ty yelling at him for abusing fine whiskey, telling him he ought to know better.

He should. Know better that is. Mixing thoughts of a woman and whiskey was sheer lunacy.

In truth, thinking about Cat Parker was the ultimate madness. She wasn't his type—no, not at all the kind of woman that usually appealed to him. But appeal to him she did. In spades.

Damn, he couldn't imagine a man more ill-suited for her than himself. However, he could easily imagine what her reaction would be when she learned what he was—a gunslinger.

He rubbed his thumb back and forth across the empty glass, picturing the look of horror and disdain on her face. Oh, it would be there, he had no doubt about that happening. The question was, why hadn't he told her what he was before now?

He refused to consider that the answer might be because he was coming to care for her. Just a little bit. Yeah, just a little bit too much, he thought, angrily getting to his feet.

Although by her evasive actions earlier, he wasn't the only one hiding something. The lady most definitely held a few secrets of her own. Was he interested enough in her to bother to uncover what those secrets might reveal?

A smile curved the corners of his mouth. The answer to that was clear enough that any fool could see it. He was more than interested enough. Although he told himself she merely intrigued him, he knew better.

Cat Parker was one heck of a tempting distraction. However, she was one he had to follow through with—at least for now. She'd aroused his curiosity, not to mention his desire. She'd left him no real choice in the matter.

He would pursue Cat, but cautiously.

Glancing down at the cluttered desk top, his gaze rested on a recent stack of wanted posters. Thoughts of Cat Parker had effectively distracted him from his concern for the town, but now his duty returned full force with the sight of those papers.

Picking up the wanted posters, he flipped through them. Each one in the pile bore the face of a gunfighter; some wanted for murder, some for robbery. Most of them young guns looking to find a reputation or a bullet.

All of them were looking for a showdown. Why did they

insist on trying? And many of them were headed straight for Millwood and him.

What had he brought to Millwood?

He laid the blame squarely where it belonged—on himself. His decision to quit the killing and hang up his guns had brought trouble to the town. It endangered the lives of those he'd come to care enough about to protect. But he couldn't go back to that life.

He'd grown tired of moving from one range war to the next. From one town to the next. There always seemed to be someone ready to hire a good gun. He had more than enough money saved up if he chose never to work another day in his life. His services hadn't come cheap. And at last he'd found a place to call home—to set down roots. If he lived long enough.

He hadn't thought his decision to retire his guns would bring the hornet's nest that the sheriff had referred to, but he should have at least expected this. He shook his head and tugged his Stetson lower.

How could anyone have imagined his decision to hang up his guns would bring every young gun within two states around running for the innocent town of Millwood. They were so eager to make a reputation for themselves—with his death.

If he had known, would it have changed his decision? No, he couldn't keep on the way he had been living. It was past time to start a new life for himself.

A picture of Caitlan Parker sprang to his mind. He laughed aloud. As if the fine Eastern beauty would want a life here in a small Texas town. Much less a life with a gunslinger—reformed or not.

He grabbed the bottle of bourbon, then stopped himself. He'd had his one allotted drink. He never allowed himself more than one.

Tugging open the bottom drawer of the desk, he replaced the whiskey bottle. Ty would have his hide if he left it sitting out.

As he started to push the drawer closed, it stuck at an angle. Jiggling the drawer to right it, he shoved again, but it wouldn't close. He bent down to check it out and found a clump of old paper wedged tight behind the whiskey bottle. He yanked out the paper.

Curiosity demanded he take a look. He unfolded the crumpled page, straightening it with his hand. Then he stared down at the rumpled paper and wished he hadn't given in to that curiosity.

A younger version of his own face looked back at him from the poster, below the bold printed words "Wanted Dead Or Alive." The charge of "Murder" jumped out at him. A long-ago memory of the Indian village swamped him.

Garrett resisted the sudden impulse to wad the poster up and throw it away or hide it out of sight forever. What good would it do? Ty had obviously already seen it. The question remained in Garrett's mind—what did his friend plan to do about it?

The instinct to flee came on strong and hard. As he fought it back, curling his one hand into a fist, the door swung open.

Sheriff Ty Friedman stepped inside, then stopped dead still.

Garrett met his questioning gaze straight on. For the space of an instant neither man moved or spoke.

"Find something of interest?" Ty asked, taking a step into the room and finally breaking the tense silence.

Garrett merely held up the wanted poster of himself.

"Nice likeness." Ty nodded at the paper.

Garrett dropped the poster onto the top of the desk, instinctively freeing both of his hands. "Why?" He fired out the single word like a rifle shot.

"Why do I have it, or why'd I keep it?" Ty's voice was casual, but held an edge to it.

"Both," Garrett snapped.

"For the first, it's part of my job."

Garrett tensed, his right hand going to rest atop his gun out of years of habit.

"You gonna draw on me?" Ty accused.

"No. You know I've never drawn down on any lawman." Garrett raised his hand off his gun butt.

"I knew." Ty merely raised one eyebrow, then continued, "For the second reason, I was waiting for the right time to show it to you."

"Think it's the right time?"

His friend smiled. "It better be."

The tension left the room like air escaping.

"First time I've seen it." Garrett glanced away from him and back at the wanted poster.

"Figured as much."

Garrett looked back at the other man, a question in his eyes.

"It came out years ago. It's never been posted in this town. Or many others either." Ty stopped and rubbed his chin. "As far as I know, most folks, lawmen included, believe the story that Lieutenant Jacob Garritson died in that Indian raid way back."

Garrett's breath left in a rush. He hadn't realized he'd been holding it. That long-ago day still lived in his memory. He'd nearly died from a wound received that day, but he hadn't.

"Couldn't see no sense in putting up a wanted poster for a dead man. Could you?" Ty walked forward and clasped Garrett's shoulder.

"What about when I came to town? Didn't you recognize me?"

"I did. But I'd heard the rumors about that raid. So, I waited and I watched."

The corner of Garrett's lip quirked up. "I thought at the time you seemed a mite interested in my activities."

"Like I said, I watched. And I began to like what I saw."

"What's that?"

"A man who cared about this town and its people. A man by the name of Jake Garrett."

Garrett stiffened. "And now?"

"Far as I'm concerned"—Ty gestured to the poster—"that man's dead."

"Thanks."

"Then say it by taking the job as my deputy. Then at least you'd be getting pay for what you're already doing now."

"Ty, you know I can't. Not yet. Not until this hornet's nest is over and done with."

"And then?"

"We'll see." Garrett tugged his hat low and, turning on his heel, walked out the door.

Cat shut the door behind her and turned the lock. Only then did she allow herself to relax. She sagged weakly against the wood. What was happening to her?

Where had her normal, everyday competence gone to? It had most assuredly fled the moment she'd stepped off the train in Millwood.

And met Jake Garrett again, her conscience whispered.

That's when everything started going wrong.

Sighing in frustration, she pushed herself away from the door. Out of habit, she glanced about the room, instinctively checking for anything that might have been disturbed.

An uneasy feeling crept over her. Chill bumps broke out over her arms and spread up to her neck, then slowly inched down her back. Had someone visited her room in her absence?

Something drew her gaze to her carpetbag. She crossed to it and stared at where the bag sat on the chair. It appeared the same, but she had to be certain. As she touched the clasp, a comforting warmth spread from her fingertips to her shoulder.

She shook off the strange feeling and opened the carpetbag. Carefully, she removed the items, checking each one over for tampering. She found nothing out of the ordinary. Her guns were cleaned and oiled like she'd left them. The pink ribbon remained about Jesse's two letters.

The unusual feeling persisted in spite of these reassurances. Cocking her head, she surveyed the area. The window remained closed and locked. A look through her clothing showed nothing out of place either. Each and every one of her gowns hung in the armoire just as she'd left them. Still, something *felt* wrong.

A brief, but thorough, search of the remainder of her hotel room turned up nothing amiss. Cat stood in the middle of her room and slowly shook her head. It must simply be her nerves.

Between her masquerade, and spending time in Garrett's presence, her nerves were stretched too taut. Not to mention her meeting with Bill Thomas.

At the recollection of her old friend's warning, a touch of fear swept through her. How had an outlaw gang come to know her name? And why would it hold any interest to them?

Perhaps Bill had misunderstood. Yet a part of her intelligence refused to accept that possibility. No, he had been quite certain of his information. Certain enough to risk a visit to warn her.

Now it fell upon her to warn the town of Millwood. Somehow.

No, she couldn't, not without the danger of certain discovery.

Cat kicked at the floral rug in frustration. She couldn't *not* warn the town either.

Innocent people could be killed if she did nothing. But what was she supposed to do? And how could she give any warning without exposing herself?

Whirling about, she began to pace the confines of the room. Back and forth, back and forth between the window and the door. A sudden picture of Garrett filled her mind, stopping her in mid-step.

He could be one of those killed if the outlaw gang rode into town without warning. The thought gave her no comfort. She wasn't so certain that she wanted to see Jake Garrett dead. Not now.

Not after she'd seen him again, spoken to him again, been kissed by him again.

She jerked out of her wayward thoughts. Of course she still wanted him dead. She'd promised it upon Jesse's grave. Then she'd renewed that vow at her father's grave site a few months later.

It was too late to turn back now. She had a promise to fulfill. To Jesse. And to herself.

She also had a town to save.

Cat crossed back to the window and stared out at the scene below. A wagon rumbled down the street while a man and a woman waited to cross until the dust cleared. Two women, one a statuesque blonde and the other a petite redhead, stood outside the Long and Short Saloon, taking in the afternoon sunlight. Down the street, two little boys played with a golden puppy at the front of an alley.

Whirling away, she strode to her carpetbag and withdrew the packet of letters. Whispering an apology to Jesse, she tore a strip from the back of one of the envelopes.

Without giving herself a chance to change her mind or rethink her decision, Cat tucked the paper into her reticule and headed for the door. At the last moment, she recalled that a lady didn't venture out into the bright sunlight without protection, and she grabbed up her silk parasol. Not daring to stop again, she slipped out of her room and walked down the stairs to the lobby.

She crossed to the desk with her head held high in a pose that dared anyone to question her intentions. Pausing at the desk, she smiled at the clerk and picked up the pen beside the register as if it were something she did all the time.

Her heart thudded in her chest. Why, it sounded so loud that she was surprised that the young clerk didn't remark about it. She flashed him another smile, and he reddened and turned away, busying himself with adjusting the notes in the pigeon-holes behind the desk.

Cat barely restrained her own smile. Now he wouldn't be able to see what she was doing. Without giving pause, she wrote out a brief warning on the scrap of paper, leaving it unsigned.

The slightest sigh of relief escaped her lips as she replaced the pen beside the register. Checking that the desk clerk's attention was still focused elsewhere, she turned away from the desk and closed her eyes for the instant it took her to regain her poise.

Careful not to make a betraying noise, she folded the missive and placed it in her reticule.

Now all she had to do was deliver it to the sheriff's office without anyone seeing her.

Chapter Eight

"Ma'am? Please wait up."

At the unexpected sound of a voice behind her, issuing the request, Cat's breath caught in her chest. She couldn't answer him, couldn't even move a limb. She waited for certain disaster to come to her.

She'd been found out.

She gritted her teeth, anticipating the humiliation and unveiling that was headed straight for her.

"Ma'am," the desk clerk called after her again. "Miss Parker."

Feeling like a wooden toy, she turned about to face the approaching young man. She licked now parched lips, still unable to answer his summons.

"Yes?" Cat finally got the single word out past her uncooperative mouth.

"Ma'am, you forgot your parasol." The young man held out the frilly silk and lace object to her while he kept his gaze nearly glued to the wood floor.

She stared at him, then looked at the lady's parasol in his hand, dumbfounded, almost as if she didn't see it.

That was what the uproar was all about?

A silly bit of fluff? She hadn't been found out. Her masquerade remained intact, if she could manage to recover her senses and act like a lady would in the commonplace situation.

The clerk stepped closer, offering her a shy smile, the frilly parasol extended in one hand. "Ma'am? Are you all right?"

His question released her from the trancelike state. She forced a brief laugh, then followed it with a smile.

"Oh, how silly of me. Did I leave that here?" She lowered her lashes in what she hoped passed for demure embarrassment. "I declare, the beautiful sunshine outside distracted me."

She feared she was overdoing her role. In truth, she knew she was chattering, but didn't seem able to stop herself. She was plumb giddy with relief.

As she took the parasol from him, she flashed him another wide smile of thanks. The young man reddened and looked down at the floor. However, she swore she could feel the eyes of every other person in the lobby staring right at her.

So much for slipping out unnoticed.

Although she felt the scrutiny of the others directed at her, she pretended complete unawareness of the stir she'd caused. She smoothed the parasol with hands that trembled ever so slightly.

"Why, thank you so much," she added.

With an airy wave, she turned toward the door again. This time she made it almost halfway across the room before reaction set in, and she was certain that everyone could see the way her hands shook now.

Cat hesitated, thinking of the risk involved if she continued in her present course to deliver the note to the sheriff's office, of all places to go in the state she was in. She stood held in place for a minute, not certain she could continue.

Another picture of Garrett swept through her mind, his tall, lean body riddled with bullets and lying in a pool of blood. She closed her eyes, but the horrifying image remained with her.

No, she objected.

She wanted him dead, but not . . .

No, not . . .

She nibbled on her lower lip in confusion. She imagined she heard him moan and covered her mouth with her hand.

She glanced about. Realization shamed her; it had been her own voice she'd heard moaning, not his.

Horrified at both the picture and her own reaction, she knew she had her answer. She had to give the warning. She had no other choice.

She lowered her hand and tightened her fingers about the strings of her drawstring bag. Still worrying her lower lip, she drew in a breath for courage, raised her chin, and walked the remainder of the way across the lobby to the hotel doorway.

Pausing at the open doors, she sent up a prayer for heaven's assistance before she stepped outside into the bright sunlight.

Tamera snapped to attention as she distinctly heard the plea for heavenly intervention from Cat Parker. The young lady was praying?

She could scarce believe her sensitive hearing. Could this be the turnaround in the woman's behavior that she'd been hoping for and praying for herself?

With a smile on her face, Tamera left Garrett sitting at a card game in the Long and Short Saloon and flew to the hotel. One look at the nervous expression on Cat's face told her something was very wrong. She'd never seen her this worried before.

Tamera's heart sank at the sight. Cat was worried, not repentant. Obviously, she had not relented in her plan to kill Garrett.

Disappointed, Tamera decided to remain nearby and find out exactly what the woman was up to this time. She tried to see into Cat's mind, but she found an extremely strong-willed woman met her attempt. Well, she would simply follow her instead.

Cat strolled down the boardwalk as if she had no particular destination in mind. However, Tamera knew otherwise. She could feel the determination coming from Cat in waves of near desperation.

Tamera noticed that Cat's gaze kept straying to the sheriff's office. How unusual. She would think the lawman's place of business would be the last the young woman would be interested in checking.

Perhaps a little assistance was in order.

Tamera flew across the street and into the office. She found Ty at the desk working on some papers. A quick whisper convinced him that it was past time for his rounds. Grabbing up his hat, he left the building and strode down the street.

Now to see what Miss Cat Parker was up to, Tamera thought to herself with a smile.

Cat nibbled on her fingertip, her gaze returning to the sheriff's office yet again. She couldn't very well simply walk in and hand him the note.

As she continued to wait and watch his doorway, the sheriff walked out into the street. To Cat's relief, he didn't even spare her a glance before he walked down the street in the opposite direction.

She took a second to close her eyes and send up a prayer of thanksgiving. Then, gripping her reticule and her courage, she lifted her skirt and stepped off the boardwalk. Her heart pounded with each step she took that drew her nearer to the sheriff's office.

She glanced over her shoulder; an uneasy feeling of being watched plagued her. Although she couldn't find a soul observing her, the feeling remained.

What if the lawman returned too soon?

Fear of discovery lent her speed, and Cat ran across the dusty street. She hoped no one noticed her rush or if they did, they attributed it to an approaching horse and wagon.

Stepping onto the boardwalk in front of the sheriff's office, she shot a cautious glance up and down the planks before she crossed into the vacated office.

"Hello?" she called out in a soft voice in case someone waited inside.

She glanced around the room. "Anyone here?" she asked, her voice uneven.

Her query was unanswered. She sighed aloud in relief and tiptoed across the flooring to the desk. Her heart nearly in her throat, she reached into her drawstring bag and withdrew the note.

Pushing aside the scattering of papers, she paused to unfold the note, then laid the warning faceup on the very center of the desk. There was no way it could be missed.

Cat whirled about and barely stopped herself from racing to the doorway. Instead, she forced herself to walk at a ladylike pace to the door.

At the open doorway, she drew in a ragged breath of relief. She'd done it.

Now what she wanted to do was run back across the street and straight up the stairs to her room. However, she knew that might well draw unwanted attention to herself and her recent actions.

Her throat felt like it was filled with cotton. A cool drink would be wonderful now. She'd take an everyday stroll down the boardwalk to an eatery and order a ladylike lemonade. She truly wished it could be a bracing shot of whiskey. In fact, she licked her lips in wishful thinking and stepped out the door.

Garrett paused at the batwing doors of the saloon and looked up and down the street before exiting. A practice born of habit, he never forgot to employ it.

A grin tipped his lips this time. His habit had allowed him to catch a glimpse of Cat down the street. He stepped toward her, then noticed she was leaving the sheriff's office. Ty had passed the saloon on his rounds almost ten minutes ago. His office would be quite deserted.

What had Cat been doing in the sheriff's office? As he neared where she stood, he noticed the look of guilt spread across her face.

What was she up to now?

He intended to find out.

As Cat turned away from the door and walked down the boardwalk, Garrett hurried his stride to catch up with her. Near enough to ensure he couldn't lose track of her, he slowed his pace and fell into step a safe distance behind her.

At least he thought he was a good, safe ways behind. Then the impossible happened. Cat reached the edge of the board-walk, and as she began to step down, she appeared to lose her balance. She wavered, then fell backward. There was nothing for him to do but be certain he broke her fall. He couldn't chance her hurting herself.

In a lightning-fast move he lunged forward, and Cat fell right into his waiting arms.

Garrett stared down at her. Her startled green gaze met his, and for the space of a heartbeat she didn't even blink.

Cat could feel the heat of Garrett's body pressed intimately against the full length of her back. Her skin warmed beneath her gown as if the fabric wasn't even there separating them.

She gasped in shock at the path her thoughts had taken.

What was it about being near Garrett that did this to her? It seemed all she had to do was get near him, and her usual competence deserted her. Totally. Completely. Absolutely.

The unwelcome heat of a blush stole up her neck and flooded her cheeks with what she knew to be a betraying shade of pink. Anger at herself followed right on its heels.

"Unhand me," she ordered through gritted teeth.

A muscle twitched in response in Garrett's jaw, and she stared at it in fascination. His eyes narrowed an instant later at her insult.

"Whatever you say, ma'am."

He let his arms fall to his sides, releasing her.

Cat landed on her backside with a thump. A cloud of dust rose up about her. To add to her indignity, she sneezed.

"Bless you." Garrett tipped his hat to her. Then he stepped around where she sat sprawled on the dirt and walked away.

Cat gritted her teeth, biting back the hasty words that nearly dared to break free from her restraint. A lady most assuredly didn't scream insults after a man on a public street.

If she had her Colt right now, she swore she'd shoot him.

Cat sputtered in fury, muttering dire threats at Garrett's departing back. Pushing herself to her feet, she dusted off her gown. Head held high, she caught up her skirt with one hand and her parasol in the other and strode across the street to the hotel.

She didn't stop calling down every wrath she could imagine on Garrett's head until she reached her own room. She slammed the door behind her with a determined swing of her arm. The sound echoed in the hallway.

"I should have let you die in the robbery from those outlaws," she mumbled.

No, shooting was too good for him. He should be strung up. Hanged. Then he should be shot.

She threw her parasol across the room where it thudded harmlessly to the floor.

"I'll get you for this, Jake Garrett," she swore to the empty room.

The remainder of the evening was filled with her repeating the litany of ways the callous gunslinger should meet his maker. Cat was still in a fury when she at last crawled into bed.

Cat's sleep that night was troubled by strange dreams. She awoke feeling disoriented and out of sorts. A headache plagued her, and she held her head in her hands for a minute. Plumping her pillow behind her back, she sat up and looked about the small room.

Oddly enough her first thought upon looking over the sun-filled space was that the hotel room had a bleak and dreary appearance. Perhaps she should move to the boardinghouse.

Cat glanced around the room in amazement. It felt as if

someone had actually said the words aloud. She almost expected someone to step out from behind the chair in the next breath.

Nervous and suddenly on edge, she looked over the room again, making certain it was empty of any unwanted guests. The room remained as empty as when she'd gone to bed the night before.

She shook her head, both to clear it and to dispel the errant thought of relocating. The hotel room suited her fine. She didn't plan on sticking around town much longer anyway. She didn't have a single good reason to move to a boardinghouse.

No, not one.

As soon as she challenged Garrett to a gunfight and shot him, she would be leaving Millwood. Forever.

Tossing back the covers in abrupt determination, she climbed out of bed. She would spend part of the morning rearranging her few possessions in the room.

And avoiding Garrett, her conscience accused.

She shushed it.

She never wanted to lay eyes on him again.

Chapter Nine

"What do you think, Ty?" Garrett leaned over the desk and reread the note warning of an outlaw gang.

His friend shoved his hat on his head. "I think we'd better take this seriously. But it beats me who could have left it here."

"When did you first find it?"

"I found it when I came back from rounds yesterday afternoon. I'd have told you sooner if you hadn't been away on a ride."

"I had some thinking to do," Garrett answered.

He refused to admit to himself, much less to his closest friend, that the subject of his thoughts had been Cat Parker. The woman could get under his skin worse than an insect bite.

And she was about as irritating. Not to mention unsettling.

Ty's words suddenly came back to Garrett. Rounds yesterday?

"Are you sure?" he asked.

Ty frowned in confusion. " 'Bout what?"

''When you found the note?'' Garrett's words were sharper than he intended.

''Of course I'm sure. What kind of a fool do you think I am?'' Ty retorted.

Garrett ignored the remark. The sheriff had been on his rounds yesterday when he'd seen Cat outside this very office.

No, he discarded the idea.

Cat could not have left the note. What would a fine lady from back East know about an outlaw gang? Besides, if she'd left the note, it would've been written on fancy scented parchment not scribbled on the back of a torn scrap of paper.

Wouldn't it?

Garrett thought on it for a moment, then discarded the possibility again.

However, a vague inkling of something not being quite right remained behind. He shoved it aside and faced his friend.

''Garrett?'' Ty called out.

''What?''

''That's the second time I've called your name.''

''Just thinking. So, what are we going to do?''

''I'm going to deputize me a few extra men. And post guards in the bank.'' Ty reached in the desk drawer and picked up a badge.

Before Garrett could refuse, he tossed it at him.

''Pin it on,'' Ty ordered.

As Garrett opened his mouth to refuse, his friend raised his hand.

''Either stay out of this, or pin it on.''

Left with that choice, Garrett clenched his teeth and pinned the badge to his shirt.

''As soon as this is over—''

''I know,'' Ty answered for him. ''You're giving it back.''

He shook his head, and Garrett heard him mutter something about fools. He chose to ignore the disparaging remark for both their sakes.

His sixth sense was causing the back of his neck to tingle.

Glancing about the room, Garrett rubbed the spot, then resettled his hat firmly.

Something strange was going on.

Tamera leaned over Ty's shoulder and read the note. She shivered at the overheard conversation.

Outlaws? Coming to town?

Whatever was she to do?

She would not let them harm a hair on Garrett's head. The instant he'd pinned on that shiny badge, her feathers had unsettled in a most disorderly fashion. Her wings still stood out at odd angles.

She simply must calm herself. Or she'd never be able to think up a plan to stop those . . . those . . . outlaw bandits.

Why imagine, an outlaw gang coming into town to rob these nice people. And possibly harm Garrett. Well, she would simply not allow it. That's all there was to it.

She tossed her head in determination, and her halo slipped to one side where it rested on the edge of her white curls. As she took a deep breath to calm herself, her gown slid off one shoulder.

"Oh, feathers!"

She slapped her hand over her mouth. But it was too late.

Garrett turned to glance at Ty. "What did you say?"

"I didn't say anything."

"I could have sworn I heard something," Garrett muttered.

Tamera held her hand tighter over her mouth before anything else could slip out. Oh, dear. She'd have to be more careful.

The reprimand gave her an idea. This time a small, tinkling giggle escaped.

Garrett nudged his hat back on his head and fired an edgy glance about the room.

Tamera tugged up the errant neckline of her gown and flew out of the room as fast as her wings could carry her. A burst of laughter followed along.

Wait until the outlaws got a peek of what she had in store for them.

By the time the group of five men reached the edge of Millwood, angel Tamera was ready for them. In fact, she waited in ill-concealed excitement.

These men wouldn't get close enough to lay eyes on her charge, much less harm him in any way. Or anyone else in the town. Not while Garrett and the people of Millwood were under her protection, she vowed.

Tamera fluttered downward, directly in the path of the approaching riders. The horses began to edge aside nervously, even before her toes touched the road.

Taking a deep breath, she closed her eyes and let out a righteous scream of indignation.

Every single one of the five horses reared in terror. Two of the animals turned and bolted back down the way they had come, heedless of their riders pulling on the reins. A third horse stood still, shaking, its eyes rolling in fear.

Tamera reached out and thumped the horse solidly on the rump with her thumb and forefinger. The animal bucked wildly, throwing his rider into the air. The outlaw hit the ground with a satisfying thud. The instant he scrambled to his feet, he yelled and ran off after his horse.

She dusted her hands together. Three down and two to go.

All about her pandemonium reigned. The men's shouts could be heard all the way to the center of town. Behind her, she could see people gathering in the street to watch.

Oh, dear.

Sucking in a deep breath, she blew it out directly at the two remaining horses and outlaws. A whirlwind of dust rose into the air. It nearly unseated the two riders, and they had to grab for their pommels in a desperate bid to remain on their mounts. Two hats flew into the air in unison and rolled on the wind out of sight.

The men hung on desperately to any part of their saddles

they could grab hold of as their horse's turned and wildly raced in the direction the hats had taken.

Tamera tossed her head, resettled her halo, and dusted off her hands.

"And good riddance," she called out at their departing backs.

The storm stilled, and all about her grew ominously quiet. She held her breath, waiting.

"Tamera!" a voice shouted.

"Oh, feathers," she whispered to herself.

She threaded her fingers together in her gown's folds and cringed at the censure in St. Peter's voice. Sighing, she flew for heaven and another sure-to-be stern lecture from her superior.

Garrett stood alongside Ty and watched the strange storm dissipate into nothingness. The odd sensation at the back of his neck returned with a vengeance.

"Now, what on earth spooked those horses that way?" he muttered.

"Never seen the likes of a windstorm like that before, did you?" Ty asked the men around him, including Garrett.

Each one shook his head in stunned response.

They stood in the center of town, watching the riders head down the road away from them at a speed that was almost inhuman.

Ty slapped Garrett on the back. "I don't care how they left, so long as they left."

Garrett merely raised his brows. Something damned unusual was going on. He intended to get to the bottom of whatever was behind it. And Miss Cat Parker seemed the perfect place to start.

He turned on his heel and strode down the street, headed in a direct line for the only hotel in town. Cat's hotel.

Cat saw him coming from her vantage point in front of the hotel. She curled her fingers tighter on the revolver hidden in the folds of her skirt. As she watched Garrett walking closer, it seemed as if he were headed right for her.

He was!

Her eyes met Garrett's, and she raised her chin in a subtle gesture of defiance, forgetting for the moment all about being a fancy Eastern lady. He didn't even give pause, only sending her a nod of acceptance to her challenge.

"Oh, shams," she muttered under her breath.

Whirling about, she turned and ran inside the hotel, and straight up the stairs.

She was not running, she told herself. She had merely made a tactical retreat. She retreated all the way to her room, slamming the door shut in her wake.

Not daring to risk even a brief pause to catch her breath, she dashed across the room and tucked her revolver deep in the recesses of her carpetbag, hiding it from Garrett's observant gaze. She turned around and faced the door. Waiting.

A loud knock pounded on her door. Although she'd expected it, she still jumped guiltily. She stared at the wooden panel, hesitant to open it, yet knowing she had no choice.

Dare she hope Garrett didn't know anything about the warning note? She didn't believe that would be a safe assumption. She could be certain the sheriff had showed it to him. Now what?

Another knock sounded; this time it rattled the wood. She knew she'd better open the door before he knocked it down.

Smoothing down her skirt and tucking up a wayward curl, she crossed to the door. She paused for an instant and plastered a smile of welcome to her lips. How long it would last she dared not wager a guess. But she'd try her darnedest to keep it there.

The moment she swung the door open and met Garrett's hardened gaze, she knew her smile would be short-lived.

"Why did you run, Cat?" he asked in a deceptively low voice.

It didn't fool her for an instant.

She lowered her chin and stared at the floor in a false gesture of meekness. A sentiment she was far from feeling.

"I . . . I was upset by all the dust—"

"The truth, Cat," he ordered.

This time she knew she couldn't give him a falsehood. Not without him seeing right through it. Not in the mood he was in.

"I was frightened," she stated, raising her chin and meeting his gaze head on.

Her statement was the truth. Just not all of it.

She had been afraid. Afraid that he'd catch her with her Colt .45 in her hand at the wrong time.

Swearing, Garrett pushed the door aside, stepped into the room, and swept her into his arms. He kicked the door shut with a booted foot.

Cat was too startled to utter a single sound. Much less a protest.

Garrett buried his face in her neck, and she could feel his ragged sigh. "What were you doing outside during that?"

"Watching," she whispered, unable to get her full voice back under control.

As he set her from him, her voice returned along with her senses.

"Everyone else in town was looking, too," she fired at him in defense.

"Cat, you could have been hurt."

She opened her mouth to tell him she could take care of herself and had been doing so for three years, then shut it before the words could escape. How in heavens was she supposed to explain that?

"Mr. Garrett?" A young man's hesitant voice came from the other side of the door.

Cat recognized the desk clerk's Texas accent immediately.

"What?" Garrett yelled in response.

"Is everything all right with Miss Parker?"

"It's the clerk—"

Garrett cut her off. "Everything is fine." The words were clipped and short.

"Well, Mr. Garrett—" the young man cleared his throat before he continued—"Sheriff Ty told me to come and tell you there's going to be a dance tonight."

"Very well. Tell him thank you."

"Mister—"

"I'll be down in a minute," Garrett snapped in a voice that dared to be defied.

They heard the sound of running footsteps at this.

A smile tugged at Cat's lips. "Did you have to be so harsh with him?"

"Yup."

She shut her mouth on whatever else she'd been going to say. The look in Garrett's eyes said it all.

Heavens.

She took a hesitant step backward, knowing the wisest course was to put more distance between them.

His next words stopped her in mid-step.

"Cat, come to the dance with me tonight."

It was a thinly veiled order. One she could no more refuse than she could willingly stop breathing.

She merely nodded in response.

Garrett smiled, then tipped his hat to her. He stepped back and turned away. A moment later the door shut on his departing figure.

Cat stared at the closed door. What had she just agreed to? And why hadn't she told him no?

Because she couldn't, a little voice taunted her with irritating persistence. Her conscience nagged at her, making matters worse.

Within no time at all, the town was buzzing with the news of the outlaw gang's sudden departure and obvious change of plans. Even Cat heard all about it from the hotel desk clerk. It seemed no one could talk of anything else. Thankfully, the strange goings-on took precedence, and the warning note was never mentioned.

Cat fluctuated between eagerly preparing for the dance and devising a half dozen different refusals to send to Garrett. Finally, after she'd nearly paced a path into the flooring, she made her decision. She'd go with him. But she wouldn't enjoy herself.

No, not the tiniest bit.

She pulled her favorite new gown from the armoire. One glance at it, and she smiled. It was a beautiful ivory silk creation. The skirt was richly embroidered with silk of the same creamy tint. She ran her hand almost lovingly down the skirt and trailed her fingers across the ruffled flounce at the hem. Suddenly impatient, she laid the gown across the bed and began to undress.

Almost three-quarters of an hour later, she was ready. She stood before the mirror, staring at herself in awe and disbelief. Why, she was almost beautiful.

The gown would make any woman feel so, she told herself. The bodice hugged her breasts snugly, but not too tightly. It gave her body a shape she'd never quite noticed before.

Nervous, she tugged the fine material upward. It didn't budge. If anything, it dipped a little lower. She gave up, instead smoothing down the skirt. She'd have to get used to the way a lady's clothes fit—if she stuck around here long enough.

Cat worried her lower lip, nibbling at it. She jumped and nearly bit it when a knock sounded at the door.

He was here.

She swallowed down her nervousness. There was no reason to be nervous, she told herself. However, her nerves were having nothing to do with the false reassurance.

Her heart sped up, and her palms grew damp. She resisted the urge to wipe her hands on her skirt. Instead, she swept up her wrap and reticule and wiped her palms on the drawstring bag. At the same time, she checked that her derringer was safely tucked inside. There wasn't any chance she was leaving this room without it—not when an outlaw gang had expressed interest in her.

At the feel of the little gun, she felt much more ready to

face the evening ahead. She slipped on her gloves and walked across the room. She could swear her knees were knocking together.

Cat opened the door with a sudden show of faked bravado. She told herself she was ready to meet anything. The sight of Garrett dressed in a white shirt and dark pants nearly stole her breath away. She feared it might never return when he took her arm and led her out the door.

The town hall was gaily lit with lanterns. Cat could scarcely believe her eyes. On one table cakes, breads, and baskets of sweets practically overflowed. Another table held a bowl of punch.

Garrett laid her wrap aside and swept Cat into his arms and out onto the improvised dance floor. The soft strains of a waltz filled the air about them. Cat assured herself that the money she'd spent on a rushed set of dance lessons in Fort Worth had been money well spent.

No one would ever be able to tell that she'd never danced up until a month ago. Not if she kept track of her feet, and counted off each and every step silently to herself.

Studious, she counted one, two, three. It was the only way she could dare even hope to remain unaffected by the feel of Garrett's strong arms about her. An unusual warmth flowed through her body, and she was smart enough to know that it had nothing to do with the dance steps, and everything to do with being held by Jake Garrett.

When at last the music came to an end, Cat scarcely held back her sigh of relief, although a small part of her almost moaned aloud in disappointment.

A Virginia reel was announced next, and once again Garrett caught her hands in his. Her heart raced straight for the toes of her slippers at the contact.

Thankfully, keeping up with the steps and moves took all her concentration. Well, almost all. There was still room for errant thoughts of how handsome Garrett looked and how well he danced. She'd never known he could dance. Much less so well.

Maybe there was a lot more she didn't know about him, a little voice of conscience hinted to her. She brushed it aside and nearly missed the next step. Garrett caught her hand and drew her along with him under the arch made by another couple.

When the dance ended, Cat was out of breath. Whether from the contact with Garrett or keeping pace with the music, she didn't know. And she wasn't certain she wanted to know the true answer.

At last Garrett left her side to go and obtain a drink of punch for her. Cat released a sigh of relief. However, no sooner had he walked ten paces away, than several men converged on her.

One hand flew to her throat to hold back a cry of fear while she reached inside her reticule with her other hand. Whatever could the townsmen want with her?

Her fingers securely on her derringer, she felt her courage returning full force. Her chin raised, she met the men with a tight smile of greeting.

"Ma'am, may I have the honor of this dance?" asked a tall man she remembered seeing at the mercantile.

"Hey, I was first in line," another man objected.

"Can I have the next one?" a slender man almost shouted at her.

Cat took an instinctive step backward. She stared in open-mouthed amazement at the cluster of men standing in front of her. They had encircled her because they wanted to dance with her? She shook her head in disbelief. Such a thing had never happened to her in her life.

"Miss Parker, if you would—" a fourth man spoke up, suddenly taking advantage of her confusion.

"Fellas!" A slender, dark-haired woman not much older than Cat pushed her way through the men surrounding her. "Give a body a chance to catch her breath."

The men grudgingly made way for the woman. Cat eyed her cautiously.

"Hello, I'm Sarah Miles." The woman stuck out her hand.

Cat shook the woman's hand. "I'm—"

"No need to say it. The entire town knows it by now," Sarah announced with a grin.

Cat tensed, waiting for whatever might come. She stiffened her back and raised her chin, preparing to be unmasked. If the whole town knew her name, what else did they know? And how?

"Millwood is a small town." Sarah laughed softly. "And a little too interested in everybody else sometimes. But welcome."

"Ma'am," the tall man interrupted.

"Okay, fellas. I give her up." Sarah threw up her hands at the men's persistence. She leaned closer to Cat and whispered, "Enjoy," followed by a wink and a wicked smile.

The first man to speak up took Cat's hand in his and drew her out onto the dance floor. "Name's Matt Newson, ma'am."

Cat smiled up at him, quite flattered by his attentiveness. As they began to dance, she silently counted each step so as not to trip on his feet.

It took less than twenty minutes of dancing for Cat to lose track of the names of her various partners. It seemed that no sooner had one dance ended, than she was claimed by a different partner. She'd never had such an experience in her life.

Another waltz began, and Matt whatever his name was drew her into his arms and out onto the floor. They had only taken a few steps when he suddenly stopped dead still. She saw his eyes widen at something behind her.

Turning her head, she glanced back over her shoulder and straight into Garrett's heated gaze.

"I'm cutting in."

Garrett didn't bother with the accustomed pleasantry of asking if he could. He simply did it.

He pulled Cat out of the other man's arms and into his own. However, Garrett held her much tighter and closer than any of the other men had dared to do.

"Are you enjoying yourself?" Garrett's voice was strained.

Without even considering her answer, Cat responded with a grin, "Oh, yes."

"I thought so. You've danced with every man here except for old Mr. Bates, the piano player."

She pushed back from him a bit so she could look up into his face. He appeared angry. Very angry.

"Is something wrong?" she asked in confusion.

"No," he snapped. "What could be wrong?"

Cat shrugged at his odd reaction and continued counting her steps. Although, she noticed that strangely she didn't need to watch her feet nearly as closely when she danced with Garrett. She wondered for a second why ever that could be.

Suddenly Garrett whirled her away from the other dancers and into a secluded corner. Before she could do more than glance up at him and part her lips, his head descended and his lips claimed hers. Cat forgot all about her feet.

And everything else as well.

Chapter Ten

One thought penetrated Cat's senses.

Why couldn't she truly be a real lady from New York and have only met Garrett this week?

The foolish question acted like a splash of cold water to Cat's heated body. She pulled out of Garrett's embrace with a jerk.

"How—"

"Oh, excuse me," a woman interrupted, apologizing profusely. "How clumsy of me. I'm sorry."

When she stepped back, Cat recognized Sarah Miles. But it was the glimpse of Garrett's face that held her spellbound. Fury emanated from him in waves.

Puzzled, Cat turned her attention back to him, and what she saw caused her lips to twitch with laughter. Red punch ran in rivulets down the side of his white shirt and dripped onto his dark pants.

"Oh, I am sorry to have done that." The twinkle in Sarah's eyes belied her too earnest apology. "And the punch was so cold, too."

Cat felt her lips twitch as she tried to hold in her sudden

giggle. Why, the woman had done it on purpose. That much was quite obvious.

"You really must be more careful, Garrett," Sarah remarked in a low voice. "Things can get *ruined* so easily." She glanced from him to Cat and back to him again.

Comprehension struck Cat with the force of a slap across her face. If she'd been caught in Garrett's arms—being so thoroughly kissed—by a town gossip, her own reputation would be ruined.

If not for Sarah's intervention, Cat's reputation would be in complete tatters. She raised her hands to her face in embarrassment.

How could she have allowed him such . . . such liberties!

She could have ruined far more than her name. She could have ruined her plans. And her future.

"Cat, how about a nice piece of Miss Simms's cake?" Sarah caught her arm and pulled her in her wake.

Cat followed without the slightest resistance. She could scarcely believe what she'd done.

And with Garrett.

"I . . ." Cat paused to clear her throat. "Thank you, Sarah."

The other woman waved her words away. "I've been in love before myself."

"But I'm not in love," Cat denied in a loud voice.

"Shush." Sarah patted her shoulder and continued pulling her away from Garrett. "You really must come visit me tomorrow. I run the boardinghouse two streets over from your hotel."

Cat stared at her in amazement.

"We'll have a good long talk if you want." Sarah winked at her, then handed her a slice of cake.

The remainder of the evening passed in a blur of music and an assortment of partners. None of them Garrett. Sarah maneuvered Cat and Garrett apart and carefully kept it so. While Cat realized she'd done it for the sake of her reputation, a part of her resented the interference.

She told herself it was only because she didn't like relinquishing control. However, she knew that was a falsehood. A part of her wanted to be in Garrett's arms again. If only for a brief dance.

By morning, Cat's sanity had returned, along with her anger at Garrett. How dare he compromise her in such a manner?

She was supposed to be a fine lady. However, she didn't feel much like one at the moment. She was embarrassed, tired from a restless night's sleep, and her feet hurt. Not to mention that she was mad as a wet hen in a rainstorm.

Cat paced the room in a swish of skirts. Her lavender gown whirled about her feet with her agitated steps while her eyes snapped with growing fury. Kicking the skirt out of her way, she paced the width of the room again.

Stopping, she crossed to the chair and sank down. She rubbed the bottom of one foot, then stomped the other foot in a burst of anger.

"Just who does he think he is?"

Cat clapped her hand over her mouth when she realized she'd spoken the words aloud. Now he had her talking to herself.

"Damn you, Jake Garrett."

This time she didn't care if she'd sworn even aloud.

The room suddenly felt overly warm to her. As an uneasy sense nagged her, she slowly looked around the room. She could swear someone was watching her. But that was foolish, wasn't it?

Tamera looked down from her perch atop the armoire and stared at Cat. Oh, feathers. Things were not going at all the way she planned.

As she continued to observe Cat, a frown creased her face. It seemed that last evening everything was proceeding along so well. She flinched as Cat stomped her foot again.

Oh dear, it was plain for any angel to see that Cat was angry with Garrett. And likely going to avoid him as well. That simply wouldn't do. Why, however was she going to fall in love with him if she continued to avoid him?

It couldn't be done.

Oh, dear feathers. The situation called for much more drastic measures than she'd first thought she'd have to employ.

Patience, she told herself. She must have patience. As soon as Cat left the room, she would get to work.

A little over an hour later, Tamera watched her from the window until Cat crossed the street and walked into Dena's Restaurant. A smile lit her face. Ah, good, she would have plenty of time.

Tamera flew out the open window and headed south out of town. Minutes later she fluttered down beneath a large overhanging tree. It looked like a probable site for her requirements.

In no time at all she found exactly what she needed. A pretty nocturnal creature lay sleeping serenely with her babies. She counted an unusually small litter of only three babies, then petted the mama with the gentlest of touches. The soft black fur with its distinctive white stripe running from nose to tail's end gleamed even in the shade of her burrow.

Ah, a nice protective mama skunk would provide exactly what she needed to bring Garrett and Cat closer together.

With angel speed Tamera scooped up the three peacefully sleeping baby skunks and laid them in the nest provided by her skirt without them even blinking an eye open from their nap. Next followed the snoozing mama skunk before the little animal even knew she'd been moved.

In a flash Tamera returned to the hotel with her new charges. Once inside Cat's room, she dispensed with the gowns in the armoire, packing them in the camelback trunk and delivering them to the boardinghouse along with the carpetbag. The woman would need her clothing the moment she arrived there.

Checking to see that everything was in readiness, Tamera gave the room a quick once over. Yes, all was in preparation. Only one thing left to do.

She gently prodded the mama skunk. The creature awoke with a start, obviously not pleased at the intrusion. The little animal blinked and closed her eyes again. Dropping her chin down on her paws, she settled back to her nap without a concern.

"Oh, feathers."

Tamera leaned forward and tapped the skunk on the head. The animal reared her head up.

In a flash Tamera materialized directly in front of the mama skunk. Holding her nose, she bent low over the little animal.

Tamera waved her arms, flapped her wings, and yelled, "Boo!"

The skunk jumped back, stuck up her tail, and sprayed in defense.

"Tamera!" came a booming voice.

She closed her eyes at the reproach she could hear in St. Peter's tone.

"Yes?"

"Get up here. Now," he ordered.

Tamera flew upward in a mist scented with the distinct aroma of skunk.

An instant later, she settled her feet on a cloud and faced her superior.

"I thought I smelled trouble," he remarked.

"I . . . ah . . . I—"

"What have you done now!"

As Tamera ducked her chin, a single feather floated downward.

Cat heard the commotion from down the street. Gathering up her skirt in one hand, she hurried toward her hotel.

What on earth had happened?

She stepped off the boardwalk to cross the street, then stopped. Complete pandemonium greeted her. People rushed from the hotel, dashing in all directions. A woman held a handkerchief to her nose while a man raced past her coughing with tears streaming down his ruddy cheeks.

She'd walked halfway across the street when the sheriff caught her arm and pulled her back.

"Ma'am, pardon me, but you shouldn't go any closer," he suggested in a firm voice.

Cat's eyes widened in fear; then the wind carried a scent

across the short distance to her, and she almost sighed aloud in relief. Then she wrinkled her nose in distaste.

"Polecat," she gasped, then quickly pulled out her kerchief from her reticule and covered her nose.

Ty led her back across the street. Chaos still reigned at the hotel. People rushed out the open doors, and two men jumped off the boardwalk.

"Sure seems like it," Ty answered. "The hotel won't be liveable for a while."

"But, I—"

"Ma'am, Missus Sarah likely has room in her boardinghouse if you'd like to stay there. It's a fine place for a lady to stay."

"Thank you. I—"

"But I wouldn't waste any time jawing about it if I was you," he interrupted her. "Spare places are going to fill up real quick around here."

Cat glanced up at him and saw the twinkle of laughter in his eyes.

"Sorry, ma'am, but we haven't had this kind of excitement in Millwood for some time. Bet old Henry won't be wearing his red underwear for quite a while."

Ty's lips twitched again; then he broke into laughter.

At the sudden picture of the hotel owner in the clothing he'd mentioned, Cat joined his laughter. She dabbed at the corner of her eye with the kerchief.

"Sheriff, if you would direct me to—"

He caught her elbow, and she fell silent. Good heavens, this was the first time the law had ever laid a hand on her in a gesture of friendship. Imagine that.

"Right this way, ma'am." He looked down at her, and his lips twitched again.

Cat smiled back at him with a genuine smile. "Thank you, sir."

Within minutes the sheriff handed her over to Sarah Miles with a brief explanation of the occurrence at the hotel.

"Guess I'd better head back there. They are gonna need

some help corralling that skunk." He grinned, then added, "But I'm all for letting it slip out on its own come nightfall."

"Shame on you," Sarah teased.

Ty nodded to them. "Goodbye, ladies."

Sarah looked Cat up and down thoroughly. She wrinkled her nose in distaste.

"Come on. Into the tub with you."

Cat sighed at the thought of a bath. She'd dearly love to wash off the smell of skunk, however faint it happened to be. Thank goodness she wasn't in the hotel when it happened.

"I'll show you to your room." Sarah touched Cat's arm, then stepped back. "On second thought, why don't you wait out on the front porch while I get the water ready?"

Cat smiled in understanding. "I'll be outside when you're ready for me."

In a short time, Sarah called out and led Cat up the stairs, careful to stay several steps ahead of her. She opened a door and waved Cat inside.

"If you'll toss your clothes out into the hall after your bath, I'll see they're taken care of for you."

"Oh, thank you." Cat turned back to her new friend. "But my other clothes—"

"Are already here."

"What?"

"They arrived this morning in your trunk, along with a carpetbag. That's how come I saved you a room."

Cat stared in openmouthed amazement. "I didn't send my things here. Or anywhere."

Sarah shrugged. "Well, they're here nonetheless."

A little girl of about three ran up to them, her dark curls bouncing. "Mama, mama." She stopped and covered her nose. "What stinks?"

Sarah laughed, and added, "My daughter, Amanda."

"But, Mama—"

"This is Miss Parker. We need to let her take her bath, darling."

The little girl frowned and looked from her mother to Cat

and then to the open door. ''But, Mama, look what I found.'' She held out a white feather.

''That's nice. Now come along, Amanda.''

''But, Mama, that nice old lady brought the trunk. I saw her.''

''Come on, sweetie.'' Sarah scooped up her daughter and walked down the hall.

She stopped to call back over her shoulder, ''Don't forget to toss your things out.''

''I won't,'' Cat answered. ''Thanks.''

Sarah and her daughter hurried on down the hall. Amanda waved over her mother's shoulder. Cat waved back, then stepped into the room.

The tub stood in one corner of the room, and fragrant steam rose in wisps. She wrinkled her own nose at her gown. Quickly she slipped out of the garment, then dropped it across a footstool. Cat hoped the pretty gown wasn't ruined.

She turned away from the door. The tub drew her like a catfish to a fishing lure. As she neared the bath, she saw the thick bubbles, and sent up a silent thanks to her hostess.

Cat stepped into the heated water, then sighed and lowered herself into the foaming bubbles. It felt wonderful. And smelled even better. The scent of roses enveloped her, washing away the faintest hint of skunk.

She raised one leg and ran a handful of water along her calve. She wiggled her toes in pure pleasure.

Could life get any better than this? She'd always loved a scented bath. To her, it was the height of luxury, and one she indulged in.

The door swung open, bringing in a cool draft of air. Cat shivered against the chill and sat up to glance at the door.

''Sarah . . .'' Her voice trailed off.

Garrett stood silhouetted in the opening. His hat sat low on his head, and he nudged it back. A wide grin tipped his lips upward.

Cat gasped.

He entered the room with complete disregard for her present state of undress. The door clicked shut behind him.

"What do I have here?" he asked in a leisurely drawl.

Cat almost stood to her feet in anger; then realization struck her. She scooted lower into the tub, peeking up at him from the froth of bubbles.

"Garrett," she squeaked out his name.

"Waiting for me to join you, Cat?" he asked. His voice held the soft touch of smoothest velvet.

She shook her head, unable to speak. One curl fell free to lay against her bare shoulder.

A slow, sensual smile eased over Garrett's face. "Why else would you be waiting in my room? In my tub," he stated.

Cat's mouth dropped open. It took her two tries to force out a sound. "Your room?"

"Yup."

Garrett tossed his hat across the room. It landed brim up on a chair. Cat watched it rock back and forth. Finally, she returned her gaze to him.

"Your room," Cat repeated.

"Yup."

Garrett crossed the room to stand beside the tub.

"Mine," he answered.

Chapter Eleven

Cat sat up in the tub, the water running down her shoulders. She didn't remember when she'd been so mad.

"Get out," she ordered, her voice rising.

Garrett leaned closer. "Nope."

Cat gritted her teeth. She swore if she could have reached her derringer, she'd have shot him right then and there.

"Would you like some assistance?" Garrett held out his hand.

"No," Cat sputtered. Then realizing where his gaze had fixed on the expanse of skin below her shoulders exposed by the water, she scooted lower into the tub.

"I could wash your back," he offered.

"No."

Garrett shrugged, then propped one foot on the edge of the tub.

"Get out of here," Cat ordered again.

He merely raised his brows.

Cat's anger rose right along with them. "Garrett." She gritted the name out past clenched teeth.

"Yes, my dear?"

His voice held pure innocence, tinged with the softest hint of seductiveness she'd ever heard before in her life. It threatened to evaporate her temper as surely as the air hurried along the disappearing bubbles.

"I—"

"I could rinse your back, or—"

"No." She finally managed to regain control of her voice.

Garrett reached down and touched her shoulder. She slapped his hand away.

A smile of daring lifted the corners of his lips. It was all the spark her temper needed to set it off. Lifting her hands suddenly, she threw a handful of water and bubbles directly into his face.

His smile vanished. The water ran in rivulets down his cheeks and dripped off his chin. Their eyes met in a new challenge, and neither moved or even dared take a breath.

A knock at the door broke the silence. Cat jumped guiltily.

"Are you about ready?" Sarah asked, tapping on the door again. "I've got you a fresh gown."

"Leave it," Garrett called out, never taking his gaze off Cat.

The door swung open in the next instant. Sarah stood in the opening and took in the scene before her without a word. She held the clothing in her arms, and ignoring Garrett's dismissal, she walked across the room.

"Sorry to borrow your room, Garrett." Sarah dropped the clothes on the foot of the bed.

His bed, Cat thought. She glanced from the bed back to Garrett.

His room. His tub. And his bed.

"Any time," he answered, his gaze remaining on Cat.

Cat swore she could feel the water's temperature beginning to heat under his stare. It was as if he knew if he stared long enough, the bubbles would up and disappear. And they were in danger of doing exactly that.

"I didn't expect you back so soon." Sarah faced him, her hands on her hips. "Now, if you'll leave, we will be finished in no time."

"After you, ladies," he stated.

Sarah laughed as if he'd made a joke, while Cat inched lower into the tub, her cheeks heating with a furious blush of anger combined with humiliation.

Garrett lifted his foot off the tub and placed it on the floor, but didn't step away from the tub.

"Out with you." Sarah swatted at his shoulder, then shoved him toward the door.

Cat stared in shock, her eyes widening. No one ever pushed Jake Garrett. As she waited, every muscle tensed, he turned and picked up his hat from the chair. Then, tipping it to them, he strode to the door.

"I'll *see* you later, Cat." He chuckled, then shut the door behind him.

Cat sat straight up in the tub and threw the washcloth at the door.

Without saying a word, Sarah held a towel out to Cat. She almost snatched it from the woman's hand.

"Sarah—"

"Cat, dear, I'm sorry. I didn't think Garrett would be back so soon. He's never here at this time of the day. He's usually helping out Ty. And I . . ." She lifted her hands, then dropped them to her sides.

Cat wrapped the towel about herself tightly and glanced back at the door as if she expected it to open again and Garrett to stride back into the room.

"This is his room." Cat's words were a statement, not a question.

"The largest tub is here. In Garrett's room," Sarah explained.

Cat noted that her voice wavered ever so slightly. Surely Sarah hadn't planned this encounter on purpose? No, the very idea was ridiculous. Wasn't it?

Cat opened her mouth to ask, but snapped it closed before she could utter the insulting words. The thought wasn't worth mentioning. She was only seeking someone else to blame for her reaction to Jake Garrett. It wasn't the other woman's fault that she couldn't control her own destiny whenever Garrett was around. It seemed that things just happened whenever he came near.

"Shams," she muttered under her breath, forgetting her friend's presence.

"What did you say, dear?" Sarah asked, her eyes wide in confusion.

Cat realized her mistake and forced herself to smile in sweet innocence. "I swear I don't know when I've been so embarrassed." She patted her cheeks with the corner of the towel.

She lowered her head, but didn't have to fake the humiliation she felt. It was genuine.

Even worse was the fact that she'd been sorely tempted to give in to Garrett's offer to let him "wash her back."

"As soon as you're dressed, I'll show you to your room," Sarah offered.

Cat smiled her acceptance and held her tongue. She would have to watch herself very carefully from now on. How could fate have placed her in the same boardinghouse as Jake Garrett? Could things get any worse?

Sarah crossed to the bed and gathered up the underclothes and handed them to Cat. Blushing to the roots of her hair, Cat dropped the towel and hastily slipped the chemise over her head. She intended to be long gone from this room before Garrett could possibly return.

As Sarah shook out the blue gown, she eyed it appreciatively. "This is beautiful."

"Thank you." Cat wasn't sure what else she was supposed to say to the compliment.

"You will be the envy of the town ladies, I swear." In spite of the words of warning, a grin lit her face. "With a little lace added to the bodice of this, you'd win the approval of the town matrons. And the interest of every available man in town." Sarah looked from the gown to Cat and giggled.

"Sarah, I—"

"Of course, I'd be delighted to help you."

"But, I—"

"Think nothing of it."

Sarah brushed off the rejections Cat had been trying to make. Shams, Cat swore silently, the nice woman thought she was asking for her assistance. Now what?

"As soon as you're dressed, we'll go have a look at the rest of your wardrobe. I'll see what else you need fixed up."

Cat closed her eyes with a silent groan. She had a feeling that trying to stop Sarah Miles when she had her mind set to do something would be like trying to stop a runaway team of horses. Very determined horses.

What could it hurt to go along with the friendly landlady? Perhaps it could help establish her in the town as a fine Eastern lady, and put Garrett off his guard at the same time.

Cat smiled her thanks, and the next instant the blue gown was plopped over her head.

Sarah kept up a steady stream of chatter while they finished. Cat was truly beginning to like the woman. Before she'd finished fastening the back of Cat's gown, she'd told her of being widowed only months before Amanda's birth. Cat's chest tightened, and she wanted to reach out to her in some way, but wasn't sure how.

Before she could think of an appropriate comment, Sarah continued on as if she hadn't revealed anything of importance.

"Oh, dear, you must meet Ruth and Judy. They run the Long and Short Saloon together." Sarah held up a hand to cut off anything Cat could possibly say. "They are really quite respectable, you know. Both married ladies, too."

Cat frowned, wondering what that had to do with anything, but she didn't have long to wonder.

"Being happily married, neither has an interest in a certain tall, dark man." Sarah winked.

Cat gasped.

Undaunted, Sarah continued to regale Cat with the town gossip. She soon learned that Miss Simms, the old maid schoolteacher, was thinking of going home to Minnesota to live with her newly widowed sister. Cat pondered this bit of news for a moment. If that happened, the town would need a new teacher. . . .

Cat chased the idea right out of her mind. Imagine her a teacher. It didn't bear thinking about. The idea had only been planted in her mind after hearing about Dena leaving her teaching position to run a restaurant, and then the notion had popped up again when Cat had needed a quick lie to answer Garrett's questions.

She didn't have the qualifications to be a teacher in the first place. Why, sure she knew how to read and write. And she had taught Mr. Baker's daughter to read, but . . .

"Cat?" Sarah tapped her on the shoulder.

Jerking her head up, Cat quickly apologized, "I'm sorry, I was—"

Sarah stopped her explanation with a smile. "Yes, he does provoke daydreaming in the ladies about town," she remarked with a knowing wink.

"Who?"

"Why, that dark-haired man we've been talking about. Jake Garrett. Who else?"

Who else indeed.

Cat opened her mouth to deny it, but her landlady waylaid her before she could utter a single word of protest.

"Yes, well, he is something to look at. Isn't he? Not my kind of man, but now you and he do look fine together. You'd make a—"

"No," Cat snapped.

Sarah blinked several times. Then a slow smile lifted her lips. "Of course, you're right, dear. It doesn't do for a lady to appear too eager."

"I am not—"

"Come along, I'll show you to your room. If you're ready?"

In truth, Cat was more than ready. The talk of Garrett had made her too conscious that she was standing in *his* room.

She had no intention of being caught anywhere near his room when he returned. No, absolutely not. She scooped up her reticule from the floor beside the tub. Sarah led the way to the door, chattering happily all the while.

By the time they had taken three steps away from Garrett's

doorway, Cat had learned that Sheriff Ty Friedman had never been married and was being considered for the upcoming post of marshall.

As Sarah stopped abruptly at the first door they came to, Cat nearly plowed into her back.

"Here we are." Sarah unlocked the door and swung it open to reveal a bedroom, tastefully decorated.

Cat couldn't do anything but stare in shock.

Sarah faced her. "Is something wrong with the room?"

Cat shook her head, unable to utter a word.

The room had been painted a crisp white and matched the white iron bed. A brightly colored patchwork quilt lay over the soft feather mattress while lace curtains were pinned back from a window. It was a beautiful room. One any lady would feel pleased to stay in. There was only one thing wrong with it.

The bedroom revealed by the open door sat directly beside Garrett's own room.

"Is there a problem with your room, dear?" Sarah asked in concern.

Cat blinked, then looked from the open doorway to the closed door of Garrett's next door. She forced her gaze back to the open door. Her room?

She shook her head in denial. It couldn't be. There had to be some mistake. Perhaps another room was available. Perhaps she could ask for one facing the south?

Sarah took her silence in stride. She reached over and patted Cat's shoulder. "Well, I'm glad there's no problem. Your clothes are already hanging in your room ready for you."

"My room?" Cat's heart sank. Shams, *this* room had already been readied for her.

"Yes, thankfully I had one room left when Ty brought you here. Why, with the hotel being unlivable, there isn't a spare place in town left now."

Sarah walked into the room. "Why, that tenderfoot Mr. Winston came asking for a room, you know." She wrinkled her nose. "I didn't like the looks of him one bit. Reminded me of a little weasel with his skinny body and bowler hat."

Cat barely contained her gasp. The Pinkerton man.

"I sent him on his way. Heard he hopped the next train out of town." Sarah patted her shoulder. "I know we're going to be friends. I'm glad I had a room left for you."

"Mama?" a little voice called out. "Come see my pretty feather."

Sarah turned away. "I'll leave you to get settled now."

Cat remained in the hall, digesting this latest bit of information. This was the last room available in the town. She couldn't ask to be moved to another room, farther down the hall. A lot farther down the hall.

Things had most assuredly gone from bad to worse. Her room was next door to Garrett's. Only a thin wall separated them.

She closed her eyes and swallowed. Gulped would describe it better. Garrett would be living on the other side of the wall from her.

The hotel couldn't reopen soon enough for her tastes.

"So, how long will the hotel be closed?" Garrett asked Ty, leaning back in the chair.

Ty smiled at him over the rim of his glass of whiskey. They had retired to a back table at the Long and Short Saloon after Garrett had slammed the door to the sheriff's office, nearly shaking it off its hinges.

"In a hurry for it to open?"

"Hell no. I mean yes." Garrett pushed his hat low over his eyes and rubbed the back of his neck. An ache had seemed to lodge there the second he turned his back on Cat in his tub and walked out of his room.

His room.

"It's my room," he muttered. "I pay my rent."

"Hear tell you've got a new neighbor." Although he tried, Ty couldn't keep the smile off his face.

Garrett slammed his feet to the floor, shaking the table, and shoved his hat to the back of his head. "What do you know about this?"

Ty shrugged in pretend innocence. "All I did was take a certain lady to the only place in town with a room available—"

"Yeah, my room," Garrett snapped. "Thanks a lot."

Ty leaned forward. "What are you talking about?"

Sighing, Garrett propped his feet back up on the corner of the table. He ignored the frown of disapproval Judy sent him from the bar.

"Well?" Ty prompted.

"Oh, nothing of any importance. I merely returned to my room at the boardinghouse and found the lady in my room—"

"What?"

"In my tub."

"Well, well. That's the way it is."

"Isn't."

"Oh?"

"Seems Sarah didn't expect me back so soon. So, she loaned my room for a bath. Cat wasn't too pleased with my appearance."

"Ah, so Sarah's at it again."

"At what?"

"Her matchmaking," Ty declared.

"She wouldn't dare." Garrett's eyes narrowed dangerously.

"Not only would she. She has. With dang near every eligible lady to come to town."

"Why me?"

Ty poked his finger at Garrett. "You were handy, and she likes you. That's all the reason that interfering woman needs. I swear, since her husband up and died, she's stayed too busy for her own good."

"Somebody needs to put a stop to her."

"Go ahead," Ty suggested. "The rest of us are scared who she'll stick us with if we upset her."

"You can't be serious?"

"She even tried getting me and old Miss Simms together."

"The schoolteacher?"

"The same." Ty nodded once.

"What did you do?"

"I found reason to hightail it out after some outlaws for the better part of a month. She gave up."

"Coincidence," Garrett declared.

"What about Ruth?"

"Friend, now I know you've been in the sun too long. Ruth's married."

"Exactly. Who do you think set her up?"

"Sarah?" Garrett asked in disbelief. His sweet widowed landlady seemed so nice.

"What about Judy?" Ty persisted.

Garrett frowned. "Don't tell me Sarah is responsible for her getting married six months back."

His friend nodded, then continued, "And Smitty the blacksmith. She fixed him up, too."

A chill snaked its way down Garrett's spine, and he scooted his back tighter into the chair. He turned his gaze to the batwing doors, watching.

"Just don't say I didn't warn you," Ty announced.

"She's crazy."

"No, she simply believes in love." Ty sighed loudly.

"So, why don't you keep her occupied?" Garrett suggested with sudden inspiration.

"Who, Miss Parker?"

"No," he snapped. "Sarah."

Ty rubbed his chin. "Might be worth a—" He shook his head again. "No. No way."

Garrett hid his smile behind his glass. He recognized the look in his friend's eyes. It was interest. Pure and simple.

He should recognize it. He'd seen it in his own eyes often enough since Cat Parker arrived in town.

"Hear tell the ladies in town are planning a pie and box supper this coming Saturday," Ty informed him. "There's posters up all over town."

"You know I avoid those things."

"Maybe you should try this one. You could bid on her box

supper." Ty sat back in his chair, a smile of encouragement on his face.

"Whose?" Garrett asked.

"Miss Parker's. Who else?" Ty snapped back at him, then grinned widely. "Never know what you might buy yourself."

"That's what I'm afraid of," Garrett grumbled. But the idea had been planted. Perhaps this would be one town social event he would plan on attending.

Cat managed to avoid running into Garrett for the next three days. She did so by learning to listen at the connecting wall so she could tell when he'd left his room. However, this also meant that she heard nearly every move he made.

Watching for Garrett and avoiding him, until her senses fully returned and listened to her orders, was taking its toll on Cat. She'd become jumpy.

Not to mention that she had to listen to Sarah singing his praises every time they talked. The woman was a tireless matchmaker. Nothing Cat could say would discourage her—except the truth. That she'd come here to kill him.

Since Cat knew without a doubt that she could never reveal her plan to anyone, she was forced to listen to her landlady and smile agreeably. Cat swore her jaws were beginning to ache from so much smiling.

However, Sarah was also a source of endless information. Through her new friend, Cat learned that Garrett was helping Ty while refusing to wear the badge of deputy. Yet. That fact bothered her more than she was willing to admit.

It didn't change her plans, she told herself. No, not one little bit.

She closed her bedroom door behind her, then almost tiptoed past Garrett's room. Her conscience nagged her. She admitted she was reluctant to encounter Garrett. She assured herself it was merely due to her embarrassment at being found naked in his room.

As she passed that room, she purposefully averted her eyes.

Even so, she could feel the heat of a blush creeping up her cheeks. She rushed down the hall to the stairs.

The only good news she had to smile about was confirmation that the nosy Pinkerton man had indeed departed town when he was unable to obtain lodging after the skunk incident. This she'd also learned from Sarah through Ty. It seemed that the sheriff had begun courting Sarah.

Cat couldn't help smiling. About time the woman got some of her own back. Maybe if Ty kept Sarah busy, she'd forget about encouraging Cat and Garrett. Although she feared she knew better than to even dare hope for that to happen.

She'd reached the bottom step when Sarah came into the hall from the kitchen.

"Oh, Cat, I'm so glad I caught you. Can you cook?"

The twinkle in her friend's eyes warned her. A decidedly uneasy feeling crept over Cat.

She opened her mouth to respond that of course she could cook; she'd fixed all the food for her pa and the farmhands when they could afford hired help. Which had been only at harvesting season.

Recalling what her thoughts could reveal, Cat slammed the door on her past life. She was supposed to be a fine Eastern lady, not a farm girl from Illinois. Were ladies from New York supposed to know how to cook? she wondered. She gnawed on her lower lip in a quandary of how she should answer.

Sarah took her hesitation as an answer. "Oh, don't feel badly about it. I can teach you cooking, but just to be safe, I'll fix you up a box supper this time. And no one will be the wiser. The cook's identity is supposed to be a secret, you know." She winked conspiratorially.

Cat stared back in confusion. "Box supper?"

"Why, yes." Sarah planted her hands on her hips and eyed Cat in open challenge. "You are going."

"Where?"

"To the pie and box supper this Saturday night. I won't allow a refusal."

Cat inwardly cringed. Memories of the one and only box

supper she'd attended back in Shelbyville haunted her, and she closed her eyes. She'd been a clumsy fifteen-year-old in a faded calico dress that hit her above the ankles. Pa had bought her box supper after no one bid on it.

"No, I—"

"Yes, you will." Sarah caught her arm. "There won't be any argument. And don't you worry, I'll fix you a box supper that will guarantee that Jake Garrett makes a bid."

"He won't," Cat said in a voice laced with old sadness.

"Oh, I believe he will. Especially when he knows whose box he is bidding on." Sarah winked, tugging Cat into the kitchen.

"But no one is supposed to know who—"

"He'll know all right. Garrett has his sources. And he will most definitely be bidding on you."

Chapter Twelve

Saturday dawned bright, and clear, and sun-filled. Cat stared out the window of her room and groaned. Why couldn't it be pouring down rain?

"Shams."

She'd hoped for rain. Prayed for rain.

If it had rained hard enough and long enough, the box supper would be canceled. Bright sunlight taunted her, reminding her that the function would go on exactly as planned.

Cat covered her face with her hands and groaned again. By yesterday afternoon, she bet everyone in town knew exactly which box supper was hers. Sarah had grudgingly agreed not to tell anyone. However, Cat had forgotten about Amanda.

It sure seemed that the warning "don't say anything in front of little ones that you don't want repeated" was borne in truth. Amanda had proudly told practically everyone in town who would listen all about Cat's box supper, including the fact that it contained a lemon pie—a rare treat here in Texas.

Cat knew Sarah had put the child up to it. But what could she do about it now?

Perhaps Garrett wouldn't hear about it. Of course, she didn't believe that any more than she'd ever believed in fairy tales.

"Hey, Garrett," Ty called out from across the street. "Wait up."

Garrett turned and waved to his friend, then leaned back against the hitching post to wait his approach.

"So, did you hear?" Ty reached his side, grinning widely.

Garrett tensed. It made him a mite uneasy when a man smiled too widely. "Hear what?"

"Miss Cat Parker is bringing a pie and box supper tonight."

Garrett could feel his friend's eyes watching him for the slightest reaction. He calmly gave none.

"I heard," he answered.

"Do tell? Now I wonder how you could have heard 'bout that?"

"Do you know that you're the fifth person who has told me as much in the last hour?"

Ty slapped Garrett on the back and broke into laughter.

Garrett didn't feel the least like laughing. "Sarah's gone too far this time," he announced.

"I gave you fair warning, didn't I?"

"I think she's got the entire town in on this matchmaking thing of hers."

"Don't be so sure of that," Ty warned.

"What do you mean?" A decidedly uneasy feeling began to plague Garrett.

"Hear tell that you might have some competition bidding on that lemon pie."

"Lemon pie?" Garrett licked his lips before he could stop himself.

"Yeah. And fried chicken with potato salad."

"Hold up, we don't even know if she can cook. It might not be edible."

"Not to worry. Hear tell that Sarah did all the cooking

herself. Miss Parker it seems can't cook, being from New York and all," Ty explained.

Garrett nodded; he could have figured as much by himself.

Ty patted his stomach. "I might even have to throw out a bid or two myself."

Garrett glared at his friend in answer.

"Also heard that several men in town are planning on bidding on that supper so they can have the lady's company tonight." Ty rocked back on his heels, obviously waiting for a reaction.

"Then they can have her." Garrett tugged his hat lower, shielding his eyes from the bright sunlight. And his friend's perceptive eyes.

"Umm. We'll see." Ty cleared his throat, then asked, "Any more visitors in your tub?"

"Shut up, Ty."

A short burst of laughter met his order.

However, the remark had hit its target. A picture of Cat sitting up to her shoulders in frothy bubbles filled his mind. He'd been able to think of little else since he'd entered his room to find her bathing in his tub several days ago.

It was enough to put a man off his feed.

Fried chicken and potato salad was sounding better and better. He shook off the thought. He could eat Sarah's cooking every evening at the boardinghouse. However, he knew the meal his friend had described wasn't the only lure. Cat Parker presented one heck of a temptation.

Thanks to her, he no longer had any peace, even in his own room. If he wasn't picturing Cat there, he was listening to her stir next door to him. The thin wall did little to stem his imagination. Late at night, he lay in bed, envisioning her in her bed.

A rivulet of sweat trickled down his temple. Garrett wiped it aside and shoved his hat back on his head.

"Any word on when the hotel's reopening?" Garrett asked abruptly, his voice edgy and uneven. It couldn't be soon enough to suit him.

"Did you hear tell that word is they've got that skunk trapped?"

"Good."

"Old Charles is going in after it today to bring out the traps. If he's caught it, the hotel should open next Monday."

"Good news at last," Garrett grumbled.

Somehow the news didn't sound so good to him after all.

Word of the hotel reopening soon was far from good news to Tamera. Why, the hotel couldn't open yet. It would ruin everything she'd set up.

She absolutely forbid it.

Once the hotel reopened, Cat would move back in there. And away from Garrett. Although she had to admit her plan of putting them together at the boardinghouse wasn't working as well as she'd hoped. Cat persisted in avoiding him at every opportunity.

Imagine that.

No, things were not proceeding well at all. Cat ignored her subtle hints, and although she'd encouraged thoughts of Cat in Garrett's mind, he hadn't taken one bit of action yet. Well, if the man didn't do something soon, Tamera would have to take some action of her own.

However, first things first. She had to ensure that the town's only hotel stayed closed. And that was just what she intended to see to. A glance at Garrett next to Ty assured her that her charge would be safe for the short time it would take her to check and empty those animal traps herself.

Tamera flew down the street and into the hotel. Then she began her search. The downstairs traps proved to be empty. Good. She hated the things. Imagine the horror of trapping a poor animal.

"Tsk, tsk," she muttered.

If she didn't have other things to do, she'd give Charlie something in those traps of his all right. Sighing in dismay at her lack of time, she flew up the stairs. She proceeded to go from room to room, checking the deserted hotel. Where had the little mama skunk herself gotten off to? She couldn't find her anywhere.

Suddenly she noticed the whiff of fresh air blowing in from an opened window. All scent of the skunk had dissipated. Oh, that wouldn't do at all. She slammed the window tightly closed.

Turning away, she fluttered into the next room and stopped in midair. There on the floor lay the mama skunk trapped in a cage.

Tamera flew straight to the pinned animal.

"Oh, you poor thing." She lifted the animal free. "And where are your babies?"

She set the skunk down on the floor, and immediately the animal dashed out the door. Tamera followed right behind her. Two doors down she found the mama checking over her three babies.

A loud sound from downstairs alerted Tamera. The sound of footsteps on the stairs warned her, and a noise outside the door nearly panicked her. The men were coming. They couldn't find the poor mama skunk and her babies now. Why, the little things were tired and quite helpless.

In a flash Tamera scooped up the animals into her arms and disappeared into the next room. As the group of men thumped from room to room, checking the traps, she fluttered from room to room, always one ahead of them. She held tightly to her little charges. Mama skunk seemed to understand the need for subterfuge and snuggled into her rescuer's arms.

"Traps are empty," old Charlie yelled out. "Every last one of 'em."

"Maybe that polecat up and left," another man volunteered.

"Ain't never seen the likes. It's as if that critter's moving around by magic," Charlie mumbled, scratching the back of his thick neck.

"That's foolish talk."

"What do you call what's happening?" Charlie demanded, an edge of fear in his words. "That little critter is staying one step ahead of us all the time."

"It's plain good luck. Nothing more," one man answered.

"Humph," Charlie grumbled.

"Looks to me like maybe we can't find that skunk 'cause it ain't here no more."

"That's good news," Henry proclaimed. "It means that I can open the hotel again come—"

Tamera shut out the rest of the man's words.

Absolutely not. The hotel would not open anytime soon.

Tamera eased the mama skunk onto the floor and leaned forward. "I helped you. Now it's time for you to help me."

The dignified little skunk looked into her face. Her little eyes blinked as if in agreement. The sound of the men's voices could be heard clearly from the hallway outside the room now.

The door swung open to admit the men. Then, as if in a pique, the skunk stamped her front feet and turned her back on the door and the stunned men. Suddenly she lifted her tail and—

"Whew!" Charlie yelped. "Get outta here, boys."

The sound of retreating footsteps brought a smile to Tamera's face.

The hotel wouldn't be reopening anytime soon.

Sarah caught Cat's hand and led her to the door of the schoolhouse. Cat glanced into the room. Everything had been scrubbed to a fare-thee-well. The school practically sparkled.

Still she continued to hold back in reluctance, one hand tightly clenched around the handle of her basket. The last place she wanted to be was at the pie and box supper. Her nerves refused to steady themselves no matter how much Sarah had assured her that the evening would be a resounding success.

Cat had never been so happy to keep her past a secret. Thank goodness her new friend knew nothing about the one and only box supper she'd attended years ago. And what a failure she'd been. She tightened her grip on the woven basket.

"Stop worrying," Sarah whispered to her, then pushed her into the room ahead of her. "You look beautiful in that dress."

The blue gown had undergone a minor transformation under Sarah's needle. A delicate ruffle of imported lace rimmed the bodice. It lended the gown an aura of innocent respectability while drawing any male's attention directly to the lace and precisely what it edged.

Cat brushed at the new trim with her fingers. She glanced about the room, telling herself she wasn't looking for Garrett. No, she wasn't.

"Dear, you don't need to draw any more attention." Sarah caught her elbow and pulled her hand away from her bodice. "That lace I sewed on does its job just fine, if I do say so myself."

Cat felt her face heat with embarrassment. Thank goodness the lace edging had raised the bodice of her gown because she was certain she was blushing all the way to her toes. "I—"

Before Cat could say another word, one of the two young girls in charge of collecting the food baskets grabbed Cat's box supper from her hands. Although Cat reached out to stop her, the girl carried the basket straight up to the table, then bent low to whisper her name to the woman seated there.

"She'll write your name on the list and give the basket a number," Sarah explained to her as another young girl took her basket.

Cat resisted the urge to tell her friend that she recalled exactly how the pie and box supper worked. It worked terribly. She barely held back a shudder of dislike.

"Now, if you'll excuse me a minute," Sarah said, "I really must go and have a word with Miss Simms."

Sarah left Cat standing inside the door and hurried across the room to speak to the older woman at the table. So, that was the old maid schoolteacher, Cat thought to herself, eyeing the tall, slim woman whose brown hair was streaked with gray.

As Cat's basket was unpacked and the lemon pie set out on display, a murmured "ohh" sounded from around the room. If nothing else, the luscious dessert attracted attention. Cat crossed her fingers in the folds of her blue gown.

In a remarkably short amount of time, Sarah returned to her

side. "I've got it," she announced triumphantly with a wide grin.

"What?"

"The number of your supper, of course."

"But, they are supposed to be secret." Cat caught her mistake and quickly added, "Aren't they? I thought that was what you told me yesterday."

Sarah leaned closer and winked. "I promised Miss Simms that I would see that her basket sold. In exchange for a couple of numbers."

"You didn't."

Raising her chin, Sarah answered, "I most certainly did so."

"But—"

"I must warn you, she can't cook worth a tinker's damn. Now, help me find somebody to buy her supper."

Cat volunteered, "Garrett could. If he comes to the social."

Sarah shook her head. "He's bidding on yours."

She scarcely held back her smile at her friend's announcement. Not only was Garrett planning on attending the pie and box supper, but he was intending to place a bid on her supper.

"But how will he know which one?" The question slipped out before she could stop it.

The smile on her friend's face warned her.

"Because, I will make *certain* he knows your number." Sarah tapped her fingertip to her lip. "It wouldn't hurt for him to have a little competition."

An uneasy feeling settled in Cat's stomach. She wasn't sure she liked the idea of Garrett getting competitive over her.

"Oh, look, there's Matt Newsom." Sarah waved him over, then caught Cat's elbow and held her anchored in place so she couldn't sneak away.

Cat forced a smile to her lips. Within mere minutes she was amazingly once again surrounded by townsmen. She looked from Matt, to George, to a third man whose name she couldn't remember. Maybe wearing a pretty, ladylike skirt instead of breeches had its merits.

From the corner of her eye she caught Sarah holding up her

fingers to signify the number ten. Cat's gasp of surprise drew her friend's attention, and she merely shrugged and winked at her.

"Miss Parker." Matt drew her attention back. "I certainly look forward to dining with you."

"I believe that honor will be mine," George put in.

Cat glanced from one to the other. Then she looked over at her new friend. Sarah's smile had I-told-you-so written all over it.

When Cat spotted the sheriff entering the schoolhouse, she couldn't resist the idea that sprang into her mind.

"Excuse me for a minute." She held up her hand to forestall any complaints. "I will be right back."

Slipping away before anyone could waylay her, she walked across to the lawman.

"Sheriff."

"Miss Parker, you're looking lovely."

She waved the pleasantries aside and spoke quickly. "Bid on number eleven."

His head jerked up, and he took a step backward away from her. "Miss—"

"Eleven," she repeated. "That is if you'd like to share supper with Sarah Miles."

A smile spread across his face. "Thank you."

Smiling back at him, Cat turned away and returned to Sarah and the group of men. Now her friend could get a little taste of matchmaking from someone else for a change.

"What did you say to him?" Sarah asked in suspicion.

"Me?"

"Cat."

She shrugged in a delicate movement, then whispered, "Why, I merely told a certain lawman to bid on number eleven."

"You didn't," Sarah hissed.

Cat merely smiled in answer. What was it they said about what was good for the goose? She winked at her friend.

A movement at the doorway caught Cat's gaze, and her breath left in a soft whoosh.

Garrett stood silhouetted in the open doorway, his dark clothing setting him off from every other man in the room. No, she corrected the thought, no matter what he wore, Garrett would stand out. He had a taut alertness about him that was unmistakable.

While he didn't approach her, Cat could feel his eyes on her. The feeling continued throughout the play put on by the school children. By the time it was finished, she was as edgy as a long-tailed tomcat around a roomful of children.

It was not a feeling she appreciated.

Smitty, the blacksmith, was introduced as the auctioneer, and a cheer sounded around the room. Cat curled her fingers into her palms. She tried to appear calm and composed, but her heart pounded so loud in her chest that she was surprised that everyone didn't turn to tell her to hush.

The door slammed closed, and Cat jumped. Her gaze quickly turned to the doorway out of ingrained habit. A short, skinny man in a bowler hat stood inside the schoolhouse room.

Cat swallowed and stared at the Pinkerton man. Her mouth felt like someone had wiped it dry.

Miss Simms hurried across the room to greet the newcomer. Sarah poked Cat in the side.

"What is he doing back in town?"

Cat only shook her head. She couldn't utter a word if her life depended on it. She watched in stunned disbelief as the Pinkerton removed his hat and bowed low over Miss Simms's hand. She could hear the woman giggle from across the room.

"Would you look at that?" Sarah poked her again. "Maybe we've found our buyer after all. Come on."

Cat jerked her arm from her friend's grasp. "What are you doing?"

There was no way on this earth that she was going to willingly draw any attention to herself around the man who had been trailing her.

"We're going to sell us a box supper. Miss Simms's to be exact."

Before Cat could elude her hold, Sarah caught her elbow and dragged her along in her wake.

"Mr. Winston, isn't it?" Sarah asked in a voice laced with friendly welcome.

"Ladies." He rolled the brim of his hat between his fingers.

As Miss Simms stared at the floor, his gaze never left her face. Cat figured she could pull out her derringer and wave it in his face, and he wouldn't even notice it. His full attention was centered on the tall woman beside him.

Sarah leaned closer in a most unladylike manner and whispered above his ear, "Celia brought supper number one. In case you'd like to place a bid."

"Thank you. I do believe I will be bidding tonight," he answered.

Miss Celia Simms blushed and giggled like a schoolgirl. Mr. Louis Winston grinned widely and took both her hands in his. Together they walked away to a corner of the room, leaving Cat and Sarah staring after them.

"Well, I'll be danged," Sarah muttered.

"Sarah," Cat chastised her.

Her friend merely shrugged one shoulder. "Who'd have ever thought that little weasel would go all soft-eyed over Miss Simms? Oh, come on. The bidding is getting ready to start."

Louis Winston led Miss Simms to the front of the room and stood only a few feet away while she stood beside the blackboard, ready to write down the numbers and amounts. He stared at her in rapt attentiveness.

Sure enough, when number one was announced and the basket held up, the Pinkerton put in the first bid, and the second, and the third. In fact, he was the only one to bid on the schoolteacher's supper. Cat didn't think he even noticed.

As the next number was announced and the bidding began, Cat observed the statuesque blonde from outside the saloon whispering to the man beside her.

"That's Ruth and her husband," Sarah leaned closer and informed her.

Just then, Ruth jabbed her spouse sharply in the ribs. He yelped and raised the bid on the current supper. The rest of the room burst into laughter.

"No husband worth his salt better miss bidding on his wife's supper," Sarah whispered.

As each new number up for bid was announced, drawing ever closer to Cat's supper, she grew tense. She caught herself rubbing her hand back and forth over her stomach to calm it, and stopped herself. That was certainly not a ladylike action. Without thinking, she drew her lower lip between her teeth.

Garrett's gut clenched at Cat's motion. He knew firsthand how tender her lips happened to be. And how sweet. And how tempting.

As number ten was called out, he ignored the flurry of activity and stared at Cat. She looked beautiful today, if possible even more so than the last time he'd seen her. No, he corrected himself. The last time he'd laid his eyes on her, she'd been in his tub. Naked, except for a layer of bubbles.

He tightened his gun hand into a fist. If he didn't get better control of himself, he'd stride right across the room and take her into his—

A sharp jab to his side abruptly halted his thoughts. One hand going to his gun, he turned to face his attacker.

"Bid," Ty ordered him.

Garrett blinked at his friend.

Ty gestured to the auctioneer and the basket. "Go ahead and bid."

Garrett noticed the rush of activity. Matt Newsom and George Benton were trying to outshout each other in their eagerness to bid on the current lady's supper. He watched in open enjoyment.

Another jab in his ribs caught him unaware.

"Aren't you going to even bid?"

He turned to Ty with a frown. "Why should I?"

"That's number ten."

When Garrett didn't react, Ty poked him again.

"That's Miss Parker's."

Garrett turned his full attention to the front of the room. He raised his hand in a challenging bid.

Cat listened to the furious bidding over her box supper. A smile curved her lips. Who would have ever thought her supper could create such interest?

She ran her hand down her skirt. Yes, there was definitely something to wearing these fancy outfits.

"Sold to Jake Garrett," the auctioneer announced.

Cat snapped her head up, and her gaze met Garrett's. He smiled and tipped his hat to her.

"See, that wasn't so bad, was it?" Sarah asked her. "Soon the real fun begins. Supper shared with our buyers."

Cat's mouth suddenly went as dry as burned toast.

Now came the hardest part—sharing the box supper with Jake Garrett. When the final bidding concluded, she felt him approaching her, even before she saw him.

Garrett smiled and gave her his arm. Cat hesitated a moment.

"Shall we eat outside?" he asked, gesturing to where Miss Simms and Mr. Winston were slipping out the door.

Sarah stepped closer. "Absolutely not. Cat's reputation would be ruined." She took Cat's other arm and led her and Garrett toward a table. "Why don't you two join Ty and me?"

Cat almost sighed her relief at her reprieve. Right now, her emotions lay too near the surface to be alone with Garrett. She didn't trust him. Or herself.

She helped Sarah unpack the suppers, carefully setting the lemon pie on the table. Garrett glanced from the treat to her and grinned widely.

"I didn't think you could cook," he whispered when she sat down.

Cat bit back her response that of course she could cook. And darned good, too. She forced herself to lower her gaze in the ladylike, demure gesture she was coming to hate. The constant remembered deception played on her nerves. For a brief moment, she wished things could be different, that she could be herself. But, the past had changed everything. She had no choice now.

From the corner of her eye she saw Garrett bite into the fried chicken.

Unable to live with one more unnecessary lie, she spoke the truth. "I didn't cook the box supper. Sarah did."

"I know."

Garrett smiled at her over the piece of crispy chicken in his hands. He took another bite. Smiling in return, Cat began to eat her supper. She could hear the low voices of Sarah and Ty from down the table.

"Cat, come for a ride with me? Tomorrow afternoon." Garrett touched her fingertips with his.

Her breath quickened and she knew she should refuse, but she didn't.

"I'd like that," she answered, ignoring the little voice of warning in the back of her mind.

A feeling near to anticipation came over her, and she tried to deny it. She refused to believe she might be looking forward to the outing with Garrett. She was merely pleased her plan was proceeding so well. After all, spending time with Garrett would keep him off guard.

That had to be the reason.

She couldn't be falling for him.

Chapter Thirteen

Garrett patiently unraveled another portion of his horse's mane from the strands of tail braided into it. Six months ago, he'd have already been facing down the man responsible for the prank. And he'd be doing it with a gun.

Now, today, he'd reacted differently. It brought fully to his attention how much he'd changed since his few months in Millwood. Maybe he was getting ready to settle down with a nice woman. He jerked his drifting thoughts up sharply. What *nice* woman would have him?

He reached down and grabbed up the brush, shoving the answer to the question into oblivion. His horse nickered, and he patted his neck.

"Easy," Garrett murmured softly to him. "Bet you'd like to get hold of who did this, too?"

Garrett set to work on another portion of mane. He wasn't more than half done. He'd be the first to admit his patience was growing thin about now. If he caught the culprit who had braided his mount's tail into its mane, he'd . . .

"Morning," Ty spoke from the doorway of the livery stable.

Garrett merely nodded and kept working.

"Busy, are you?"

Garrett took note that his friend's voice held a betraying thread of repressed laughter. He held his tongue, waiting.

"Looks like you've been at it awhile." An undercurrent of humor could be heard in the words.

"Well, let it out, or you'll bust." Garrett turned to face his friend in time to see his lips twitch with laughter.

Ty looked up at the hayloft above, his lips twitching worse. "Seems you're up and mighty busy early today, aren't you?"

"Yup." Garrett knew the sheriff was waiting for an outburst from him, but remained stoic.

"Any special reason you care to tell me about?" Ty asked.

"I was planning on an early morning ride, then a leisurely breakfast before I spent the afternoon in a lady's company."

"Plans change some?"

Garrett brushed at a patch of detangled mane. From the corner of his eye he observed his friend throw a quick glance to the horse's tail. The movement was a dead giveaway.

He'd found one of his culprits; he'd be willing to place a bet on it.

Garrett turned suddenly and faced his friend. "You wouldn't know who happened to think that braiding the tail into the mane was a good idea, would you?"

Ty burst into laughter, unable to hold it back any longer. "Can't say I do. But, I can think of a half a dozen suspects. It usually happens to whoever wins the bidding on the best girl's box supper."

"Yup. Figured you'd say something like that. Next time, see it isn't braided quite so tight, will you?"

"Me?" His voice held the epitome of innocence.

"Who else was likely the one in charge of this?" Garrett accused, but his grin belied any true anger.

Ty slapped him on the shoulder. "But wasn't her supper worth it?"

"That it was." A smile curved Garrett's lips and stayed there.

Stepping back, Ty leaned against a stall. "Miss Simms's

new beau left on the train a bit ago. Hear tell she's a mite upset with him. A body could hear them arguing all the way to the station.''

"The Pinkerton man's gone?"

Ty nodded. "It's a shame he couldn't have stuck around awhile. Miss Simms just might have managed to lasso him." He paused to rub his chin. "Then Miss Parker could stay on in town as the new schoolteacher."

Garrett's head snapped up at the remark. It was worth considering. The hairs at the back of his neck prickled, and he threw an assessing glance about him. Nothing there but his friend. However, the feeling persisted.

Maybe he'd speak to Cat about teaching in Millwood when he met her this afternoon. One never could tell.

Tamera's thoughts were following the same trail. She shifted position from her listening post atop the stall rail across from where Garrett stood brushing his horse.

If Cat Parker were to be established in town as the new schoolmarm, all respectable, she couldn't very well kill anyone, could she? Much less Garrett.

It seemed a little heavenly assistance was in order. Whatever Miss Simms and that little man Winston had words about surely could use some smoothing over. She tapped her foot against the board, nearly upsetting herself from the rail. She wavered, then caught herself from falling. However, her halo rolled over her shoulder, hit the floor, and rolled down between the stalls.

"Oh, feathers!"

Tamera scrambled down on her hands and knees and followed the errant golden circle. It came to a rest against the horse's back foot. She eased forward and snatched up the halo.

Garrett's horse shied to one side, nearly knocking him over.

"Easy," Garrett soothed his mount. He glanced about the stalls again. Something had disturbed the animal. And him as well.

Tamera slapped her halo atop her head and backed away. She'd nearly done it that time. Her charge was beginning to sense her presence more and more. She supposed it came from him being a gunslinger and being more observant to his warning senses than most people. She'd have to be more cautious in the future.

However, for now she had another task to attend to. She would find Miss Simms and convince her to follow her heart.

Easier said than done.

Fifteen minutes later, Tamera glared down at the schoolteacher from her perch atop the desk. Whatever was wrong with the woman?

She'd whispered the bit about following her heart into the woman's ear until she feared her halo would fly off. Her feathers ruffled in dismay. Her brilliant idea was not working.

All Miss Simms had done in response was wave her hand about like she was shooing away a pesky fly.

Why did the teacher have to be so stubborn?

Tamera sighed and stood to her feet. She didn't want to resort to this, but she didn't have a choice. She needed the woman's attention off her class paperwork.

"Miss Simms," she said aloud.

The woman jumped and dropped the papers from her hand. They scattered across the floor.

"Who's there?" she asked.

Silence.

The teacher slowly looked around the room as if examining every nook and cranny.

Tamera sucked in a big breath and released it all at once, straight at the papers on the wood floor. The papers lifted into the air, then resettled.

Miss Simms let out a shriek.

Tamera reached out a hand and knocked a tin pitcher off the desk corner. It clattered to the floor.

This time Miss Simms threw up her hands and screamed, "Ghosts."

Tamera stopped in mid-breath. *Ghosts?* Oh, no, she hadn't

meant to scare the poor woman silly. She'd only wanted to get her attention. She closed her eyes tightly and winced.

The sound of running footsteps pounded in her ears. Tamera groaned. She hadn't meant to chase the poor old dear away in terror. Why, she'd—

"Out! Out! Out! Do you hear me?" Miss Simms's voice could have been heard in heaven itself.

Tamera's eyes snapped open and widened in disbelief. The teacher had grabbed up a broom and was running about the room brandishing it like a weapon. Suddenly she drew closer and *swatted* Tamera solidly on her backside.

Gasping in disbelief, Tamera flew for the door. No one ever struck an angel. Well, she most certainly was not finished with Miss Simms.

The teacher swiped the broom through the air again, and this time Tamera took the wisest course of action. She left.

Miss Simms followed her right out the door and into the street, narrowly missing running her down in her haste. Tamera sidestepped her, then fell in behind the teacher and followed close on her heels, but not too close. The woman still held the broom clutched to her bosom like a weapon.

Miss Celia Simms stomped down the street, turned at the corner, and marched right into the sheriff's office.

"Sheriff?" she yelled out, shoving the door hard enough to make it bounce off the wall.

Ty jumped to his feet, his hand drawing his gun in an instinctive gesture.

Miss Simms stepped back, her one hand on her heart, other hand gripping the broom handle. "Don't you dare point that thing at me after what I've been through."

"Sorry, ma'am." He reholstered his gun, and apologized again.

She waved away his words. "Well, I want to know what you intend to do about this." She shook the broom at him.

"I've already apologized to you. Twice."

"Not that." She slammed the broom handle against the desk.

"I want to know what you're going to do about the pranksters playing games in *my* schoolhouse."

"Ma'am—"

"Oh, very well, come with me. I'll show you."

With this, she turned and marched out the door. There was nothing for Ty to do but follow in her wake and try to make sense out of her ramblings about flying papers, and sticky fingers, and tin pinchers. He scratched his head and decided that maybe he and his buddies hadn't been the only ones having some fun this morning. But did he have to be the one on the receiving end this time?

Two hours later, Garrett stood looking out the window of the sheriff's office at the sunlight without really seeing anything outside. Of course, there wasn't any doubt that he'd do the favor Ty had asked of him. It seemed Miss Simms had the entire town in an uproar, and Ty had his hands full settling things down here. It was up to Garrett to handle the problem outside of town.

"I appreciate this," Ty said, breaking into his thoughts.

Garrett glanced at his friend in time to catch the small object he tossed at him. A deputy badge.

If Ty wanted him to wear the badge, there was trouble.

"Telegram said the outlaw gang that's been stirring up things around these parts has been seen headed for Madison. I need you to meet up with the posse there, see if you can spot any of the men who rode in here."

"Consider it done."

"But I need you to be wearing that."

Garrett rubbed his thumb back and forth over the face of the badge in his hand.

"Well," Ty cut in, "you going to polish that thing or wear it?"

"I'll wear it." Garrett held up his hand to forestall his friend's sure-to-be vocal congratulations. "For this one job."

Ty crossed the room and slapped him on the shoulder. "I knew—"

"Then when I ride back in here, you get this back. Until I'm ready to wear it full time."

"All right. I'll take what I can get."

Garrett pinned the badge onto his vest.

Ty's grin widened. "But I'm betting that once you've pinned it on, you won't take it off."

"You'd lose your money."

"You think so?"

"I know so."

Garrett settled his hat firmly on his head and strode to the door.

Ty's serious voice stopped him. "Don't go trying to be no hero. You hear?"

"Yup."

"All you gotta do is help track that outlaw gang that nearly hit our town. You're only lending a hand to the posse from Madison."

Garrett nodded his agreement. He had his own reasons for wanting to go to Madison himself. This would be as good a chance as he'd get to check out Cat's story about that teaching position. He wanted to believe her, but some nagging sense of doubt ate at him.

"See you tomorrow?" Ty asked.

"Tomorrow."

At the door, Garrett stopped and turned back around. "Would you mind telling Cat that I won't be able to take her riding today? Explain things to her for me?"

"Sure enough. Hey, maybe I can help out your case with her a little while I'm at it," Ty teased.

"Just relay my message. Nothing else."

Garrett turned and strode out the door, shutting it behind him on his friend's laughter. He was in a hurry to get this job over with and get back to Millwood. And a certain lady.

* * *

Cat adjusted her bustle for the fifth time in as many minutes. The soft pink muslin gown with its slightly fuller skirt was the closest thing she had to a riding habit. It had never crossed her mind when she'd purchased her new wardrobe that she would need a special outfit of clothing to ride a horse.

She nervously ran her hands down the skirt. Her petticoat whispered beneath the muslin gown. Would it do for an afternoon ride? She didn't have much of a choice at this late date.

Her feet still ached from last night, and she frowned down at her kid slippers. What she wouldn't give for her old boots hidden away in the bottom of her carpetbag. However, she was certain fine ladies didn't wear well-worn boots with a fancy dress.

Turning away from the temptation of the carpetbag's contents, she walked across to the window and peered out. She didn't know what she expected to find outside. Maybe Garrett approaching? A rush of disappointment swept over her at the view.

Garrett was almost an hour late.

Forgetting her aching feet, she stomped one foot in a burst of anger. Who did he think he was asking a lady out and then daring to be late to pick her up?

Her anger soared, only to dash to the bottom of her toes at her next thought. Maybe he wasn't coming. Maybe he'd changed his mind.

Once again she was a skinny teenaged girl with all those old self-doubts. It didn't matter that she now wore fine pretty gowns instead of too-short faded calico dresses. Inside she hadn't changed that much.

This wouldn't be the first time Garrett had promised to come for her and never shown up. Pain ate away at what self-confidence she'd worked hard for and mastered through the years. She slowly walked over to the oval mirror and stared at her reflection. She couldn't help wondering what it was about her that sent the men hightailing it away in the opposite direction.

She looked harder at the reflection of the finely clothed woman in the mirror. Oh, she could attract a man's attention, especially dressed as she was in pretty gowns. But why couldn't she hold their attentions? What was wrong with her?

She whirled away from the mirror. Thrusting the old hurts into the back of her mind, she crossed to the window again. She leaned her forehead against the cool pane and looked out at the town below. However, no matter how hard she looked, she couldn't make Garrett materialize and come for her.

Anger rose in her again. Rejection warred with it, and they combined forces. Who did he think he was, breaking promises to her like this?

She might not even go out riding with him if he arrived for her. It would serve him right if she refused.

A tiny part of her ignored this possibility. She drew her lower lip between her teeth and began to worry.

Tamera let out a deep sigh that came from the bottom of her toes. She'd made such a mess of things. Cat was mad at Garrett, and when the sheriff couldn't find evidence of any pranks, Miss Simms began telling the whole town that the schoolhouse was haunted.

She shuddered at the thought. She'd received a stern lecture over that incident.

She could still hear St. Peter shouting at her. "You're supposed to guard one man. Not disrupt an entire town."

She imagined she could still hear the echo of St. Peter's voice chastising her. He'd boomed the words at her in a volume that would shake the heavens.

"Oh, feathers," she grumbled under her breath.

How was she to tell her superior that she'd now lost track of Garrett? He'd only gone out on a ride. At least that's what she'd thought she understood, but then she'd gotten sidetracked with Miss Simms and the sheriff.

She shuddered at the memory of that disaster. Then she squared her shoulders with sudden resolve. There was nothing for it but to set about locating Garrett and taking care of him before anything else happened.

The sun beat down with springtime insistence. Garrett urged his horse on. He was hot, tired, and beginning to wish he'd listened to Ty.

But no, he'd had to go off on his own when he'd run across the outlaw gang's trail. Of course, that trail had taken a turn and led *away* from Madison.

He squinted up at the sun. He'd give it another half hour; then he'd turn his horse around and head to meet up with the posse.

He glared up at the sun again. For this he'd given up a leisurely ride with Cat Parker. He was a fool. Plain and simple.

Last night, she'd been so sweet when she'd confessed in a nervous voice that she hadn't cooked the box supper he'd bid an outrageous sum to buy. He'd resisted the urge to draw her up into his arms and carry her out of the schoolhouse. He smiled at her imagined reaction if he had acted on the impulse.

She was the prettiest thing he'd laid eyes on in a long time. And the most stubborn. Beneath that ladylike demeanor, she had a will of iron. If he'd carried her off like he wanted, she would likely—

Suddenly, some sense of self-preservation told him to get the hell out of there.

A chill snaked its way down Garrett's neck. He could have sworn he heard someone whisper a warning aloud. He sent a quick glance over his shoulder and caught a faint movement behind a nearby rock.

Ambush.

A betraying noise to his left alerted him, and he whirled his horse about in time to avoid the bullet that thudded into the ground. Damn.

He'd let himself fall right into an ambush any fool could

have avoided. If he'd had his mind where it should have been instead of daydreaming over a woman. . . .

Turning, he bent low over his horse's neck, making himself as small a target as possible. This time a bullet zinged past his ear.

Garrett ducked lower and spurred his horse, urging any additional speed out of him. He could hear hoofbeats behind him. The next bullet caught him in the back, knocking him out of the saddle.

He hit the ground with a bone-jarring thud. He attempted to get to get to his feet, but before he could succeed, the men were on him.

A booted foot slammed into his side, and he nearly blacked out from the pain that stabbed through his body. It robbed him of his breath.

Paralyzed with pain, for a moment he couldn't move. He could feel the blood seeping through his shirt. A picture of Cat flitted through his mind. He reached for his gun belt with one hand and struggled to get to his feet, to face his attackers.

"Hey, Lazarus, shouldn't we be riding out?" a man's voice asked.

"We'll ride when I say so."

Garrett heard the men speaking as if from a long distance off. He struggled to remain conscious. Forcing his eyes open, he blinked against the sunlight and concentrated on reaching his gun.

Someone delivered another sharp kick to his ribs, and he doubled over. Blackness swept over him in rolling waves, then receded.

"Not such a fast gun now, are you?"

The words tinged with hatred penetrated Garrett's pain-filled mind. He struggled up from the dark void enveloping him.

"Lazarus?" a man called out. "Come on."

"Not yet," the man shouted back.

Then, his voice drew nearer to Garrett's ears, and a whiskey-scented breath fanned across his face. "Now we're even."

A final kick to his side sent waves of pain to drown out the words.

The sound of horses riding away stirred Garrett, and he attempted to sit up. Searing pain swept through him, sending him into the dark void that awaited his return.

He gave in to the darkness of unconsciousness.

And certain death.

Chapter Fourteen

Cat removed the gloves she'd smoothed on only minutes before. She tossed them atop the bed beside her pink lace parasol. Tipping her head back, she stared at the ceiling of her room. The boardinghouse was as quiet as a tomb with Sarah and Amanda out visiting. She sighed, it was past mid-afternoon.

Jake Garrett was long past late for their ride.

A vague uneasiness gripped her. Had something happened to him? Or had he merely changed his mind and been too cowardly to come and tell her so?

Caitlan Parker. Garrett needs you.

The words seemed to come from within the room, making Cat jump. They sounded over loud in the small room. She whirled about to confront the speaker, but found the room empty, except for herself.

She rubbed her hands up and down her arms, a sudden chill overcoming her. Slowly, she turned in a circle and surveyed her surroundings.

Crossing the wooden floor, she laid her ear against the wall separating her and Garrett's rooms. Nothing. Not a single sound came from the other side of the wall.

He hadn't returned from wherever he'd gone to early this morning.

She whirled away from the wall, angry with herself for her foolish action. Surely she would have heard him enter his room if he'd come back. She always did. In fact, she could hear each and every sound he made moving about next door. It had caused her sleepless nights and unspeakable dreaming.

Frustrated, she kicked her skirt out of her way and began to pace. Surely *someone* knew Garrett's whereabouts. A bad feeling settled like a lump of greasy food deep in her stomach.

Something was wrong.

Cat knew it with absolute certainty.

Grabbing up her gloves and reticule, she determined to find out exactly what was going on. Garrett's friend, the sheriff, would be a good place to start.

Her worry for Garrett outweighed her usual reluctance to get within spitting distance of any lawman. Minutes later, Cat walked into the sheriff's office, her head held high and a winning smile on her face. He looked up at her entry with surprise.

"Good afternoon, ma'am," Ty said, beginning to rise to his feet.

Cat forestalled his movement with a wave of her gloved hand. "Do you know where Jake Garrett is?"

Ty shoved back his chair and jumped to his feet. "Oh, ma'am, I'm sorry. I got busy with Miss Simms's problem and forgot to give you his message."

"Message?" Cat had trouble forcing the word out. She was certain her tongue had stuck to the roof of her suddenly dry mouth.

"Yes, ma'am. He had to ride out to Madison on a job for me. Won't be back until tomorrow. He asked me to tell you he apologized."

Garrett hadn't run out on her a second time.

Cat's knees weakened at the realization. Garrett had ridden out for the sheriff.

"Thank you, Sheriff," she answered. More than you know, she added silently.

"Ty. Call me Ty, ma'am. Nearly everyone in town does."

"Well, thank you ... Ty." She couldn't help the slight hesitation on using his name. Imagine her being on a first name basis with a lawman.

Madison. She recalled the town of Madison. She'd come through there on her way to Millwood. It was also the name of the town she'd told Garrett that she'd planned on applying for the teaching position.

With a wan smile, she turned away and walked back to the door. A sudden chill crept down her back, almost the same feeling she got when someone was drawing on her. One hand on the knob, she halted and turned back to face the sheriff.

He stood exactly where she'd left him. His gun remained in his holster. She frowned.

"Something wrong, ma'am?"

Yes, the word echoed in her mind. Every one of her instincts was shouting that something was most definitely deadly wrong. If the trouble wasn't directed at her, then it had to be Garrett.

"Sheriff ... ah, Ty," she amended and tried to smile. "You said Garrett rode to Madison?"

"Yes, ma'am. Due north of here." He cocked his head, studying her. "Now, you wouldn't be thinking of heading out after him, would you?"

"Me?" She faked a shocked tone at the impudence of his question. Actually it was the accuracy of his remark that had startled her.

As he continued to stare hard at her, she placed her hand on her chest, and added with a slight shudder, "Heavens no."

"Well, that's good. It's some rough country out there for a lady."

Cat banked the rush of anger that rose up at his assumption. She'd ridden across rougher land than what lay between here and Madison, but there was no way the lawman could know that.

"If he's not back by mid-morning, I'll ride out myself to check on things," he assured her.

A little voice whispered to her that morning might be too late. Her throat caught at the implication of the wayward thought.

Garrett could be lying out there hurt. Or worse.

She couldn't hold back her question. "But if something has happened—"

"If you'll pardon me for saying it, ma'am, I don't think there's anything a little bit like you could do to help him. Garrett knows what he's doing."

Cat stopped herself from responding like she wanted to; instead she decided the best thing to do was take care of matters herself.

"Thank you, Ty," she forced the words out.

"Now, don't you worry."

That was exactly what she was already doing.

However, she had no intention of sitting idly by while the hours crept past—not when the growing sense of urgency was eating at her.

Cat closed the door behind her, resisting the urge to slam it so loud the windows of the office would rattle. She wasted no time in returning to the boardinghouse. She had things to do, and fast.

Inside her room, she set to work. She ripped off her gloves and threw them on the bed, then hurried to where her carpetbag sat on a chair. Kicking off her shoes, she reached down into the bag and lifted out her boots. She quickly carried them to the bed.

Hiking up her skirt, she yanked off her silk hose and dropped them to the floor. She sat on the edge of the mattress and replaced the hose with the thick socks that had been tucked inside her leather boots. Then she pulled her old comfortable boots on.

She wasn't about to ride out on any trail in fancy satin or kid slippers. No, she wanted the comfort and safety of her old boots.

Without pausing, she crossed back to the carpetbag and withdrew one of her Colt revolvers. Checking it, she slipped it into the deep pocket of her skirt. Later, when she'd left Millwood behind, she'd transfer the gun to the saddlebag.

She glanced down at her feet. Only the toes of her boots showed beneath the hem of the gown. Well, it would have to do. She wasn't riding out without her boots on, no matter how it might look to anyone. Riding in this fancy lady's getup was going to be hard enough as it was, but she didn't dare change into her breeches.

Cat turned and headed for the door; then she stopped a foot short. Crossing back to the bed, she made her decision.

At the last moment, she raised up her skirts and unfastened her bustle. Yanking off the annoying contraption, she tossed it on the bed. She wouldn't be needing any lady's bustle where she was headed.

It took her another few precious minutes of daylight to find the livery stable and then talk the blacksmith-auctioneer into letting her have a horse.

"Ma'am, I don't have any of those fancy sidesaddles you ladies use," Smitty explained with a heavy sigh.

She barely bit back the "thank goodness" that sprang to her lips.

Instead, she smiled sweetly at him and said, "Don't worry. I'm sure I can make do with one of those other saddles."

The only thing she knew was that she never could have even gotten up on one of the ridiculous-looking sidesaddles, much less stayed on it.

Without thinking what she was doing, she reached for the nearest saddle.

Smitty stepped to her side immediately. "Oh, no, ma'am. I'll get that for you."

As he saddled a mount for her, she quickly checked that her revolver was safely hidden and that the bulge in her skirt wasn't noticeable. Then she set to finding out the information she would need to find Garrett.

"Is this an even riding horse?" she asked, her voice full of innocence.

"Yes." Smitty straightened in indignation.

"I wasn't meaning to insult you," Cat rushed to apologize and appease him. "It was something the sheriff, Ty, said about Garrett's horse having an odd gait." She nibbled her lower lip in pretended confusion. "Or a shoe. Or something."

"Ma'am? Why would you be discussing things like that?"

His eyes widened at her wording, and she realized the mistake immediately. Quickly, she attempted to smooth it over.

She covered her lips with her fingertips. "Oh, dear, I've gotten it all mixed up now. There was something I was to tell that posse if I met them coming this way." She laid her hand on her chest. "Oh, dear, maybe I got it wrong."

"Oh, no, ma'am." He rushed to assure her in her obvious distress. "Garrett's horse has a heavy buildup on the left side of the shoe. It's special to straighten—" He paused, then added, "You just tell them that."

Cat hoped her relief wasn't too obvious. "I will."

Smitty frowned at her. "Now, remember, it's on the left side of the shoe. It'll show in his tracks. They'll know what you're talking about. You got that?"

"Yes, I've got it."

Thankfully she had something to go on, a way to track Garrett. But she couldn't dare let on that she planned to use that bit of information for herself. Of course, she'd relay it to the posse, too. If she ran into them.

She felt a brief sense of relief. This was something she knew about. Her pa had taught her to track with the best of them. Surely she could find Garrett soon.

Cat picked up Garrett's trail right outside of town. It wasn't hard to do; she knew from the sheriff that he'd been headed due north.

Thankfully, no one was around to question her skill in tracking. It was something she didn't want to try to explain. Most assuredly a fine New York lady wouldn't know beans about tracking a rider. Much less about how to spot a horse sporting a modified shoe.

The terrain was as rough as the sheriff had told her. Cat rode as hard as she dared push her mount. The distance and the hours sped past. Fear nibbled at her confidence. It would be dark soon.

She had to find him by then, or . . .

In the distance she spotted what looked to be a lone horse grazing. Nearby lay a figure on the ground. Turning her horse, she kicked the mare, urging her on. Worry tagged along beside her, making Cat fearful of what she might find.

As she drew nearer, she realized her fears had been justified. A man lay sprawled on the rough ground.

Garrett.

Her throat threatened to close off, but she nudged her horse on, hurrying to reach him. Near enough at last, she pulled her horse up.

Cat leaped off her mount and raced to Garrett. Blood stained the front and side of his shirt. Kneeling beside him, she sent up a brief prayer that he was alive. Hardly daring to breath herself, she lowered her head against his chest and listened for a heartbeat.

It was there. His heart pounded strong and steady beneath her ear.

Tears of relief burned her eyes and trickled down her cheeks, but she ignored them. She had to see to his wound and then find shelter before darkness fell. The temperature would drop drastically by then. Fear gnawed at her stomach, making it churn.

She forced herself to her feet. With a glance back down at him, she turned and ran for her horse. Grabbing up her canteen of water, she dashed the short distance back to Garrett's side.

She knelt beside him for a moment looking into his face. His skin was so pale, the only color coming from the dark stubble along the lower half of his cheeks and along his jaw. She nibbled her lower lip. She wouldn't let him die.

She wouldn't.

For the first time she was truly thankful for the confining petticoats she wore. She drew up her skirt, unconcerned with showing her ankles. There was no one but her to notice. Quickly she tore several strips off her petticoat and then used them to wipe away the dried blood from around Garrett's injuries.

When she got her first good look at the bullet wound, it nearly turned her stomach. It was worse than she'd suspected.

Cat closed her eyes a moment and got a hold of her courage. As she opened her eyes, her back straightened in determination. Drawing a small knife from her boot, she noticed that her hands trembled.

She tried telling herself this was no different than treating her pa or one of the farmhands she'd tended to before, but somehow she knew this was very different. The man lying so still beneath her hands was Garrett. She drew in a deep, steadying breath and set to cutting away his shirt and checking for the whereabouts of the bullet.

Minutes later, Cat sat back on her haunches with a sigh of relief. It appeared, as much as she could tell, that the bullet had passed clean through him.

This time her hand more than trembled when she reached for the canteen. She cleaned the wound as best as she could with what she had close at hand. Using her knife, she tore several more strips of her petticoat. As she knelt forward, it hung in tatters, tangling below her knees. She ignored it, instead concentrating on pressing a pad made of the strips tight against Garrett's chest.

Struggling, she lifted him toward her until his unresisting body lay against her breasts. She placed another pack of bandages against the wound on his back and began winding a strip of fabric about his back and chest to hold the bandages in place.

When she had finished, she gulped in several deep breaths. She held Garrett close against her, not daring to lay him back down. She wasn't sure she'd have the strength to lift him up again.

After a moment's rest, she squatted back on her haunches and placed her arms under Garrett's arms and around his back. As gently as possible, she dragged him to his feet. Standing at last, she sucked in air and continued to drag him across to where her horse stood.

It took three tries before she could maneuver Garrett's unconscious body onto her mount. She'd only managed to drape him halfway across the saddle, but it would have to do.

Sliding her foot into the stirrup, she carefully swung herself up behind him, resting one hand on his back. The sun had set, and darkness was beginning to envelop the area. If she didn't find shelter soon, it would be nearly impossible to see to make camp. She guided the mare over to where Garrett's horse grazed, then caught up the reins and drew his horse along behind her.

After nearly a half hour of riding, Cat had nearly given up on finding a shelter of any kind. She decided she'd have to attempt to make a lean-to with what few supplies she had at hand—a blanket, bedroll, and the contents of Garrett's saddlebags. However, she had no idea how she would explain a New York lady possessing that knowledge.

As she topped a small knoll, she spotted an old line shack. She sent up a silent shout of thanksgiving along with a prayer that the place would be empty. Nudging her horse, she headed for the welcome shelter.

Outside the small one-room shack, she ground tethered her horse and walked cautiously to the door. She knocked, then pushed the door open. It was vacant.

Sighing her relief, she turned back to her horse and Garrett. She quickly tied the horses to a rail, then studied on how to best get Garrett down from the mount without making his injury worse.

Her decision made, she slipped her shoulder under the front part of his body, then began to ease him from the horse. The force of his weight brought his body down faster than she anticipated, and she staggered under the impact. Reaching out, she grabbed hold of the saddle to keep herself upright.

Garrett sagged against her, his chest nearly crushing her. Straightening her own body up as much as possible, Cat shifted him to her right side and clasped her arms about his upper torso. Gritting her teeth and nearly heaving with the exertion, she half carried, half dragged him into the line shack.

By the time she'd gotten Garrett across the floor and onto

the lone cot, every muscle in her body ached. She dropped onto the floor beside the cot, needing to catch her breath a bit before she could continue any further. Right now she didn't think she could stand if her life depended on it.

A few minutes later, she levered herself to her feet, and her shoulders nearly screamed out in pain. She found a blanket beside the cot, shook it out, and pulled it over Garrett. Then, daring one more look at him, she set to doing what needed to be tended to before nightfall.

Nervous, Cat checked out the area around the shack. A small fear remained that whoever had shot Garrett might be searching for him. The isolated location of the shack reassured her as to their safety. If need be, she had her Colt, and Garrett's guns, and ammunition. She could likely send someone packing in a hurry. She prayed it wouldn't come to that.

Shielding her eyes out of habit not necessity, she scanned the darkening horizon. Relief filled her that it came up empty. No riders in sight. Once it became fully dark, the shack would be nigh to impossible to see.

Her survey of the surrounding ground located a corral and small lean-to for the horses. It had been so well concealed that she'd found it merely by luck. Within minutes, she had the horses unsaddled and readied for the night.

She returned to the line shack to find that Garrett hadn't moved. A quick search of the shack revealed a small supply of food, a lantern, and matches. She lit the lantern and set it beside the cot.

A check of Garrett's makeshift bandages found that his wound had begun bleeding again. A closer look at the gaping wound revealed the worst—it needed to be stitched up to stop the bleeding. And there was no one else to do it but her.

Cat assured herself she could do this. How much different could it be from the tending she'd done on the hated farm? She forced back the rejoinder that she'd never tended to a man's gunshot wound on the farm.

Much less a wounded Jake Garrett.

Well, it had to be done, she told herself. Another search of the small one-room shack yielded a bottle of whiskey. She uncorked it, wiped off the top, and poured a generous amount over Garrett's wound.

Tipping the bottle to her lips, she took a bracing swallow of the liquor herself. It burned all the way down, and she coughed, bringing tears to her eyes. She wiped at them, then set to work.

Once the water was heated, and the lady's needle and thread was withdrawn from her reticule in the saddlebags, Cat sank onto the floor and took several deep breaths.

Closing her eyes, she sent up a prayer for help, and gathered up all the courage she could find. Her hands shook so much that it took her three attempts to thread the needle. At the first prick of Garrett's skin, she cried out herself. Biting her lip, she raised her chin and did what had to be done.

Finished at last, Cat stared down at the pan of bloodied water; her hands were shaking so badly that she dropped the needle onto the floor. As she reached to pick it up, she burst into tears.

Angry with herself, she brushed the tears away, but more came to replace them. Cat, who never cried, couldn't seem to stop them now that they had started. Resting her head against the cot, she willed the tears to end.

She blinked and brushed a dark curl away from Garrett's forehead. His skin was hot to the touch.

Fever.

The single word frightened her to the very depths of her soul. She'd known people to die of a fever. Her ma had. She tenderly brushed a strand of hair from his temple.

"Don't you dare die on me, Jake Garrett," she whispered in a voice hoarse from crying. "You hear me?" She brushed away a tear. "Don't you dare die."

Chapter Fifteen

Cat smoothed the cool, wet cloth across Garrett's face, willing him to wake up, to talk to her, to smile at her. Even to yell at her. Anything as long as he was all right.

Had his fever cooled any at all in the time she'd been placing the cool compresses on his forehead? She couldn't tell if his skin indeed felt cooler, or if she only wished it so much that she'd begun to believe it.

Not daring to chance falling asleep when he might need her, she made a pad of the second blanket. Placing it on the floor beside the cot, she sank onto it, curling her feet beneath her.

Cat lost track of how much time passed with her placing cool compresses on his forehead and wiping his face before Garrett began to stir. Her heart soared with renewed hope.

However, as he started to moan and thrash about on the cot, her hopes crashed. Fear leaped up in her, nearly smothering her. If he kept this up, he'd likely tear out her stitching.

"Garrett," she called his name.

He didn't act as if he even heard her. Fear for him ate at her, nearly making her frantic. He couldn't die. He couldn't.

She didn't stop to question her change of heart toward him. She merely tended to him.

She tried smoothing his forehead and talking to him softly, but neither worked. He continued to kick at the blanket covering him.

Finally, Cat climbed onto the narrow cot with him. She stretched out, clasping her arms loosely about him. As she continued to whisper assurances to him, he began to calm. In a few minutes, he fell into a restless slumber.

She gently kissed his shoulder and sent up another prayer for his life. She was almost afraid that if she dared to close her eyes for even a moment, he'd slip away from her.

Although her mind knew that his sleep was a good sign of passing the most serious point and showed returning health, her heart feared to trust it. She vowed yet again not to let him die.

Finally, too exhausted to fight it any longer, her eyes drifted closed, and she fell asleep.

Cat awoke to the faint light of dawn breaking through the faded curtains of the small line shack. She turned, and every muscle in her body cried out in protest. Ignoring her own aches, she gently laid her hand on Garrett's forehead. When she found it cooler to her touch, she said a silent prayer of thanks.

His fever seemed to have broken. She noted a faint tinge of color returning to his face, replacing the fearful pallor of last night.

She recalled the chills that had racked Garrett's body during the night. They had shaken her awake, and she'd gathered up the second blanket and covered him with it. When the chills had continued, she'd finally climbed back into bed with him, holding him close to warm him. It had worked; he'd finally stopped shaking the cot, and the shivers had ceased.

He'd slept peacefully, at last, and she had brushed his hair away from his forehead with tenderness. It had been some time later before she'd drifted off to sleep again herself.

Her stomach growled in a reminder of the meals she'd missed. If she were to stand watch over Garrett and tend to him, she had to eat to sustain her own strength. And he needed food to regain his strength.

Standing to her feet, she stretched her protesting muscles. A quick search of the food supply yielded several tins, enough to make a nourishing stew.

As she prepared the food, thunder rumbled outside signaling a storm brewing. She'd hoped that if Garrett appeared better today, she'd be able to ride to Millwood for help. She paced to the window and, peering out, decided that any chance she had of riding to Millwood for help would have to wait until the storm blew out its fury.

Luckily, the rains would bring an added benefit. The water would wash away their tracks. If someone were out there looking for Garrett, there wouldn't be a single track to lead them here.

Restless, Cat turned away from the window. The wind and rain lashed the small shack, seeming to shake it to its foundation. It appeared this one was going to be a real gullywasher.

However, inside it remained snug and safe against the raging elements outside. Cat lit the lantern again, and it cast an almost cheery glow in the small room.

She wrinkled her nose. The one-room shack needed a good cleaning. Maybe later. First she had to tend to Garrett. She turned away from the small table where she'd set the lantern to meet Garrett's eyes on her.

"Garrett?" She whispered his name, almost afraid to say it aloud in case she was dreaming.

He closed his eyes, and she ran to his side. Kneeling at the side of the cot, she felt his forehead. It remained slightly warm. She nibbled her lip in worry.

Garrett opened his eyes again and stared into hers. His dark gaze looked troubled.

"Cat?"

"Yes?" She couldn't move from her spot beside him.

He blinked several times, then attempted to sit up. She rested her hands on his shoulders and eased him back down onto the cot. He didn't fight her.

"You need to rest—"

"Men . . . ambush!" Garrett suddenly pushed upward, nearly toppling her backward.

"No! You're safe," Cat assured him.

"But—"

She pressed gently but firmly against his shoulders. "Garrett, you have to lie back down."

He looked at her and blinked again. "Cat?"

"Yes, it's Cat. Now, lie down."

This time he let her ease him back onto the cot. She drew one of the blankets over him. He reached out and touched her cheek.

"You're really here?"

"Yes, I'm here. And you're safe."

She dared to rest her hand on his cheek. It was rough with stubble against her palm. But it felt wonderfully alive.

"How—" he began.

Cat interrupted him. "Save your strength. We'll talk later." She smiled at him and blinked away the sudden moisture in her eyes. "You're going to be fine."

"Umm, fine," he mumbled, his eyelids fluttering closed again.

"Garrett?"

He looked up at her.

"Do you think you could eat a little something?"

A small smile tugged at one corner of his mouth. "You cooked?"

"I cooked."

She stood and took the few steps needed to reach the wooden table and the two rickety chairs. Picking up the bowl and a spoon, she returned to her spot on the floor by the cot, then sank down onto her knees.

"Here, try some." She lifted the spoon to his mouth.

He insisted that she help him sit up first. He ate a few bites before his eyelids grew heavy. Removing the nearly empty bowl, she helped ease him back onto the cot, and he drifted off to sleep again. She let him sleep. He needed rest for now.

She set the bowl on the floor beside her and watched him sleep for a few minutes. Finally, the gnawing in her stomach reminded her that she hadn't eaten yet.

Getting to her feet, Cat returned to the table and fixed herself a bowl of the stew. It was surprisingly good, and she made short work of the serving.

She set a pan outside the door to collect rainwater, and shortly had enough to make do for a sponge bath of her own. Cleaned, she felt much more ready to face the remainder of the day. Dumping the pan of water outside, she collected both a bucket and another pan of fresh rainwater for later use.

During the course of the day, she cleaned the shack. Garrett awoke several more times; each time he remained awake only long enough to eat more of the stew she fed him. As the wind continued to howl outside, she was thankful for the shack they had found. Her ride to Millwood could wait until tomorrow. It would have to.

By late afternoon, caring for Garrett and the worrying over him took their toll, and exhaustion claimed Cat. She knew she had to get some rest or she would be of no use to Garrett or herself. She unrolled Garrett's bedroll beside the cot on the floor and stretched out onto it. She didn't want to chance disturbing him by lying on the cot with him; however, she wanted to be close in case he called out, or needed her.

Hours later, Garrett's outcry jolted her awake. She jumped to her feet and bent over him. Feeling his forehead, she bit her lip. His fever had worsened.

Cat filled a bowl of cool rainwater and laid cool compresses over his forehead again. His restlessness lessened under her gentle hands.

Sometime later, he opened his eyes and stared at her. Cat's smile sprang freely to her lips. He was all right. The horrible fever that had held him . . .

He raised his arm and laid a hand on her cheek. He blinked at her. "Laine?" he whispered.

His use of the old nickname sent a jolt through Cat that would have staggered her and brought her to her knees, if she'd been standing instead of already kneeling beside him. As it was, she couldn't move from her spot by his bedside.

Memories of the past, of that fateful day, held her in their powerful grip. Three long years ago, she'd been known as Laine. No one had called her by that name since her pa died. No one even knew her by that childish name anymore. When she'd left the farm, she'd left that name behind, taking the shorter nickname of Cat.

A hand of anticipation closed around her heart. If he'd called her by the old name, then surely it meant he'd recognized her.

Remembered her.

"Garrett?" She spoke his name with an undeniable quiver of expectancy in her voice.

A spark of hope flared in her. Garrett had remembered at long last. He'd . . .

His eyes met hers and held her in place.

"Go away," he said, and closed his eyes.

A small cry like that of an animal in pain came from deep within her. Laying her head down on her arms, she let the tears come. There was no one to see them but her. No one to care, but her.

The next morning, Cat awoke from her makeshift pallet on the shack floor. Rain pounded on the roof of the line shack, evidence of the continuance of the storm of the day before.

She rolled to her side and sat up. Her muscles ached with each move she made. Beside her, Garrett slept peacefully. His fever seemed to have lessened. However, the worry that had etched itself into her every breath wasn't entirely removed.

She wished she could get him medical help. A part of her told her that she had doctored him as good as any town doctor could do, but still she fretted. In the past, she'd tended enough farm animals and farmhands to know how to treat them and stave off infection.

Nibbling her fingertip, she stared at Garrett in consternation. She wished he'd wake up, conscious and focused. At this second, she didn't care whether he recognized her as Laine or Cat—just as long as he awoke well.

Crossing the room, she rummaged around and found an old rain slicker. Quickly she donned it, and slipped out the door into the rain to tend to the animals. And to have a check around.

Over half an hour later, Cat paused at the door and shook the rain from the slicker. Ducking inside, she removed the gear and draped it over a chair. The closed warmth of the room felt good to her chilled skin.

Turning, she shook out her hair, then froze in place. Garrett sat, propped up in the cot against the pillow, staring straight at her.

"Morning." She forced the greeting out.

He looked at her, puzzlement etched on his face. She waited, holding her breath in a blend of anticipation and doubt. What did he remember from yesterday, and from their past together?"

"Cat?" he asked.

Cat, not Laine.

A part of her was crushed. She swallowed down the burning tightness in her throat. She wouldn't cry. She wouldn't.

It was simple to see now. In his fevered state he'd confused the past and present. Now that the fever was gone, so was his Laine. Now, once again, he'd forgotten her.

She wanted to scream at him, to lash out and hurt him the way he'd hurt her. But she knew it would accomplish nothing.

Maybe the past was best left dead and buried.

However, a part of her mourned for it.

"Cat?" Garrett repeated, a frown pulling at his brows.

"Yes?" She forced the word out past the lump in her throat.

"Did you cook again?"

"What?"

"I'm hungry."

Relief swamped over her in spite of her own personal pain. Hunger was a good sign of recovery from his bullet wound. A very good sign. She dug up a wan smile for his benefit.

"Yes, I cooked. I'll get you some."

She swore she could feel his gaze following her movements. It made her edgy, and she even spilled part of the stew down her fingers.

Concentrating, she carried the bowl across the distance separating her and Garrett.

"Cat, where are my clothes?"

She nearly dumped the stew right into his lap at his question.

"Ah . . . ah . . ." She swallowed, then said, "Over there."

She gestured with one hand to where a man's pants and shirt lay draped over the remaining chair at the little table.

"What are they doing over there?" he persisted in asking.

She felt her cheeks heating and knew they had turned an embarrassing shade of pink, and were in danger of becoming bright red if he continued.

"It seemed like a good place to hang them."

She refused to meet his eyes, instead shifting the bowl to her other hand and moving the spoon about in the stew, as if it suddenly needed a great deal of stirring.

To forestall any further questions, she scooped up a spoonful of the stew and held it up to his mouth.

When Garrett opened his mouth to say something else, she shoved the spoon inside, effectively stopping whatever he'd been intending to say.

"Here, eat some," she ordered. "It's good."

He mumbled something she couldn't understand around the spoon in his mouth. One look at his eyes and she thought maybe she ought to be glad she hadn't made out his words.

He raised one hand and pulled the spoon from his mouth. Draping his arm over the edge of the cot, he discarded the utensil. It clattered to the floor.

Cat turned her head and met his gaze. The intensity and heat she found there held her enthralled. She felt her mouth go suddenly dry in response.

In a lightning-fast move, Garrett reached over and swept the bowl from her hands. Oh, he was much more improved than she'd thought. Leaning forward, he dropped the bowl onto the floor.

Cat swallowed past the lump rising in her throat. She had to be imagining what she thought she saw in his eyes. It couldn't be desire. And heat.

No, she was imagining it, or dreaming it. Garrett was recovering from being ill. He couldn't be thinking of . . .

Her body began to warm at the errant thought. She shouldn't even be thinking such a thing.

She jumped nervously when he placed his hands on her shoulders and then drew her to him. She was held mesmerized by the look in his dark eyes. He never broke the eye contact as he drew her now unresisting body closer.

And closer.

Until she was lying partially across his long, lean body, and partways beside him on the cot. Her breasts pressed against his chest. Lowering his head, he lightly brushed his lips across hers in a feathery kiss that reminded her of the touch of a butterfly.

"Garrett," she whispered against his lips. "Your wound—"

"Never mind."

He brushed another whisper-soft kiss over her lips. Then another.

"So sweet," he murmured.

Cat ached to give in to him. But she feared for him. She couldn't . . .

"Garrett," she tried again.

"Humm?" He turned his face and nuzzled the lobe of her ear.

"Ah, we . . ." She struggled to get the words out past the desire building deep within her.

He flicked the tip of his tongue over her ear. For a moment she forgot everything but the pure pleasure of his touch.

"Cat?" he breathed against the shell of her ear. "Do you want me?"

Nothing could have prevented the honesty of her response. "Yes," she answered in a soft breath of acquiescence.

He drew her tighter into his embrace. Her fingertips felt the bandage wrapped around his chest. No, they shouldn't. They couldn't.

"Garrett . . . we . . ."

He feathered another soft kiss across her lips. The words of protest trailed off into a soft sigh of pleasure.

In truth, she found it harder and harder to form any words that made sense. She felt she had to try one more time.

"Umm . . . ah . . . Garrett . . . we should—"

"Yes, we should," he murmured against her neck.

His breath stirred the fine hairs behind her ear, tickling and at the same time thrilling her, and she moaned in response.

She really should stop him. He shouldn't be doing this in his wounded condition. Another sigh escaped her lips. She should stop him.

As if of their own accord, and with a mind all their own, her hands smoothed over his shoulders, and her arms looped around his neck. Nothing on this earth could have stopped her from loving him.

She curled her fingers into the thick hair at the back of his neck. Soft, so tempting. She gave in to the temptation and ran her fingers higher through the dark waves of hair. It would be so easy to lose herself in the feel of his hair against her fingers. To lose herself in him.

Surrendering to him, she leaned closer into his tender embrace. He trailed a fiery line of kisses along her ear, to her jaw, and across her cheek. Each new kiss demanded more than the last. His lips met hers, and his next kiss shocked her speechless with its urgency.

She tightened her hands on his shoulders, wondering for the space of a ragged heartbeat however her hands had gotten there. The muscles beneath his taut flesh bunched and rippled beneath her fingers. The feel of his bare skin bought the recollection that beneath the blanket lying draped about his waist Garrett was nearly naked. While she had on entirely too many clothes.

He brushed his fingertips across her jaw and down the slim column of her neck, stroking her. His touch fired her like nothing she'd ever before imagined in her entire life. His fingers returned to trace her jawline, holding her face tenderly for the continuance of his mind-stealing kiss.

Garrett eased his lips a tiny bit from hers. Then he brushed her lips again. And again.

"Cat," he whispered in a silken drawl of need. "Love me?"

"Yes," she answered, knowing it was true.

She loved him with every part of her being.

She slid her hands to his face and drew his lips back to hers. This time she kissed him with an untold urgency.

He slipped his hand between them and began working on the tiny buttons fastening her gown. One by one, he freed them. With unbelievable gentleness for such a hard man, he eased the gown back over her shoulders. It fell about her waist, baring her to his gaze. He released his breath in a ragged sigh that touched her in a way mere words couldn't have done.

Stopping, with his hands on her shoulders, he stared into her eyes.

"Are you sure, Cat?" he asked. He knew his heart itself stopped beating as he waited for her answer.

If she said no, he'd move away from her. He'd release her from his arms, but it would nearly kill him to do so.

She stared into his eyes a moment and gave her answer. "Yes." She breathed it softly against his lips.

It was like adding a pile of kindling to an already burning fire, making it rage higher. That was exactly what her breathy acceptance did to him.

His normally constant self-control which he'd accepted as a part of him disappeared in that same fire that burned at the coldness around his soul. The warmth of Cat's loving melted whatever bit of restraint he might have had remaining.

She eased away from him, stopping to kiss his lips once. Twice. Then she stood and let the gown fall to her feet. He swore he'd never seen anything so beautiful in his life.

Moistening her lips in nervousness, she removed her chemise. At last she stood before him, naked in the glow of the lamp light.

A ragged sigh of need tore through him. "Come here, darling."

A tremulous smile quivered on her lips for a moment, and his heart nearly stopped. He held out his arms for her, and she returned to him. She kissed him as if she'd been away from him for an eternity.

He forced himself to cradle her gently, both for her and for his own injury. In the soft glow of the lantern, her skin turned the color of melted honey. He longed to touch his tongue to her skin to see if she truly tasted as sweet as she looked.

Giving in to the longing that had almost become a need, he trailed his tongue along the slender column of her neck. She tasted even sweeter than honey. As Cat arched against him, raising her chin to allow him better access, he groaned against her neck.

Did the woman have any idea what she was doing to him? He doubted it. Cat was as innocent as a perfect Texas wildflower. Resilient, tempting, and too beautiful for words. There he was nearly spouting off poetry to her again.

She eased away from him, and he watched as she nibbled on her bottom lip in uncertainty. Worry clouded the emerald brightness of her eyes.

Concern for Garrett rolled over Cat in waves, bringing along sudden indecision. She wanted him to love her, more than she wanted to draw in her next breath. But, she would never risk harming him.

"Are you sure we should?" She finally got the words past the lump forming in her throat.

"I'm sure all right." A wicked smile curved his lips.

That smile was nearly her undoing. It could make her forget everything.

"But your wound—"

"We'll make do," he told her with an even more wicked smile that promised her they would do much better than just "make do."

In another smooth as silk move, he eased her over onto her back with him above her. Leaning most of his weight on one arm, he leaned down to take her lips in a kiss that truly stole her breath from her. Any possible objections she might have been able to find dissipated under the loving in his embrace.

Oh, how she loved this man.

"My darling Cat," he murmured softly against her lips, before taking them in a kiss that sealed her to him.

He ran his fingers across her breasts, sending desire coursing through her, almost burning her with the heat of his own desire. He circled her nipples with his fingertips, brushing ever so lightly. His calloused hands were rough against the soft skin of her breasts, but his touch so tender. So loving.

Cat leaned toward him, unable to stand any distance between them now. The dark curls of hair on his chest rubbed against her breasts, the slight abrasion sending quivers of sensations through her.

When he slid her up higher in the cot, his tongue soon replaced the touch of his fingers. Suckling, he caught her waist in his hands and drew her more fully into his embrace, imprinting her with the length of him.

She surrendered her all to him. Totally. Completely . With absolute certainty.

She forgave him everything.

Leaning up, he slanted his mouth over hers, enveloping her completely with the strong feel of him, the masculine scent of him, the taste of him. Desire flowed between them, heating the small room to the point of combustion.

He molded her body to his, cradling his hardness between her thighs. Cat thought that perhaps she might faint from the wonderful sensations that were rushing through her.

His hands were calloused, but his touch was tender. And demanding at the same time. He was asking for something she couldn't refuse.

Not a stitch of clothing separated them; not even a breath of air stood between them. She ran her hands lightly over his chest, careful to avoid his bandage. The skin seemed to tingle beneath her fingertips, and she could feel the rapid beat of his heart against her palm. She moved her fingers, and the whorls of dark hair curled between her fingers, and she sighed her pleasure against his lips.

He took her sigh even as he took her next breath away with his own touch. He caught her shoulders, drawing her back to him, running his strong hands down to her breasts, cupping, loving them. He slid his hands ever so slowly down the curve of her spine.

He caressed her skin, cherishing her, loving her. Gently, slowly, he parted her legs and slid between them. Their joining was everything Cat could ever have dreamed, and more.

It was heat, and wonderful, and a little bit of heaven on earth.

Chapter Sixteen

Cat awoke the next morning snuggled up in a cocoon of warmth. She nuzzled her pillow, and something tickled her nose. She wrinkled her nose; however, the tickling sensation increased.

She opened her eyes and focused on dark whorls of hair feathering across a very broad, very male chest. Rearing her head back, she gasped in startled surprise.

It only took a minute for the night's events to return to her in a heated rush. She realized she was lying in Garrett's arms. And she had no desire to ever leave the spot.

She glanced toward the small window. The morning sky visible through the opening was only slightly overcast. During the night, the storm had rained itself out. It looked like the gullywasher had finished and moved on. The sun would probably come out by afternoon.

She gently snuggled against Garrett. His deep, even breathing gave her comfort. There would be no ride to Millwood today either. The ground would be too wet and treacherous for him to ride over. It meant they would have to remain in the small, cozy line shack another day. And another night.

A smile tipped her lips. At this moment she couldn't think of a single reason to complain about the situation. In fact, she couldn't think of any place she'd rather be for the next day or two.

Still, if they were going to remain here another day, the little shack most definitely needed a thorough cleaning. But later. The dust wasn't going anywhere. It would wait. Until later.

However, the horses wouldn't, she suddenly thought with a pang of guilt. She needed to see to them. But she truly hated to move from this spot, snuggled up against Garrett, secure in his arms.

Nearly hating the horses for their intrusion, she eased out of Garrett's arms. She almost had to bite back her sigh of disappointment at the loss of his warmth and touch.

Assuring herself she wouldn't be a single minute longer than necessary, she eased the remainder of the way off the cot. She tiptoed across to where her clothes lay in a tangled heap.

As she scooped up her chemise, she smiled in memory of the night before. Garrett had been wonderful.

So tender.

So thorough.

So loving.

Her mind pounced on the last thought. Loving? Could he love her? Holding the soft material against her nakedness, she turned to look at him.

Memories of the night before swamped over her, making her knees weak. She gulped in a deep breath. This would never do. She had to see to the horses.

Reluctantly, Cat slipped the chemise on, then quickly finished dressing. She grimaced at the sad state of her petticoat, hanging now above her knees. However, a recollection of where most of the missing petticoat was at the moment made her smile. Reaching down she tugged the tattered garment off and draped it over the back of the chair atop Garrett's clothing.

She glanced back to Garrett, thinking on how he wore the strips of her petticoat like a knight of old would wear a badge of honor. She gazed at him tenderly for a moment, strangely reluctant to leave him for even the short amount of time her work would take her.

Garrett lay on the cot exactly as she'd left him, sleeping soundly. She had to resist the urge to cross back to him, brush away a stray curl from his forehead and place a kiss there instead. She even had to clench her hands into fists to stop herself.

"I'll be back soon, my love," she whispered in a sound that was scarcely above a breath; then she blew a kiss to him.

She hoped their activity together hadn't tired him overmuch. Turning, she shoved her feet into her boots, then hurried across to the door and slipped outside.

The sound of the door clicking shut sounded loud in the morning quiet. It echoed through the small room.

Garrett woke with a start, his senses trying to place the sound and ascertain any danger. His gaze fell on the clothing-draped chair, and he smiled in pleasant recollection of the night before. Had that loving, giving, passionate woman in his bed truly been Cat?

His smile widened to a grin as he remembered the feel of her tight around him. Yup, Miss Cat Parker from New York was most definitely one hell of a lady.

His muscles protesting, he sat up and eased his feet to the floor. After pausing a moment, he stood shakily, and thought his legs were going to fall right out from under him.

Garrett sank back onto the cot. He was weaker than he'd expected. Gingerly, he moved his arms, then his shoulders, rotating them to work out the soreness. After a few minutes more, he stood to his feet again.

This time, the room stayed steady, and his legs held his weight. He shook his head; he'd have to begin moving around to regain his strength.

He wasn't about to feel like a weak pup while Cat was within arm's reach. With a smile on his face, and nothing else, he walked across the short distance to the table and chairs.

Bracing his weight against the chair back, he reached for his clothing. First he had to move Cat's frilly garment. As he picked it up, he recognized the item for a petticoat. His eyes widened at the ragged state he found it in. Glancing down, he noticed for the first time that the bandaging around his chest matched the missing portion of her petticoat. Realization hit him.

He was wearing Miss Cat Parker's petticoat.

He lightly fingered the garment, and a smile curved his lips. The fine material was soft to the touch and silky smooth, just like Cat's creamy skin had been beneath his calloused fingers.

As he continued to finger the petticoat, his smile widened. He rather liked the notion of wearing a bit of Cat Parker wrapped about him.

He couldn't believe that she'd given herself to him. Not to him. A gunslinger with a reputation that would send any fine lady running in the opposite direction.

A pang of guilt struck him. She couldn't know what he was. He hadn't told her.

The guilt threatened to eat away at him, so he shoved it into the back part of his mind. He'd tell her. Yes, he would definitely tell her.

When, a little voice prodded him. Soon, he swore, soon. Just not yet.

He needed more time to make her love him. More time so she wouldn't be so horrified by it.

More time. Period.

He looked around the one-room shack and wondered where Cat could have gone off to, and why. He didn't like the idea of her being outside alone. No, he didn't like it one little bit.

Even if she'd slipped out to take care of her personal needs, she should have returned by now.

Perhaps he'd better go out and check on her. And scold her for sneaking outside alone.

He pulled his clothes on, stopping twice to catch the back of the chair to steady himself. He swore at the weakness that plagued his body. He couldn't afford to be weak. Weakness could cost a man his life.

A quick search of the shack didn't turn up any rain gear.

Shrugging, he walked across to the door, at a much slower pace than he liked. He opened the door and, hunching his shoulders against the slow but steady drizzle, left the warmth of the shack in search of Cat.

What he found was mud up to the heels of his boots and slippery footing with each step he took. He turned to the left and strained to see any sign of Cat in the near distance.

Garrett struggled through the quagmire for several minutes, circling to the back of the line shack. The fight against the slippery footing took its toll, and he was breathing heavy. He'd go a little farther; then he'd turn back.

Wiping the drizzle away from his face, he took another step. Then another. The toe of his boot caught in a gopher hole, and he lost his footing.

He went down hard, his shoulder taking the brunt of the force from his fall. Within moments, the mud and water seeped into his clothes, covering them and gradually chilling him to the bone.

He shivered against the cold, but couldn't seem to muster enough strength to successfully get to his feet. He tried twice, falling harder each time his feet slipped out from under him, no longer having the strength to support his weight.

Darkness wavered around him, but he fought it. Cat. He needed Cat.

With sudden insight, he realized he needed her in his life. Forever.

The darkness drew nearer, enveloping him. Cold, so cold.

With his last thought he called out to Cat.

In spite of the damp chill that insisted on penetrating even her slicker, Cat's smile remained in place. She realized she was happy. Thoroughly, completely, totally happy.

And in love.

In love with Jake Garrett.

A faint memory of the tin badge she'd found pinned on his

vest caught her attention. Garrett had taken the job as lawman for Millwood.

She stood still for a moment taking this in. It didn't really change anything. Did it?

She shook her head. It made not a whit of difference to her what job he chose to do.

Not now. Not anymore.

In truth, the lawman's badge salved any portion of her conscience that might feel guilt at betraying her vow to Jesse. She couldn't very well up and shoot a lawman now, could she? Absolutely not.

However, she had to face the truth in her heart. She could no more challenge and shoot Jake Garrett now than she could up and will herself to stop drawing breath. She swallowed the sudden knot that rose up in her throat. If anything happened to him, she couldn't stand it.

She was in love. She might as well admit it to herself. And to Garrett. Soon.

Soon, she promised.

An old ache arose as she recalled the vow she'd made three long years ago. To a dead Jesse.

A vow she could no longer keep.

"I'm sorry," she mouthed the words in silence. "So sorry, Jesse. Please rest in peace."

Whirling away from the corral, she caught up the hem of her skirt. She was nearly finished here. She could head back to the line shack in another few minutes. First, she wanted to check out the area. Then, she longed to get back to Garrett.

Perhaps he was still abed. If so, she knew just how she'd like to awaken him.

She took a few moments to assure that the corral was secure, then smiled in spite of the drizzling rainfall. She knew Garrett was waiting for her. And the thought warmed her, even in the chill that permeated the Texas air.

Eager to return to his arms, she ignored the mud and the dampness and turned her steps back toward the small shack.

And Garrett.

* * *

Cat stepped into the room, his name on her lips. She stopped dead still.

Garrett wasn't there.

She told herself to calm down and took a deep breath. Turning in a full circle, she checked the room again. However, she'd known what she'd find even before she looked. Nothing.

He wasn't in the room.

Where could he have gone? She wore the only rain gear they had between them. He would be without anything to shield him and his wound from the cold rain. Cat tightened her hand into a fist, then drew it to her mouth to hold back the cry that threatened to break free.

Turning, she raced to the door and threw it open, secretly hoping to find him on the other side. When no one stood waiting, she rushed out into the rain.

"Garrett," she called out.

No answer.

Cupping her hands around her mouth, she tried again. Louder. "Garrett!"

Once again her cry was met with silence.

He'd take another chill out in this. Was his body strong enough to fight off another fever?

Fear lapped at her, threatening to dissolve her into a worthless bundle of tears. No, she fought for strength. Garrett needed her. Now more than ever.

She had to find him. She had to.

Cat searched the area in front of the line shack. Finally she spotted the blur of footsteps where he must have slid in the thick mud. Her heart raced with jubilation.

She slowed her steps and followed his tracks, pausing once or twice to wipe away the rivulets of water that ran down her face. She didn't stop to question if they were from the rain or from her tears.

Then she saw him sprawled in the mud. Not moving.

"No." The cry left her lips without her even realizing it.

Running to his side, she knelt down beside him, her hand on his shoulder. He was so cold beneath her fingers. So cold.

She had to get him inside. Once again, she caught him beneath the arms and dragged his unconscious body. Step by step, she made their way toward the cabin. Their progress came in inches. The thick mud made her own steps unsteady. She knew one misstep and she would fall, dropping his body to the ground.

While her worry screamed at her to hurry, she knew she couldn't risk injuring him worse. It seemed she would take two steps and then lose one with the way her feet slid on the slippery earth. However, the mud made him easier to drag.

Mindless of the way her own muscles were protesting, she continued her task. Drag back one step, then another, another. Then pause a second to gulp in a breath. Then start it over again.

When her back bumped into the wooden hitching post in front of the shack, Cat nearly cried in joy. Gulping in another deep breath, she pulled Garrett's body up to the door and inside the shack.

Reaching the chair, she sank into it as weariness overcame her limbs. Her legs shook in protest. Bracing Garrett's body against her own, she forced herself to breath in and out until the weakness left her.

Pushing herself to her feet, she dragged him across the short distance to the cot. She eased him down, resisting the order from her arms to let him go. Sliding her hands to the edge of the mattress, she levered herself away, then stood and walked back to the open door.

They could ill-afford to lose any of the warmth in the room right now. She pushed the door shut with an oath, then yanked off the rain slicker and threw it to the floor.

What had made Garrett go outside? He'd been getting well.

Worrying over the damage he may have done, she hurried back to his side. He hadn't moved. It seemed as if he hadn't even breathed. She laid her ear against his chest and sighed in relief at the strong heartbeat she heard.

Dammit, she was doing it again. It seemed as if the past was determined to repeat itself. Dragging him in unconscious, fretting he'd died on her, and now tending to him. Again.

Stripping his mud-soaked clothes from his body, she noted how his skin had turned clammy. She bit back the fear at her observation as she dropped the clothing to the floor, not caring where it lay.

She dried his cold skin with the remainder of her petticoat. Easing his unresisting body back onto the cot, she covered him with both the blankets.

Quickly, she whirled away from him, not giving in to the temptation to never let go of him again. She had to get a fire going. He would need as much warmth as the shack could provide.

Cat gathered up the firewood from the pile beside the wall and quickly laid a fire in the hearth. Striking a match, she urged the kindling into a flare of flame. Nursing the blaze, she assured the fire was burning strong before she left it to return to Garrett.

Kneeling by the cot, she rubbed her hands up and down his arms, trying to instill some measure of warmth back into him and replace the cold that held him. She grabbed up one of the blankets and returned to the hearth with it. Holding the blanket in front of the blazing fire, she warmed it, then rolled it into a ball to retain the heat.

She crossed back to Garrett and replaced the other blanket with the newly warmed one. She carried the second blanket over to the fire and heated it as well, then returned to spread it atop the blanket already stretched over him.

Pulling one of the chairs near the fire, she stripped off her gown and draped it over the chair. She faced the wet skirt to the heat to dry it. Next, she pulled her hair free, shaking out the moisture. Thankfully it had stayed mostly dry beneath the slicker.

Her chemise remained dry as well. Rubbing her arms against the cool air on her bare skin, she grabbed up the damp petticoat and shook it in front of the fire. The fine material dried rapidly, and she wrapped it about her like a blanket.

Crossing back to the table, she dragged the remaining chair to the cot. Exhausted and aching, she sank down onto the chair, scooting it as close to Garrett's side as possible. She'd stand guard over him. And wait for him to wake.

Sometime later, her worst fears became truth. Garrett mumbled and groaned, then began kicking against the warmth of the blankets. He thrashed, and nothing Cat said or did could calm him.

His fever had returned.

Getting to her feet, she retrieved a bowl of cold water and bathed his face. She began applying the cold compresses again, worry eating away at her confidence.

During the long course of the night, she cried over him, prayed for him, and raged at him to get well.

By morning, Cat was exhausted. And more worried than she'd ever been in her life.

The weather had cleared. A day too late, she bemoaned. If only it had been like this yesterday, maybe Garrett wouldn't have gotten chilled. Then he wouldn't have been taken with the fever again.

She stood and stretched her aching muscles. Crossing to the other chair, she pulled her gown on over her head and fastened it. She smoothed the tangles from her hair and blinked away the burning tears.

Taking in a deep breath and uttering a prayer, she turned back around to Garrett. She walked to his side and was about to reach for the cloth on his forehead when he opened his eyes.

Relief rushed through her in waves. Dizziness followed in its wake.

''Oh, thank heavens you're awake.'' Cat reached out and brushed her hand across his forehead.

Garrett raised up and snatched her hand, yanking her down until his face was even with hers.

His lightning-fast movement caught her off guard, and she cried out.

''Cat?'' Garrett blinked and stared hard at her, as if struggling with something.

She had the sudden uneasy feeling that he was confused by seeing her standing there in front of him.

His next words confirmed her fears. ''What are you doing here?''

''Here?'' she repeated the word, dread rising up in her chest.

''With me.'' He frowned at her, none of the tenderness of the day before in his face.

''Garrett?'' His name was less than a whisper of sound on her numbed lips.

She knew her voice wavered with fear, but she couldn't help it.

He shook his head, then refocused the intensity of his dark eyes on her again.

''Where am I?''

A chill swept through her, enveloping her, far stronger than the gully washer that had battered them for two days. The coldness enshrouded her, chilling her clear to her bones.

She didn't realize she was shaking her head until Garrett spoke again.

''What's happened?'' he demanded.

Cat stared at Garrett in stunned disbelief. The realization of what his words meant hit her with the force of a hard, fast blow to the stomach. It nearly doubled her over with its intensity.

He didn't remember the night before. He didn't remember their lovemaking.

Pain hit Cat hard enough that she stepped back from it. And from him.

Tears scalded her eyes, but she wouldn't let them fall. She would never let him see her cry over him. Never.

She tried to swallow, but her throat ached with the effort. Pain slashed through her from every part of her being. Not again, she cried out in silent agony.

He had made tender, wonderful, passionate love to her again—and forgotten it.

Chapter Seventeen

Cat wanted to strike out at Garrett. She wanted to hurt him like she was hurting. But she didn't. She held it in. Turning away, she didn't reply with a single hurtful word. She simply walked out on him.

The door to the line shack slammed with a resounding thud behind her. She stomped through the mud puddles, the murky moisture splattering the hem of her gown. She couldn't have cared less.

Damn bushwacker.

That's what he was.

She stomped to the corral and leaned against the rail. He wasn't any better than a damned bushwacker. She didn't give one whit if she swore or not.

He'd sneaked up past her defenses. He'd seduced her yet again. And, worst of all, he'd stolen her heart plumb away.

How dare he make love to her *twice,* and then forget it ever happened.

She kicked at a stick. She should have had more sense than to have given into him. Again. This time she'd been older. And supposedly wiser. Ha!

So much for intelligence coming with the years. She hadn't learned a thing in the last three years. She was still as much in love with Garrett now as she'd been the day he left her three long years before.

Cat clamped her hand over her mouth as if that action could call back the thought. No, she wasn't in love with Garrett.

She wasn't. She absolutely forbid it. She couldn't still be in love with a man who had forgotten her, put her so completely from his mind that he didn't even recognize her anymore.

Added to this, he even forgot their lovemaking that happened only yesterday!

"Damn you, Jake Garrett."

As she rested her hands atop the fence railing surrounding the small corral, Garrett's horse nickered to her, and she glared back at him.

"Don't you try and get into my good graces. Not after what your owner up and did."

She slammed her palm against the wood rail. Well, she was through taking care of Jake Garrett and his horse. He would just have to manage on his own from now on.

Miss Cat Parker from New York was back. She would play the role of well-bred lady to the hilt. And with a touch of vengeance.

Lifting the hem of her mud-stained gown with a gesture bespeaking dainty precision, she turned and with head held high walked back to the line shack.

Let him take care of the horses.

He was recovering fine. He was his hard, coldly cruel old self. This *lady* wasn't lifting a finger to help him a whit from this moment on.

Not without seeing that he paid for it most dearly. Before she finished with Jake Garrett, he would learn what misery meant.

She paused at the door a moment to gather all the practiced poise about her that she could possibly muster up. Then she opened the door and stepped into the room with all the snobbish disgust she could rally.

It wasn't difficult to do. She merely took all her anger at Garrett and directed it instead at the below acceptable quarters before her.

Turning up her nose in a gesture of dismay, she swept into the room like royalty. Purposely averting her gaze from where Garrett lay on the cot, she refused to even let the memories of their time together on the mattress enter into her mind. No, absolutely not. If he could forget all about what happened, so could she.

The little voice of her conscience called her a liar.

Anger rose up in her, threatening to choke her if she didn't do something. Since shooting Garrett wasn't a possibility any longer, she had to chose somewhere else to direct her anger.

"I swear I cannot abide this filth a moment longer," she announced.

Taking care that he couldn't see the pain and humiliation she felt, not to mention the raw anger, she crossed the room and picked up a broom. She attacked the mud-tracked floor with a vengeance, taking her frustrations out on it instead of the man who now sat on the side of the cot, watching her in complete amazement.

She wielded the broom like a weapon, and within minutes, dust hung over the room like a heavy cloud in the air.

"Hell, Cat. Are you trying to choke us to death?" Garrett broke into a spasm of coughing.

The coughing couldn't be good for him; it might open up his wound, she thought, then squelched the unwelcome concern that sprang up for him. Right now, she felt he deserved any discomfort she could provide him.

She gave the floor another swipe with the broom, sending up additional dust. Unexpectedly, Garrett yanked it from her hands.

"That's enough." He threw the broom into a corner. Then he walked across to the door. Swinging it wide, he propped it open with a chair.

The fresh air cleared away the dust in a short amount of time. However, it did nothing to improve Cat's disposition.

She fully intended to pay him back in every way imaginable for his cold-hearted actions. He'd be sorry. Before they reached Millwood, Jake Garrett would rue the day he met her. And even more the day he dared to forget her!

She may have loved him enough to make love with him, but now she was just plumb mad, and planning how best to get even. Garrett's life would be plumb miserable before she was through with him.

Her eyes burned with tears, and she blinked to force them away. One slipped free. Brushing away the foolish tear, she turned her back on Garrett. She was concentrating so hard on keeping the awful tears at bay that she didn't hear him cross the room to her. When he caught her shoulders with his hands, she jumped.

His touch warmed her, easing slowly through her body, warming her clear through as if it were attempting to chase out the coldness that had enveloped her ever since she learned the awful truth that he'd forgotten their lovemaking. She drew in a breath and fought the betraying warmth with every part of her being.

She would not give in to him. She couldn't. If she did, Jake Garrett would break her heart as surely as she breathed.

A tiny voice whispered to her that he'd already done precisely that.

Garrett turned her around to face him, and the confusion she saw in his dark gaze was nearly her undoing. She bit down on her lower lip to stop any words of concern from breaking free.

She couldn't let herself care for him. She couldn't. And she wouldn't.

"Cat, the cleaning can wait. What's gotten into you?" he demanded.

"I . . ." She hated the tremble in her voice. It betrayed too much.

She tore her gaze away from his, focusing on the center of his chest instead. It wasn't helping her any. The feel of his hands on her was doing strange things to her breathing.

"Cat?"

Garrett drew a step closer, and she knew she had to stop him. If he continued to touch her, continued to draw nearer, she wouldn't be able to resist. Her wounded heart simply wasn't that strong.

What she wanted to do was throw herself into his arms and make him remember. Make him want to love her again.

She forced herself to pull her gaze away from his chest and stepped away from him. Her movement broke their contact. She wanted to sigh in relief, but couldn't do so. A part of her still wanted his touch.

Longed for his touch.

Needed his touch.

She wrapped her arms about her waist to keep herself from reaching out to him. "I can't abide dirt." The explanation rushed from her lips.

"Cat, we have to talk."

His simple words stopped anything else she might have been going to say or do.

"What are you doing here? And how did you get here?" He reached for her hands again, but she balled them into fists.

"You were supposed to take me riding," she accused. Her voice rose on the last word; however, it had nothing to do with their scheduled rendezvous and everything to do with the pain he'd caused her.

Garrett shook his head. What on this earth was she talking about? They hadn't been able to make their ride because he'd gone to meet the posse for Ty. A sliver of unease crept up the back of his neck.

"I had to do something for Ty. Didn't you get my message?"

He couldn't believe she was so angry over that. After all, he'd left her word, and he hadn't done it on purpose to upset her. But the lady was mad as a wet hen over something. And come to think of it again, how had she gotten here? Wherever the hell here was.

"Yes, I received your message."

Her answer jerked his thoughts back.

That was all she said to him. It didn't make any sense. He

struggled to piece together the events before he'd awakened to find her beside his bed.

He remembered riding out for Ty and running into the ambush. He recalled the burning pain of being shot, the man standing over him. But he had no recollection of Cat in any part of it.

A sudden thought jolted him.

"What day is this?" he asked her, his eyes never leaving her face.

She thought a minute. "Thursday, I think—"

"What?"

He grabbed her arms, not realizing he'd done so until he saw her flinch. Releasing her immediately, he smoothed his hands up and down her arms.

He didn't blame her when she suddenly stepped back from him as if she couldn't stand his touch. He hadn't meant to be so abrupt, or to frighten her.

"Sorry," he said.

What had he thought, that a lady like Cat would welcome his touch, and fall into his arms here in a dirty line shack? Not likely.

"You said Thursday?"

He'd ridden out for Madison and the posse on Sunday. That had been days ago.

She nodded. The way her teeth worried her lower lip told him she was nervous about something. Being here alone with him?

"How did you get here?" he asked her.

"When you didn't come for me, I rode out to meet you," she announced.

Garrett thought the words had an odd ring to them, as if they weren't the truth. Or at least not the whole truth.

"Why?" he demanded.

Her chin raised, and he noticed the flare in her eyes for a moment before it was doused.

"No man goes off and forgets me."

He felt as if she'd thrown down a challenge to him, but for the life of him he couldn't figure out what it was all about.

"You mean to tell me you rode out here after me because I didn't meet you?" His usually even voice rose with the words.

Cat merely nodded once at him.

"And you—"

"Found you lying on the ground."

Although her surprising announcement still held a hint of challenge, he saw that she gave a slight shudder.

This time Garrett shook his head. Cat had been the one to find him?

If so, then that meant she'd somehow gotten him here to the line shack and cared for him. The possibility was too preposterous to believe. Not from a fine lady who didn't even know how to cook.

He opened his mouth, but Cat forestalled him. She didn't like the look of speculation she'd seen in his eyes. If he put all the pieces together, her masquerade would be over. And right now, she'd bet his fury at her deception would shake the rafters.

Oh no, she wasn't finished with her little masquerade yet. She'd still find a way to make him pay. But for now, she'd better repair the damage, and fast.

"You don't remember getting here?" She hoped her voice didn't give away how desperately she was waiting for his answer.

"No, I remember riding into an ambush, then not much else."

His answer suited her purposes fine. If he couldn't recall making such passionate love to her, then she had every right to use that memory lapse of his for her own benefit. Didn't she?

"You came to enough to get us here." She waved her hand to the inside of the shack.

A pang of conscience pinched her, but she shoved it aside. She had to convince him she was still that helpless Eastern lady.

"I . . ." She lowered her gaze to the floor and raised one shoulder in a delicate shrug. "I just followed your instructions."

Silence met her explanation. It stretched out in the close confines of the cabin. She felt her gaze drawn to his and couldn't refuse.

She could tell that something else was bothering him. His dark eyes were studying her. She almost held her breath waiting to learn what it could be now.

"Cat?" He paused to reach out and catch her hand in his. She felt his touch all the way to her soul.

"Cat," he began again, "who took care of my wound?"

She gulped. "I did." The honest response slipped out. She rushed to tack more onto the end of it before he could get suspicious. Obviously a fine lady wouldn't know the first thing about tending to a gunshot wound. "I just followed instructions."

Her answer was pretty much the truth. She had followed instructions—her own. However, she knew he would assume they had been *his* orders.

She couldn't let him see through her disguise. Not now. The truth would be too humiliating for her to bear. She clenched her teeth together and waited.

She could tell by one quick glance at his set face that he wasn't finished yet.

Shams. Why couldn't he leave it alone?

"Cat, who stitched me up?"

She wavered a moment at his too-pointed question. He took it for something else.

"Are you all right?" He patted her hand. "Don't faint."

Faint? Her? The very idea was laughable. Caitlan Parker had never fainted a single solitary time in her entire life. No, not once. And she was proud of the fact, too.

"I don't—"

"You don't have to feel bad about it. Ladies faint," he hurriedly assured her.

Cat's temper rose at his impertinent assumption. So, he naturally assumed she succumbed to fainting spells. Well, then let him believe it. And see if he'd swallow her answer while he was at it. Anger made her rash.

"Why, Garrett, I could never stitch . . ." She let the words trail off, and accompanied them with a shudder. "All that blood." She shuddered again and looked down at the floor.

He patted her hands in a comforting gesture.

"Oh." She pulled her hands from his hold. Waving one hand in front of her face, she rushed the lie out, "No, you did that yourself."

She was concentrating so hard on the floor that she nearly missed his gasp. A smile teased her lips, but she fought it back.

"How—"

"Garrett, please? I'd rather not discuss it."

"Cat—"

"Please, this is all too much for me."

Cat whirled away and hurried to the kitchen area. She began picking up and setting down the tins of food. Anything to keep her hands busy and distract Garrett.

"Cat—"

"What?" she snapped.

"Ah, can you . . . do you need help with that?"

Her pride rebelled at his near patronizing tone. The man thought she couldn't open a few tins and heat up the food. How much intelligence and skill did that take? She was certain even a fancy lady who had never cooked a day in her life could accomplish that without too much assistance.

"I *think* I can handle it," she answered in a sugar-sweet tone.

As she heard him turn away and cross to the cot, she set to work readying a makeshift meal of more stew. Several minutes later, she spied a container of cayenne pepper. She stared at it a full minute as a devilish idea formed in her mind.

So, he didn't think she could manage to heat a little stew, did he? Well, she'd heat it all right.

Grabbing up the container, she paused. Then she set it back down and reached for one of the bowls. After dipping out a serving for herself, she picked up the cayenne pepper again. This time she liberally sprinkled the stew with it, then stirred.

She held back her smile and scooped up a bowl for Garrett, then carried both bowls to the table. She carefully set hers down and took the doctored bowl to Garrett.

Not saying another word, she returned to the table and sat down. She didn't have long to wait before Garrett let out a yelp.

"What the hell?"

"What?" she asked, her voice pitched to perfect innocence. "Is something wrong with the meal?"

"Cat, what did you put in this?"

She shrugged. "A little of this, a little of that. I used what was left."

Raising a hand to her lips to hide the grin that threatened, she faked a sniffle or two. "Don't you like it?"

Garrett cleared his throat before he answered. "Yup, it's . . . it's fine. You did well, Cat."

He quickly focused his attention back on the bowl in his hands.

Cat licked her lips and took another bite from her own bowl. Personally, she thought it was delicious.

Angel Tamera leaned back in the spare wooden chair and covered her mouth with her hand to hold back her giggle. Cat could most assuredly give out as good as she got.

She glanced over at Garrett and sighed. Her feathers ruffled up in disturbance. Just look what happened when she was called back to heaven for a few days.

"Oh, feathers."

These two couldn't begin to take care of themselves and fall in love properly without her attending to them every minute. It hadn't been her choice to leave, but St. Peter had insisted. She'd been with Garrett until he followed Cat outside. That was the moment St. Peter had chosen to call her to heaven.

Although he'd sent a replacement, the slight time delay had allowed Garrett to stumble and fall into the mud.

Tamera frowned. Look at the mess these two had made of things. There sat Garrett trying to choke down the peppered stew, while Cat sat clear across the room from him.

Although at this moment, her sentiments did tend to follow in Cat's favor. Imagine the man *forgetting* something as wonderful as their love. How could he have forgotten what had happened between him and Cat?

Well, she had better do something or Cat might just kill him with kindness.

She would simply *have* to do something to help with the situation. Starting with Garrett's memory lapse.

Perhaps a few dreams of Cat would help. She'd whisper Cat's name into his mind as he drifted off to sleep and let his memory take over from there. He should have a most enlightening night's sleep.

Once Garrett fell asleep, Cat unrolled the bedroll, swearing beneath her breath at him the whole time. She called down every curse imaginable, and then some, upon his head.

Kicking the bedroll with her foot, she dropped down onto the floor. Funny, it hadn't felt this hard before when she'd used it as her bed. Now, however, it felt as hard as Jake Garrett's heart.

Thankfully in the morning they could ride back to Millwood.

Morning couldn't come soon enough for her.

Cat's anger had not abated one bit by the time she awoke the next morning. Much less her humiliation. The sun shone outside the window in direct contrast to her own stormy mood.

The one room seemed to have shrunk in size overnight to Cat. An uncomfortable silence filled the shack.

She knew even before she raised her head or sat up that she would find Garrett watching her. And he was. Intently.

For the space of a heartbeat, her throat tightened, and she

thought, he remembered. One look into his eyes, and she knew otherwise.

"Good morning." She forced herself to be civil and play the part of a polite lady.

Garrett ignored her effort. "What are you doing on the floor?" he demanded.

Cat raised her chin at his demand. "I was sleeping."

"Why?"

Purposely ignoring his true question, she answered, "Because it was nighttime and I was tired." She delicately hid a pretend yawn behind her hand. "How did you sleep, Garrett?"

The flush that colored his cheeks for an instant made her discomfort of the night spent on the hard floor almost worth it. Almost, but not quite.

"You should have taken the cot."

"You were already asleep on the cot." She yawned again, this time not quite raising her hand in time to cover her mouth. "And a *lady* doesn't wake up a gentleman to demand his bed."

The look of guilt that covered his face at her announcement warmed her heart. Good. He deserved to feel guilty.

Then why did she feel the pangs of guilt herself over what she was doing to him?

"I'm sorry," he said.

She held her breath, waiting for more. That's all she got from him. She pushed herself to her feet and shook out her skirt. Frowning at the gown, she noted that it had passed any possibility of repair long ago.

"Cat?"

She ignored the question in Garrett's voice. Let him wonder if she'd accepted his meager apology. Much less forgiven him.

When she didn't answer, he cleared his throat. "How do you feel about breakfast?" he asked.

"Hungry," she answered. Let him deal with that response.

"Me, too."

For an instant the soft drawl underlying his words was nearly her undoing. She felt her body being drawn to him.

He likely wouldn't remember it if she did go to him, she

snapped at herself. That was all it took to break the spell his voice had woven about her.

"Cat, have you ever cooked a breakfast?" he asked, hesitancy evident in his words.

She had to look down at her hands to hide her face from him. She'd cooked more breakfasts than she could count. However, the fine Eastern lady from New York whom she happened to be at this moment had never done such a thing in her life.

"Well, I can scramble an egg in an emergency."

She peeked a glance up at him and fluttered her eyelashes.

"Do you see any chickens around here?" he asked.

"Now that you mention it. No. Why?"

"Because that's where we would have to get any damned eggs." His voice had raised, losing the seductive drawl of earlier.

Cat forced herself to lower her gaze in a gesture of demure embarrassment. It was as fake as the wan smile of pure innocence she gave him when she looked up.

"Cat, I'm sorry. I didn't mean to take it out on you."

It wasn't her fault that he'd had his night's sleep plagued by dreams of her in his arms. Naked in his arms. In those dreams he had made love to her. Their lovemaking had been passionate. And completely unbelievable.

The dreams had left him feeling guilty, and uncomfortable, and wanting her more than ever before.

"There's some jerky in my saddlebags. We'll have to make do with that." His words came out harsher than he'd intended.

He tried to smooth things with her. "I'm eager to get to Millwood."

The pain of his remark cut through her, leaving her feeling like he'd stabbed her. He couldn't wait to get away from her, could he?

Fine. They couldn't get to town soon enough for her either.

After they had eaten the jerky and washed it down with some bad-tasting coffee, she helped him pack up and saddle the horses. However, she ensured that she fumbled just enough with the saddles and saddlebags to make him swear under his breath several times. She knew before it was time to mount that he was frustrated with her clumsiness. That should allay any suspicions he had about her taking care of the horses.

"Cat, tell me something?"

Her tongue stuck to the roof of her mouth. Good heavens, what would he want to know?"

"How did you take care of the horses?"

"Don't you remember that either?" she asked in pretend innocence. Meanwhile she crossed the fingers of one hand in the folds of her skirt.

"No, I can't seem to," he responded after a moment.

Cat bit the inside of her cheek to keep her grin locked in. He was making it so easy. She couldn't resist.

"Of course you probably don't."

"I'm sorry, but most everything after I ran into that ambush is pretty fuzzy," he explained.

Giving him an answer would be like giving candy to a child; he'd likely accept it without a doubt. Just like yesterday.

"I followed your instructions. Did I do it right?" She couldn't resist adding the question.

"I'm sure you did fine, Cat."

Garrett led Cat's mare over to a rock for her.

Cat looked from him to the rock and back to him. "What's that for?"

"To help you mount. I'm afraid I can't be of much assistance right now."

"Oh."

"Cat, how did you get onto the horse in the first place?"

"Smitty helped me up." That part was true.

Garrett nodded, then stared at the saddle as if he'd only now realized something. "Cat, this isn't a sidesaddle."

"Tell me something I don't know," she snapped at him.

She was getting tired of the questions. And afraid that he might get lucky and hit upon the truth if he kept it up.

"Smitty didn't have any." She waved at the saddle with a blatant gesture of disgust. "So I had to make do with this."

Before he could think of any more questions, she made a

great show of scrambling up onto the saddle, grabbing the saddle horn, and trying to adjust her skirt properly.

"Well, let's go. I don't know how long I can stay on this thing," she announced in warning.

Garrett turned away and mounted his own horse with slow movements, careful not to strain his wound. She had to knot her hands into fists to keep from going to him.

Once he was safely on the horse, she couldn't help but ask, "Are you all right?"

"I'm fine." He glanced over at her.

Cat felt the heat of his gaze all the way to her toes. She kicked the mare, urging her toward town.

If she didn't get away from him, she knew she'd get down off her horse and go to him.

Either that or she'd take one more look into those dark eyes of his and beg him to return to the line shack and make love to her again.

Chapter Eighteen

The moment Cat and Garrett rode into Millwood, someone gave out the shout, "Garrett's back."

Ty came at a run from the sheriff's office, a rifle in his grasp. Smitty raced from the livery, his leather apron flapping with each step. Sarah came only steps behind Ty, her skirts caught up in both hands.

Within seconds, Cat and Garrett were surrounded by people. It seemed each and every one of them had a question to ask. Ty helped Garrett dismount while Sarah aided Cat in sliding off the horse. Instinctively, Cat took a step backward, closer to Garrett. Without realizing why she did it, she stood at his side, in a protective stance.

Cat looked around them at the crowd of people and heard the murmuring of questions. Questions she didn't want to face right now.

She drew in a breath and did the only thing a *lady* would do at that instant.

She fainted.

Well, it wasn't a true faint, but she thought she managed a pretty good imitation of one she'd witnessed once before.

However, it accomplished her purpose. All the questions ceased. It seemed as if the entire town held its breath for the space of a moment.

A voice yelled, "Dammit, she's fainted. Somebody get her help."

She nearly opened her eyes when she recognized it as Garrett's voice.

She heard a murmur go through the crowd surrounding them, followed by several voices protesting. It took her a moment to make sense of what was going on around her.

At the feel of Garrett's hands on her shoulders, she realized with a jolt that he intended to lift her up. He couldn't do that. It would open his wound. He'd start bleeding again.

Cat had started to open her eyes when Ty's shouted order stopped her.

"Let her be, Garrett. You can't pick her up, you fool."

Suddenly, Sarah's voice could be heard giving out the commands and taking charge. She ordered that Garrett be taken to the doc's, and the horses be taken to the livery, and that Cat be given smelling salts.

Before Cat could fully take all this in, someone stuck a vile-smelling object directly under her nose. She nearly gagged from the strong smell. Her eyes snapped open, and she coughed, struggling to shove the terrible odor away. Why, it was worse than the skunk.

"What is that?"

"She's fine, folks," Sarah assured everyone.

Cat felt that she was far from fine thanks to the vile potion.

"Cat, dear? Do you need someone to carry you?" Sarah asked, concern etched on her worried face.

Looking up at her friend, Cat felt like the worst kind of fraud at that moment. "No, I'm fine. I can walk."

"Well, then let's get you over to the boardinghouse," Sarah offered.

Nothing could have sounded better to her, Cat thought. She opened her mouth to say so, but that's not what came out.

"How's Garrett?"

Cat wanted to bite her tongue for letting the question escape. Instead she held her breath, waiting for an answer.

Sarah patted her arm and helped her stand to her feet, but she didn't respond to Cat's inquiry.

Cat tensed at the possible meaning behind her friend's action. Garrett had seemed better. His fever hadn't returned, and he'd been stronger. Surely he would recover fine. Surely he . . .

Her throat closed off the very thought of anything happening to him.

She grabbed Sarah's arm, tugging her around to face her. Cat had to swallow twice before she could get the words out.

"How is he? He's not—"

"No," Sarah assured her. "They've taken him to Doc. That's all we know right now. As soon as I hear, I'll let you know."

"Thank you," Cat whispered. Her eyes welled with tears.

She told herself it was merely exhaustion and reaction. That's all it could be. She wasn't concerned about Garrett. No, not in the slightest. Her hand trembled ever so slightly when she brushed a stray curl from her cheek.

Sarah's eyes widened, and she leaned closer. "So it's like that, is it?"

Cat knew she'd given away too much. She stiffened her spine beneath her friend's concerned touch and raised her chin. "I don't know what you mean."

"I mean you're in love with him."

Cat wanted to tell her to hush. Instead she forced the lie out. "No, I'm not."

Sarah merely smiled.

"I'm not," Cat repeated.

"Umm, let's get you home, shall we?"

She let Sarah lead her away from the curious eyes of the townsfolk and any more questions for the time being. As they walked the short distance to the boardinghouse, Cat kept repeating to herself, "I'm not in love with him. I'm not."

* * *

Cat awoke hours later in her own bed, in her own room at the boardinghouse. Looking around her, she wondered for a minute if she'd dreamed it all.

Then her gaze fell on her boots lying on the handwoven run beside the bed exactly where she'd left them after her bath. Mud still crusted the boot soles and streaked the sides of the leather.

Alongside the muddy boots lay her saddlebags.

Cat swallowed and gripped the coverlet. She hadn't dreamed any of it.

Her time with Garrett had been real.

As real as the shaft of pain that cut through her along with the sudden rush of memories.

Throwing back the coverlet, she climbed from the bed. She needed the company of someone besides herself and those memories that taunted her. The decision made, she quickly dressed and headed downstairs to find Sarah.

At least that's what Cat told herself she was doing. She refused to accept the truth that she was too anxious for word of Garrett's condition to wait a moment longer.

She found Sarah in the kitchen.

"Cat, dear, how are you feeling?" Sarah asked, pushing her into a chair.

"I'm fine." Cat felt nervous under her friend's intent scrutiny. "Really."

Sarah eyed her a minute longer, then turned away to the cake she'd just finished icing.

Cat glanced to the window, then blurted out, "Any news of Garrett?"

Sarah turned back to her with a wide smile. "Wondered how long you'd wait to ask."

"Well?"

"Doc says he's gonna be fine."

Cat felt like all the stuffing had been knocked out of her.

Garrett was going to be all right. She released the breath she hadn't even realized she'd been holding.

So much for forgetting about him.

"You did a good job of tending to him."

Sarah's comment caught her off guard, and Cat couldn't think of a single thing to say to her in response.

"Let's sit and talk awhile." Sarah brought over two slices of cake.

Cat's stomach rumbled in response, drawing her friend's laughter.

"I don't know how you two made it." Sarah glanced up from her fork to look askance at Cat.

The hint was too strong to ignore. Besides, Cat didn't have the slightest idea how to do so, and she figured if she did ignore it, Sarah would simply get bolder in her questions. And maybe ask some that Cat didn't want to hear.

"Well, let's just say that if I never see another bowl of stew it will be too soon for my tastes." Cat gave a delicate shudder.

"You cooked?"

The surprise in her friend's voice couldn't be concealed. Cat bristled at it. Why was it everyone naturally assumed she couldn't cook a thing without ruining it?

If they knew the meals she'd cooked back on the old farm in Illinois—Cat cut off the thought. If they knew the truth, they would likely run her right out of town.

She could well imagine their reaction if they knew she'd come to their fair town to kill Jake Garrett. A shudder coursed down her back at the thought.

And now? her conscience asked. What did she intend to do now?

She honestly didn't know. The bite of cake stuck in her throat. She clenched the fork in her hand. Should she go on with her plan? Could she now?

Or should she forget the whole thing and catch the next train out of Millwood?

And away from Garrett.

"Cat?" Sarah's sharp voice jolted her out of her indecisive musings.

She looked up at her friend. "I'm sorry, what did you say?"

"That's the third time I've said your name. Are you certain you are all right?"

No, she wasn't "all right" in the slightest.

Cat raised her chin and lied, "I'm fine. Perfectly fine."

She could have sworn she heard Sarah mutter, "Thought so."

Over the delicious cake and chat with Sarah, Cat answered her friend's questions with an abbreviated version of the line shack. In return, she soon realized that only the reality of Garrett's gunshot wound had saved her reputation. That, and Sarah's assurances to the town matrons that Cat was a perfect lady. Her friend had even reminded them how she'd likely saved Garrett's life.

"Everyone in town was worried for you." Sarah patted her arm.

Cat heard in detail from Sarah how the townsfolk had formed a search party and gone out hunting for both her and Garrett. However, since Garrett had veered away from Madison on the trail of the outlaws, and the storm had obliterated both their tracks, everyone had been looking for them in the wrong area.

While the townsfolk had been frantically searching, she and Garrett had been miles away from them, stranded together in the line shack.

Making love, a little voice reminded her.

As if she needed to be reminded of that. The memory never left her for more than minutes at a time. Garrett stayed in her mind.

But not in her heart, she told herself stubbornly. Not in her heart.

If he could forget about her, then she'd set to forgetting about him.

Sarah didn't help in doing so in the slightest. "So, what happened with you two?" She blurted out.

Swallowing several times, Cat told Sarah a very modified version of the truth.

When she'd finished, Sarah cocked her head and eyed her skeptically. "And pigs fly," she remarked.

Cat forced herself to take another bite of the cake. It nearly choked her. She refused to meet her friend's eyes.

"So, that's the way it is."

Her head snapped up at Sarah's observation.

"You've up and fallen in love with him."

Cat started to shake her head, but Sarah's hand on hers stopped her.

"It's no use lying, Cat. I can see it in your eyes."

Pain cut through her so intense that it stole her breath away. As tears burned the back of her eyes, she gulped in a breath to halt them. If Sarah continued to be so kind and concerned, she'd start bawling. She wasn't used to this caring from someone.

"He feels the same way about you, I'm sure." Sarah curled her fingers around Cat's hand.

She shook her head. "No, he doesn't."

"Why, of course he does," Sarah argued. "I swear when he looked at you before you fainted he was darned near making love to you with his eyes." She fanned herself with her free hand.

The pain that sliced through Cat this time brought anger in its wake. Before she could think over what she was saying or stop the words, they burst out.

"Not likely. If so, he wouldn't have up and forgot all about making love to me in that shack."

As soon as the words were out, Cat dropped her fork and slapped her hand over her mouth. The utensil struck the tabletop, then clattered to the floor.

Neither woman moved to pick it up.

"He what?" Sarah demanded, shock and compassion written across her face.

Cat couldn't take it. She pushed away from the table and ran up the stairs to her room.

* * *

"I what?" Garrett shouted.

He sat on the bed in Doc's office and stared at Sarah Miles. The woman had gone plumb crazy. That was the only answer.

"Keep your voices down," Ty ordered both him and Sarah. He slid an arm around her shoulders in a gesture of comfort. "I'm certain we can take care of this matter without the town needing to hear about it."

When Garrett opened his mouth, Sarah held up her hand to stop him.

"Are you trying to ruin her completely?"

He shook his head as if trying to clear it. The whole world had gone mad. Here stood his best friend and his landlady, arm in arm, against him.

He was being accused of the impossible.

"Don't you think if I had taken the lady to bed, I would have remembered it?" he demanded of them.

"Are you trying to get out of doing the right thing by her?" Sarah glared at him.

"Right thing, hell." Garrett stood to his feet. "Nothing happened."

He wasn't about to continue sitting there on the bed while the two of them berated him for something he didn't even do.

Sarah snapped her mouth shut when Ty squeezed her hand tightly.

"I didn't touch her," Garrett insisted.

A mental image of his dreams arose to haunt him. An uneasy feeling settled in the pit of his stomach. They had been dreams, hadn't they?

"Now, Garrett," Ty reasoned. "A fever can do strange things to a man."

He turned on his friend. "What?"

"Doc says you likely had a bad fever with that gunshot wound—"

The look Garrett turned on him shut him up in mid-sentence.

"If I had a fever, then I wasn't in any condition to be taking any woman to bed. Was I?'' Garrett attempted to reason with his two accusers. ''Much less taking advantage of her. Then forgetting all about it.''

The fact that his best friend Ty had sided with Cat galled him.

''You had the fever twice,'' Sarah informed him in a soft voice.

Garrett whirled to face her. ''What?''

Ty's response was the same. ''What?''

Sarah frowned in response. ''Are you two hard of hearing? I said he had the fever two times.''

As Garrett continued to stare at her, she held up two fingers and waggled them in his face.

''Cat said you went out to check on her once. In the rain,'' she paused, giving Garrett a chance to speak up, to explain.

He merely motioned her to continue.

''When was this, Sarah?'' Ty prompted.

''Day before yesterday, I think. She found you on the ground. Unconscious.''

Garrett narrowed his eyes, struggling to recall any such thing. He drew a blank. However, a vague feeling of mud sucking at his feet tickled at the back of his mind. Could it have really happened the way Sarah was claiming it had?

''What happened?'' he asked in a still voice.

''I don't know. Maybe you fell. Perhaps you passed out.'' She shrugged her shoulders at him. ''Anyway, that's when you took the second fever.''

Garrett took a step back, coming up against the bed. He sank down onto it. His stomach churned at the possibility that Sarah might be telling the truth as it happened.

He covered his face with his hands. Could he have taken advantage of Cat while she was caring for him? And then callously forgotten all about it?

''Garrett, it was probably the second fever that caused you to forget. That'll do strange things to a man sometimes,'' Ty offered in explanation.

The door swung open, and Garrett looked up to see Doc

Henson walk in. The doctor looked from one to the other of the three of them.

"Is there a problem?" he asked.

Garrett flinched at the question.

Sarah jumped at the opportunity presented by his timely appearance. "Doc, could a fever make a man forget things?"

"Could be. I've heard tell of it before." Doc Henson rocked back on his heels and looked from her to Garrett. "Did you up and forget something?"

"No," Garrett snapped.

"Yes," Sarah insisted.

Doc rocked forward, then back on his heels again. "Anything of interest?"

"No," Sarah told him.

Garrett opened his mouth, then shut it on his response before any words came out.

Ty stepped forward. "Doc, let's say this happened—"

Garrett's distinct act of clearing his throat interrupted him.

"Doc," Ty attempted his question again. "For the sake of argument, let's say this happened. Would that man later up and remember it again?"

"Maybe."

Garrett sighed. All he had to do was wait and see if he did indeed remember taking Cat Parker to bed or not.

"And maybe not," Doc added.

Garrett's solution crashed down around him.

The doctor glanced from one of them to the other. He rocked back on his heels again. "Well, seeing as how this is my office, I'll mosey on out and find something to check on across the street."

With this, he slapped Garrett on the shoulder. "If you recall what it was you forgot, will you let me know?"

Garrett's response wasn't repeatable. Doc chuckled and slammed the door behind himself.

Sarah tapped her foot on the floor. The *tap-tap-tap* echoed in Garrett's head. It was beginning to ache worse than his gunshot wound.

"Why do you suppose she came to you with this story?" he asked her.

The tapping stopped. Sarah leaned down until she was eye to eye with him. "She didn't."

"Then, how—"

"She let it slip. After I told her you loved her."

"You what? I what?" Garrett surged to his feet, towering over her.

To give her credit, she did take a step back from him. Garrett glared at her. "Have you gone crazy?"

"No, but you have if you don't do right by Cat," she fired back at him.

"Sarah," Ty put in, "why don't we leave him to think on it for a spell?"

That sounded like a great suggestion to Garrett. He needed time to mull this over. To examine the possibilities and see if it could be true. He didn't remember anything about most of what happened in the line shack. A disturbing thought came to him. If he didn't remember, then there was a strong possibility that it could have happened the way Sarah said it did.

He closed his eyes. He'd give almost anything to recall those days. What in heaven had he done?

"Garrett?"

He looked up at Sarah.

She laid her hand on his arm. "Will you at least please think on it?"

He couldn't think on anything else.

Once again, he dropped his head in his hands. He didn't even see Ty and Sarah leave. However, the click of the door closing echoed and reechoed in his mind. It stirred the faintest of memories.

He grabbed at the image, but it was gone as quickly as it came. It left a distinctly uneasy feeling in its wake. He had to fill that gap in his mind.

He had to.

A mental image of Cat came to his mind, chasing out everything else but her. He slowly thought over the disturbing dreams he'd had of her.

Had he? Hadn't he?

What was he going to do about her?

Cat whirled away from her window in disgust. What was she doing? Watching for Garrett to come walking down the street?

Yes, she answered truthfully.

She leaned her head back and closed her eyes. An image of him filled her mind, and she quickly opened her eyes.

She absolutely refused to let herself moon over him like a lovesick calf. Obviously she meant so little to him that he could up and clean forget her whenever he wanted. Well, maybe she'd set her mind to it and start forgetting about him.

But could she?

At the sound of a sharp knock on her door, she turned and nearly tripped over her skirt. Angry with herself and her heart's refusal to do as she said, she kicked the ruffled green-and-white-striped skirt out of her way and walked to the door.

She knew it was only a matter of time before her friend Sarah came up to check on her.

Cat swung the door open without hesitation. She might as well get this over with. Sarah wouldn't give up easy if she knew the woman.

"Sarah, I . . ." Cat's voice trailed off, then disappeared altogether.

She stared at the tall, leanly muscled man dressed in black pants and clean white shirt standing on the other side of the doorway.

Jake Garrett.

She swallowed, but her mouth remained as dry as day-old bread.

"Cat." He nudged the brim of his black Stetson back farther on his head.

She stared at him, unable to do anything else. Why was he here? At her door?

"May I come in?"

At her hesitation, he quickly added, "We can leave the door open if you'd like."

Cat found her voice long enough to utter, "Come in."

As he strode into the room, she couldn't seem to take her eyes from him. He looked leaner. Had he lost weight? Was he well?

His hair dipped over his forehead from beneath his black hat, just like always. She ached to brush the hair back. It had been so silky beneath her fingers.

She shut her eyes for a moment, trying to shut out the memory. It remained.

She quickly opened her eyes again and met his dark gaze. If anything, it was more mesmerizing than before. More intense.

She swallowed down the overwhelming dryness in her throat. He looked so wonderfully alive to her.

"How are you?" she asked him.

The minute she'd said it, she wanted to take back the inane question.

"Fine," he answered.

"How's your wound?" For the life of her, she couldn't seem to stop questioning him.

"Doc says it's healing fine."

"Good." She wished she could bite her tongue for that remark. Why couldn't she think of a single sensible thing to say to him?

"Cat," he hesitated.

An unsettled feeling stirred in her stomach. She'd never known Garrett to be hesitant. About anything.

He cleared his throat, and her stomach tumbled.

"Cat, I might as well get this out. I came here to apologize to you."

"Apologize?"

"A feeling similar to a sudden draft skittered over her.

"Yes. I need to apologize for . . . making love to you out there."

Cat felt like someone had slammed a fist into her stomach. It knocked all the air out of her lungs.

Mutely, she opened and shut her mouth, then curled her hands into fists. She didn't know when she'd been so angry. And humiliated. He had come to *apologize* for making love to her.

To apologize.

Her fingernails cut into her palms, but she only clenched her hands tighter. If she didn't, she feared she was so mad that she might just slug him.

"Cat—"

She unclenched her hands and met his eyes with a cool look in return. "You've said what you came to say. Now, would you please leave? I'm not feeling so well."

She was proud of her outward calm. No one would know that she wanted to scream at him and strike him.

No one but her.

And if he didn't leave soon, that calm demeanor might desert her.

She raised her chin and motioned him to the door.

"Cat?"

"What?" she snapped.

"I also came to tell you I'll marry you."

"You what?" she sputtered.

He took a step toward her. She retreated a step in amazement.

"I said I'd go ahead and marry you."

Oh, he thought he'd marry her, did he? Well, she wasn't about to assuage his conscience or fulfill any obligation he felt toward her.

She faced him squarely, and gave him her answer. "Like hell."

She saw shock, then anger cross his face. Instinctively she took another step back at the sudden coldness in his eyes. Her step brought her up against the washstand.

Reaching back to steady herself, her fingers brushed the

velvet material of her reticule. She felt the hardness of her derringer inside the cloth.

"I said I'd marry you." He shoved his hat back a notch.

His words pushed her anger past the point of no return. Why, he hadn't even had the manners to remove his hat!

Grabbing up her reticule, she pulled out the derringer and pointed it at him.

Garrett's eyes widened in shocked disbelief. "Cat?"

"And I said 'like hell,'" she told him between clenched teeth.

"Cat?"

"Get out."

Pointing the small derringer at his offending black Stetson, she pulled the trigger.

Chapter Nineteen

Garrett stormed to the door, retrieved his hat from the floor, and slammed the door behind him.

If he stayed, he'd throttle her.

His anger hadn't cooled in the least when he strode through the door of Ty's office.

"Well, Garrett—"

He slammed his Stetson down on the desk top in front of Ty. His friend sat forward in his chair.

"What—"

"Thanks so much for your suggestion," Garrett ground out.

"What—"

"She shot my damn hat."

Ty looked mutely at the black Stetson lying on the desk in front of him. A small, round bullet hole marked the center of the hat, inches above the brim.

"What on earth did you say to her?" Ty finally got the words out past his amazement.

Garrett sent him a look that could have frozen hot coffee. "I asked her to marry me."

Ty stepped back. "Is that all?"

Garrett narrowed his eyes at his friend. Ty was pushing it pretty far, even for a friend. Shaking his head, he picked up his hat and stuck one finger through the bullet hole.

"She shot my hat," he muttered.

The reality of her act only now hit him. Miss Caitlan Parker had pulled a pea shooter on him. And shot his hat right off his head.

He rubbed the top of his head. Maybe he was lucky he still had a head. If she'd missed . . .

A sobering thought struck him. What had the lady been aiming at anyway?

And what had he said to make her so angry?

"Garrett?" Ty shook his shoulder.

When he looked over at his friend, Ty held out a glass of his private whiskey.

"Drink it. I think you need it."

Garrett accepted the glass he'd thrust into his hand and took a swallow.

"Tell me once again what you said to her?" Ty asked, curiosity filling his voice.

Angel Tamera swung her heels back and forth from her perch on the windowsill in the sheriff's office. She was past caring that her heels repeatedly banged the wall beneath the window.

Something had to be done.

If not, Cat and Garrett were likely going to succeed in killing each other.

Imagine, the lady had actually drawn that little gun of hers and shot at Garrett!

Why, she'd sent his hat flying right off his head, too.

Tamera patted her shoulders, smoothing her ruffled feathers. Thank heavens that Cat obviously hadn't been aiming to kill him. But she'd put a nasty hole in Garrett's hat just the same.

While she in all truth had to admire the lady's spunk and her shooting ability, she could not allow this type of behavior to continue. She was getting too slow to jump up and stop bullets anymore. So, she'd just have to see this behavior didn't happen again.

No, absolutely not.

A smile lifted her lips at a remembrance of the shocked expression on Garrett's face when his hat had sailed right off his head.

Honestly, these two humans couldn't manage to do one thing right between them.

Poor Cat. Her own heart had gone out to the dear girl when Garrett had so heartlessly apologized for loving her. *Apologized.*

Why, imagine that. Offering a woman an apology of repentance for loving her. Her own feathers ruffled to such an extent at this that she had to take several deep breaths to restore calm to herself.

"Humph." She kicked the wall again.

Oh, feathers, didn't the man have any idea how to express himself to a woman? She'd never heard tell of him having this problem before Cat came along. The cause must be this thing called love. It sure had Cat and Garrett in a stir.

Well, it looked like it was up to her to straighten the mess out. The solution was really quite simple. All she had to do was ensure that Garrett remembered making love to Cat.

She tapped a fingertip on her lips. What could she do to help?

What Garrett needed was to be able to see the *real* Cat Parker—the one she worked so hard to keep concealed behind that ladylike facade. If only there was a way for Garrett to see her, truly see her, without that fancy lady image so firmly in place.

Tamera smiled to herself. Well, wherever there was a will, there was a way.

Cat whirled away from the window at the sound of a light knock at her door. At the realization that the knock was too timid to be Garrett returning, some of the tension left her.

But then again, whatever would he return for?

Hadn't he done enough?

She clenched her hands into fists. What she wanted to do was strike out and hit someone. Preferably Jake Garrett.

"Who is it?" she asked, not a hint of friendliness in her voice.

"It's Sarah."

Cat let out a disgusted sigh. She didn't want to talk to anyone right now—not even Sarah. She was too damned mad for friendly chatter.

"Sarah, this isn't a good time. I have a headache," she lied.

A mere instant later, the door knob turned, and her friend and landlady stepped into the room. Cat noticed that her eyes were practically sparkling with the curiosity of unasked questions. She wondered how long she'd be able to hold out before she asked the first one. Not long.

"Is it true?" Sarah stared at her in wide-eyed amazement.

Inwardly Cat cringed at the question, but outwardly she forced a calm smile and asked, "That depends on what you're referring to?"

"Did you shoot Garrett?"

"No, I shot his hat," Cat announced calmly, though anger still rimmed each word she spoke.

However, it was a calm she was a far sight from feeling. In fact, she could feel her hands tremble slightly every time she moved them.

Had she really shot Garrett's hat? She could scarce believe it herself. Even though he deserved it.

"You didn't," Sarah said. "Tell me you didn't." She sank down onto the bed as if her legs might not continue to hold her up.

Cat faced her and nodded. Her anger still burned too hot to allow her to lie about this.

"He had it coming," she stated, raising her chin in defiance of her friend's censure.

Sarah met her gaze a moment, then her lips twitched. "Now I truly wish I'd been here to see his face."

Cat grinned in remembrance. "Oh, it was something to see all right."

Her friend sobered. "But didn't he come and propose to you?"

Cat's smile left faster than the sunshine in a thunderstorm. A glint of anger replaced her momentary humor.

"No, he did not."

"But I was certain he was going to do ri—" Sarah cut off her comment.

"Do right by me? Is that what you were going to say?" Cat advanced on her until she stood less than a foot away. "Sarah, what do you know of this?"

Her friend glanced to the door. "I . . . I think I hear Amanda."

"No, you don't."

Cat took another step closer.

"What do you know?" Cat repeated. Her voice brooked no argument.

Sarah glanced away from her. "I . . . I heard he might be going to propose marriage."

"And where did you happen to hear this?"

Sarah lifted her hands, palms up. "When I was with Ty."

"The sheriff told you?" Cat's voice rose on this bit of news.

"Not exactly." Concentrating overhard on her hands, Sarah added, "Garrett told us."

"Now, I wonder why he suddenly decided to do that? And tell you two about it?" Cat planted her hands on her hips in demand for answers.

"Ty and I kind of had a talk with him."

At Cat's startled gasp, she rushed on, "Dear, the man had to do what's right. Why, he—"

"I know exactly what he did."

"Cat, somebody had to look out for you."

"I—"

"Haven't done such a good job," her friend pointed out in a soft voice.

"I'm doing fine on my own." Cat momentarily forgot all about her masquerade as a fine Eastern lady.

''Well, you shouldn't have to.'' Sarah jumped to her feet. ''I can't believe he didn't propose. He was supposed to propose,'' she muttered in a low voice, as if to herself. She faced Cat. ''What did he come to see you for? And why did you shoot his hat?''

''He apologized.''

Cat's two words hung in the air like a storm cloud, waiting.

''What!''

Tears blurred Cat's vision for a minute, and she furiously blinked them away. She clenched her hands into tight fists.

''He apologized. Damn him.''

Realizing what she'd said, Cat slapped a hand over her mouth. Too late.

Sarah's eyes widened at this.

Cat took a breath and blurted out the rest, ''Oh, and then he said he'd go ahead and marry me!''

Sarah's mouth opened and closed twice before she got her next words out. ''I suppose you refused?''

Cat turned the full force of her glare on the woman.

''Umm, yes, you refused. And then you shot him?''

''Not him, his damn hat!'' Cat shouted.

''Of course.''

Cat felt her anger growing again. ''He didn't have the manners to remove his hat.''

''Yes, dear.'' Sarah patted her on the shoulder and walked toward the door. ''I'll go and leave you to rest now.''

Cat didn't like the look in her friend's eyes in the slightest. It had interference written all over it.

''Sarah, don't meddle.''

''Me?''

Both her voice and her face were the picture of innocence.

Cat wanted to scream or throw something. She forced herself to answer in a nearly calm voice. ''Yes, you.''

''Why, Cat dear, I wouldn't dream of it.'' With this parting shot, she left the room.

Yeah, she'd just up and do it, Cat thought to herself in exasperation.

At the thought of Garrett returning with another so-called marriage proposal, her temper rose.

"He apologized," she muttered to the empty room.

Well, she wasn't going to let him get away with it. No, she'd . . .

She wasn't sure what she'd do, but she'd think of something.

She strode across to the window, stubbing her toe on the way. "Shams."

Glancing down, she spotted the corner of her saddlebags. Angered by the memories it brought along, she swung back her foot and kicked the bag again.

"Yeow."

She hopped on one foot, gritting her teeth against the pain in her toes.

"What in the . . . oh, no."

The heavy object her foot had connected with had been her Colt revolver. Bending down, she threw open the saddlebag and withdrew her revolver. Mud caked the pearl handle.

She squeezed her eyes shut. Shams.

Up until now, she'd always treated her guns with the utmost respect. She'd never, never left one to lie around dirty.

What had come over her since arriving in Millwood? The answer to that was simple—Jake Garrett.

Crossing to her carpetbag, she opened it and withdrew her cleaning supplies. Then she set to cleaning her guns.

"This is all *his* fault," she muttered.

She rubbed at a particularly stubborn spot of mud, then spit on the rag and rubbed some more.

Remembering their time together in the line shack, she added, "Damn bushwacker."

She rubbed the rag over the barrel.

The longer she worked, the madder she got.

Right about now, she'd like to shoot him and not his hat. Only this time, if she challenged him, it would be for herself and not for Jesse.

A sudden recollection jolted her, and she laid the rag down atop her revolver. When Garrett had come to call on her, he hadn't been wearing the deputy badge. She distinctly recalled that the shiny metal piece had been missing from his white shirt.

Garrett wasn't a lawman anymore.

That fact meant there was nothing to stop her from carrying out her original plan and challenging him to a gunfight.

No, not one thing. Except the blasted indecision the very possibility brought with it.

Could she continue with her plan? Could she do it?

She honestly didn't think so.

The next afternoon, Garrett sat across from his best friend's desk, helping Ty clean the three rifles that usually hung on the wall of the office. A dark mood enveloped him. He absently rubbed a cloth across the rifle barrel.

"Well, out with it." Ty leaned forward, his elbows on the desk top.

"With what?"

"The facts. Did Sarah tell it right?" He rubbed his chin. "Did you really tell that little gal you'd up and go ahead and marry her?"

"Yup, I offered to marry her. What—"

"But did you truly *tell* her you'd go ahead and marry her?"

Garrett thought about it minute. Put the way Ty had said it just now, it didn't sound the way he'd tried to say it to Cat.

"Well?" Ty almost shouted at him.

"I might have said that, but what I meant—"

"Dagnamit, it don't matter a hill of beans what you *meant*. What matters is what you said."

"I offered to marry her—" Garrett rubbed the back of his head.

"Don't you know anything about women?"

"I thought I did. Until she came along."

Ty patted him on the shoulder in a gesture of sympathy. "Listen to a master—"

"You? You're single—"

"Yup, been wanting it that way, too," Ty pointed out. "So listen and learn."

Garrett frowned at him, but his friend blatantly ignored it.

Instead he leaned back in his chair, raising the front two legs off the floor. "You got to sweet-talk a woman. Dagnamit, you *ask* her to marry you. You don't up and tell her you're gonna do it."

Garrett closed his eyes. His words to Cat came back to him in a clear picture. He groaned.

No wonder she'd refused him. He'd made a mess of it.

But, she'd refused him. He'd done his duty to her.

And she'd refused him.

That hurt, he realized all of a sudden. He wasn't so much angry about his hat being shot up as he was about her refusing him.

He tried to tell himself it was his pride that was hurting, but he knew better. It was his heart.

The truth of the matter was he wanted Cat Parker. And he wanted to marry her. He felt a smile curve his lips. Yup, he wanted Cat Parker.

And he intended to have her.

If she'd have him. A little voice reminded him she still didn't know he was a gunslinger.

He shoved himself out of the chair. If he wanted her, then he'd better do something about it. And he'd start by trying some of that sweet talking Ty mentioned.

Yup, he'd talk his way right into Cat Parker's heart. And her life.

Then he'd tell her about his past—just before he made love to her.

Garrett grabbed up his hat, rammed it on his head, and strode out the door. He didn't even bother saying goodbye to his friend. And he likely didn't even notice the round bullet hole in his hat.

He was going courting.

He made one stop on his way to the boardinghouse. At Dena's Restaurant. She always had pretty flowers around the inside of her establishment. Maybe she'd let him have some to take to Cat. It seemed like the right thing to do to start off his courting of Cat.

Minutes later, flowers in hand, Garrett set off for the boardinghouse. His smile seemed to be stuck on his face. He felt happy for the first time in days.

In fact, he felt so good that his wound didn't bother him in the slightest. Nope, not one bit.

He didn't return any of the greetings he received on the way to Cat. His full attention was on reaching her as soon as possible. He suddenly recalled how several other men in Millwood had expressed an interest in Cat's box supper. He knew for a fact those other men hadn't been bidding on Sarah's finely cooked meal any more than he'd been doing.

If he didn't make his move with Cat soon, someone else would. He'd bet on it.

When he reached the boardinghouse, he didn't look for Sarah and speak to her as he usually did. He took the stairs two at a time, and he didn't stop until he stood in front of Cat's door.

Straightening his hat, he raised his hand and knocked. He waited impatiently for the sound of her soft, slightly husky voice.

And he waited.

He knocked again. And waited some more.

His patience at an end, he twisted the door knob. It turned under his hand, and he swung the door open a small bit.

"Cat?" he called out, keeping his voice low.

No response.

Shoving the door open wider, he stepped inside and glanced around. She wasn't here.

Sighing in irritation, he kicked the door closed with one booted foot. Well, he wasn't leaving.

When she got back, he'd be here waiting for her.

Then he noticed the steam rising off the water in the tub sitting in her room. No lady up and left a freshly drawn bath. Not for long.

Yup, Cat Parker would be returning very shortly. He'd bet his hat on it.

A smile curved his lips, and a decidedly wicked idea sprang to mind.

Grinning widely, he walked over to the enameled tub.

Cat trudged up the stairs. She was tired of fighting with herself over Garrett.

In truth, he was winning the argument she'd been having with herself.

Upset, with herself and him, she had decided a hot, scented bath would calm her. Then he'd had her so distracted she'd completely forgotten to pick up any towels from Sarah for her bath. And she hadn't been any to pleased to have to dress again to come down the stairs to find a towel.

However, there wasn't any way on earth she would step foot outside her door not fully clothed with Garrett living right next door to her room.

No, absolutely not.

He hadn't been in his room all day. The thought struck her, and she shoved it away. She was not keeping track of his movements. She did not care where he went off to. No, not one whit.

Reaching the top step, she forced herself not to even look at his door as she walked past. Head high, she proceeded straight to her own room.

Why, he could just go to the devil for all she cared.

She opened her door and stepped into her room. Sighing, she inhaled the soft scent of roses from her bathwater. She hoped it was still hot.

Turning toward the tub, she froze dead still.

Garrett sat waiting for her. Stark naked in her bathtub!

Utter shock rapidly turned to anger. Cat held her temper in check with a great degree of difficulty.

"What are you doing here?" she asked, her teeth gritted so tightly together that they ached.

So did the rest of her. Especially her heart.

"Garrett?"

She was proud of how calm his name sounded to her own ears. Especially when she wanted to scream at him to get out.

"I was waiting for you, Cat."

His silky voice held the low edge of a drawl. It was velvet soft, and oh so tempting.

She swallowed down her impulsive response. She was not happy to see him here.

No, she wasn't.

Liar, the little voice of her conscience challenged.

If she could have, she would have used the second shot in her derringer on that blasted conscience of hers.

She met his words with silence, but it cost her all her strength.

Then Garrett held out a wilted handful of flowers to her.

She almost reached for the bright flowers. Almost, but she stopped herself barely in time.

Garrett gave her a smile that almost melted her very toes even in kid slippers. Almost, but not quite.

Cat gathered her anger about her like a shield. If he thought he could fix everything with a smile and a handful of wilted blossoms, he couldn't be more wrong.

"How's the water?" she asked.

"Hot."

"Maybe we'd better do something about that," she purred in response.

She crossed over to the washbasin and picked up the pitcher of cold water, hiding it in the folds of her skirt. She walked back, making certain to sashay her hips. As she'd hoped, his gaze was riveted to her hip movements. He never noticed the pitcher in her hands.

He sat in the tub waiting for her. In *her* tub. Anger bubbled up in her.

Suddenly, she raised the pitcher and dumped the cold water right over his head.

"Enjoy your bath. Alone."

Turning on her heel, she stormed out the door, slamming it on his shouts.

Chapter Twenty

Garrett wiped away the cold water that ran in rivulets down his face. His jaw set in anger.

She hadn't even stuck around to listen to him sweet-talk her. And he'd had it all planned out what he was going to say to her, too.

No, she'd dumped a pitcher of cold water on him. Damn cold water.

Grabbing hold of the sides of the tub, he surged to his feet.

The little minx.

As he stepped out of the water, the scent of roses wafted up to him, reminding him of Cat held close in his arms. It didn't look like he'd be holding her in his arms anytime soon, not the way things were going now.

He'd tried Ty's sweet talking, and look where it had gotten him!

She wouldn't even stop to listen. Well, he had a few things to tell her. Unconcerned for the damp tracks he was leaving on the floor, Garrett headed straight for the door and after the woman.

Cat Parker would not get away with this. He'd had enough. More than enough.

First the woman shoots his hat. His best hat.

Then she refuses his flowers. Flowers he bought and paid for. Especially for her.

And she tops it off by dumping a full pitcher of cold water on him. Very cold water.

He clasped the door knob and shoved the door open.

When he got his hands on her, he'd . . .

A gust of cool air hit his body, and he belatedly realized he didn't have a stitch of clothing on. Thankfully, no one was in the hallway. Swearing, he stepped back and slammed the door shut.

Cat nearly ran into Sarah on her race to the front door. She skidded to a stop barely in time to avoid knocking the other woman down.

"Cat, what's wrong?"

Swallowing, Cat forced a wan smile to her lips. "I . . . I was on my way out."

"With a towel in your hand?"

Cat glanced down at the towel she still held tightly gripped in one hand. She closed her eyes and sighed in frustration.

She'd left with the towel.

A sudden thought struck her, and she smiled in jubilation. If *she* had the towel, then Garrett couldn't—

A slam sounded from upstairs, followed by, "Cat." Garrett's yell could be heard all the way through her closed door and downstairs.

Cat flinched. She struggled to keep her smile in place. It wavered.

"Sorry, Sarah. I . . . ah . . . need to leave."

Footsteps could be heard overhead. Both women looked up to the ceiling.

"Right now."

After one look at Cat's face, Sarah caught her arm and tugged her along in her wake. "Through here."

Cat opened her mouth to protest and heard a door opening upstairs. She grabbed hold of her skirts with one hand and followed her friend.

Sarah led the way to her private quarters, only stopping to ensure she turned the door lock once they were both inside. She faced her visitor, a distinct twinkle of laughter in her eyes. "Now, tell me—"

Cat put a finger to her lips.

A door slammed above stairs. Her door. Garrett was coming.

"What was that all about?" Sarah bent closer and whispered.

Before she could answer, Garrett's shout filled the stairwell for an instant. "Cat!"

She flinched again, shutting her eyes.

"Is Garrett looking for you for some reason, dear?" Sarah inquired politely in hushed tones.

Cat gulped and nodded. She was almost afraid to even whisper an answer.

Just then footsteps could be heard pounding down the stairs. Two at a time. Then the front door slammed. Cat released an audible sigh of relief.

Sarah's next words snatched it away.

"Care to sit awhile and tell me what I missed this time?"

Cat sagged weakly against the door.

Sarah chuckled softly. "Come on. I've got just what you need about now."

Knowing she had little choice, Cat allowed her friend to pull her after her to a small sitting room. Avoiding her friend's curious glances, Cat studied the room. The walls were painted in a soft hue of blue, while cream lace curtains hung at the windows.

Sarah cleared her throat, and Cat jumped. Once again her friend gave a short chuckle.

"You look a bit pale. I'll fix us both a nice cup of coffee."

As she left to get the refreshments, Cat closed her eyes. What she'd like about now is a nice stiff drink of whiskey, but ladies didn't imbibe. She sighed in a sound that seemed to come up from her very toes.

What had she done?

Sarah's words about her looking pale brought to mind full force exactly what she'd done.

She'd dumped cold water over Garrett.

"Oh, dear heavens," Cat muttered, at a complete loss for words.

He was going to be furious. She just knew it. Even if his shout hadn't warned her, the look on his face had done so.

She'd done the only thing she could think of once she'd slammed the door. She'd run.

Hiding wasn't in her nature. It grated on her nerves. However, at the moment she had no intention of venturing outside the sanctuary of this room. None whatsoever!

"Here we go." Sarah walked back into the room, carrying a tray with a pot of coffee, two steaming cups, and a small bottle on it.

Sarah motioned her to one of two overstuffed chairs on either side of a small, round mahogany table. "Sit down. This will make you feel better."

As Cat watched in amazement, her friend picked up the bottle of vanilla and poured a dollop in each cup, then held one of the cups out to her.

"Try it, dear. It's delicious. But since you're not used to spirits, sip it slowly," Sarah warned.

At Cat's hesitation, she added, "I won't tell if you don't."

Cat smiled back. "Thank you."

She took the cup, trying not to appear as doubtful of the brew as she felt. She forced herself to take a small sip of the coffee.

Why, it was tasty. A touch of sweetness with a slight kick. Still not as good as a shot of good whiskey, but on the other hand, it did quite well in a pinch. Quite well. She took another sip.

"How do you like your coffee, dear?" Sarah asked.

"Ah, it's very good."

Sarah winked at her. "I thought you'd enjoy some about now."

Cat took another swallow. The doctored coffee rolled smoothly down her throat. It was warm and comforting. And it left the tiniest tingle in its wake—exactly what she needed.

So, this was what ladies drank to relax—a shot of vanilla, she thought to herself, suppressing a chuckle.

She'd heard tell of ladies putting a dab of vanilla behind their ears, but she'd never cared much for the scent herself. She much preferred jasmine or rose water. However, she had to admit, Sarah was putting the vanilla to a much better use. She took another sip.

Sarah settled into the opposite chair. "So, might I ask why Garrett was looking for you?" She scarcely held back the laughter.

Cat grimaced. She proceeded to tell her friend what had happened. Including the pitcher of cold water. She interspersed her tale with sips of the delicious, relaxing coffee.

Laughing over the story, Sarah leaned forward and refilled Cat's cup, then added another dollop from the bottle of vanilla.

"Well, I think this was a good time for you to visit me." Sarah took a swallow from her cup. "We'll have a nice long chat, and let Garrett cool off a bit more," she added with a giggle.

Cat couldn't agree more. She had the feeling that Jake Garrett needed to cool off more than a bit before she dared meet him again.

"Yes," she answered. "He's furious by now." She couldn't repress the slight shudder at the thought.

Sarah reached over and patted her hand. "Now, don't you go up and worrying about Garrett. He's not the hot-tempered type."

Cat sent her a distinct look of disbelief.

"No, dear. It's true. Jake Garrett has a reputation for always fighting fair in a gunfight. He's never let temper get in the way like some do."

Fighting fair?

Cat sipped at the coffee, deep in thought. Sarah had spoken with honesty in her voice. And a man was known by his reputation.

But, surely he hadn't been fighting fair three years ago when he'd shot Jesse. Word in Shelbyville had been that the gunslinger had drawn early and gunned poor Jesse down. It had all been over in minutes, and Jesse's closest friend had taken care of the body and burial.

Cat held back a sniffle. She could still recall crying over Jesse's grave. She took a swallow of coffee, draining the cup, and scarcely noticed when Sarah refilled it again. Her thoughts were far away.

She had to admit that maybe Jesse Stewart hadn't been the best man around, and sure there had been rumors after his death; but he'd been the only man who ever offered to take her away from the hated farm life.

"So, it looks like he will be staying here with us in Millwood," Sarah announced.

Cat jerked herself up. What were they talking about? She felt so warm and relaxed that her thoughts seemed to have developed a mind of their own.

"I'm sorry, Sarah." Cat blinked at her friend. "I was woolgathering. Who were you speaking about?"

"Why, Jake Garrett, of course."

"Garrett? Staying in Millwood?" For some unknown reason her thinking was getting muddled. She blinked again at her friend.

"Why, yes, dear. He's retiring, you know." Sarah leaned back in the chair and smiled at the news she'd relayed.

Cat stared at her a full minute. "Retiring? Garrett's retiring?"

"Yes." Sarah sat forward and refilled Cat's half-empty cup, then splashed in more vanilla. "Isn't that wonderful news?"

No, it was terrible, Cat thought to herself. Absolutely terrible.

If he was hanging up his guns, she couldn't begin to challenge him. Even if she wanted to do so. She refused to consider that thought in her present state.

Cat blinked and looked around the room. Why, she was . . . what was the word ladies used? Oh, yes, quite inebriated.

Her mind returned to the news of Garrett she'd just learned.

"Oh, shams," she said. "If he's retiring and staying, I might as well leave town."

Sarah patted her hand. "No, dear. We will have to think of another way to get you two together. That's all there is to it."

Smiling, Sarah refilled both their coffee cups. This time she added a dab extra of vanilla. For flavor.

Angel Tamera frowned down at the two women. Feathers, they were drunk. Both of them.

She clucked her disapproval. A nice lady like Mrs. Miles should certainly know better. However, she had been the one to give the alcohol to Cat.

Well, there was nothing more to be done here, with the state the two women were in now. She could hear Garrett stomping around in his room upstairs, where he had returned when he'd been unable to find Cat. He was quite safe for now.

Cat was in no condition to do harm to anyone. Including herself.

Recalling Cat's last remark caused Tamera to pause. She'd talked of leaving town. No, no, no. That couldn't be allowed to happen. The only chance either Cat or Garrett had of happiness lay in their love for each other.

Well, it was up to her to stop this foolish notion before Cat could proceed to act on it.

The train whistle pulled her thoughts away. Tamera pondered on this for a moment; then a wide smile broke out on her face.

Miss Simms's new beau was on that train.

Turning, she flew out of the boardinghouse and straight away for the train station. Sure enough, Louis Winston stepped down off the train. A stranger walked past and headed for the hotel. Tamera decided someone else would have to find him a room.

She needed to make certain that poor Mr. Winston had a place to stay. So he could begin courting Miss Celia Simms. The sooner the better.

With the teacher out of the way, the job would be open for Cat. Then she could stay in Millwood, too. It would be next to nothing to finalize plans for her and Garrett after that was accomplished.

Maybe she'd better go drop in on Miss Simms and suggest it would be nice of her to take a pie to Mr. Winston. Yes, that was definitely a good idea.

Tamera reached the schoolhouse in no time. As she'd expected, Miss Simms sat behind her desk. Once again her concentration was firmly fixed on the papers on her desk. Something needed to be done with the woman.

"Oh, Celia, honestly. You need to learn to live a little." Tamera tapped her foot on the floor beside the desk.

The moment the teacher let out a scream that shook the roof, Tamera realized she'd spoken out loud. Oh, feathers.

"I'll get you myself this time," Miss Simms threatened. "Then the sheriff will believe me."

Miss Simms reached down to the floor and grabbed up a long-handled object. Not the broom again, Tamera thought, squeezing her eyes shut.

When she opened them, a tiny squeak left her mouth. The woman had a shotgun. A *loaded* shotgun.

Tamera gave up on her plan and flew for the door. A deafening blast sounded behind her.

Thankfully, Miss Simms's shooting was as bad as her cooking. She missed, but Tamera's lower feathers tingled. She glanced down and saw they were singed nearly black.

This time she headed for heaven before St. Peter could call her. One slightly singed feather floated down to the wood floor in her wake.

* * *

The sound of the shotgun blast rattled the windows in Sarah's sitting room. She and Cat stared at each other in horror.

"Garrett!" Cat cried out, jumping to her feet.

Before Sarah could move to stop her, Cat raced out of the room and out the front door. There was nothing for Sarah to do but run after her. She didn't catch up with Cat until they had reached the main street.

By then, half the town was outside as well.

"It came from the schoolhouse," Ty shouted, leading the way, with a rifle in his hands.

"Folks, stay back," Garrett ordered from beside him.

No one listened. The people headed in the direction of the school.

Except for Cat. She stood not moving until the fact that he was alive and well sank in. Then she weaved a little. Sarah caught her arm.

"Maybe, we'd better walk there together," Sarah suggested.

"The school?"

Someone grabbed Cat's other arm, and she barely spared them a glance at first. Then, she recognized the bowler hat and stopped in place.

The Pinkerton man?

He stared back at her a moment, his eyes fixed on her face. She could swear she saw recognition there as well.

"You're her," he said in a whisper, staring into her eyes.

Cat's fuzzy mind didn't make sense of this. "What are you talking about?" He was definitely a strange man.

He stepped closer and tightened his grip on her arm. "I'm sorry to tell this, but your brother is not a nice man. Watch out for him. He's after your money," he warned in a low voice.

Cat wavered on her feet a moment and stared at him. His babble didn't make a whit of sense.

She tried to disentangle her arm. "Ah, I have to go to the schoolhouse—"

"Miss? Were the shots from the schoolhouse?" he promoted in a high-pitched voice.

Cat took a step and found both her footing and her voice equally unstable. "Yes."

"My Celia," he called out, running for the school.

Cat and Sarah arrived in time to see Miss Simms standing on the step with a shotgun in one hand.

"Celia!" Louis Winston ran to her and threw his arms around her.

Miss Simms, Mr. Winston, and the shotgun all landed on the ground in a pile.

"Oh, dear," Sarah said, then broke into giggles.

Cat looked at her friend. Oh, shams. She was drunk as a skunk. Taking charge, she caught Sarah's arm and whirled around, then dragged her back to the boardinghouse before any of the fine townsfolk could realize the condition they were both in.

Thankfully, she knew Garrett was occupied with the uproar caused by Miss Simms. Cat helped Sarah into her private quarters. Together they got her to bed and covered up before Sarah fell asleep. Cat recalled earlier she'd heard that Amanda was visiting her grandmother for the week, so Sarah would be fine left to her own devices for now.

Cat crossed to the door and cautiously peered out before she stepped into the hall. While she was certain Garrett would be busy for some time, she couldn't be too careful.

The last thing she wanted was to run into him right now in the state she was in.

Run?

A giggle bubbled up and burst free at the mere thought of running. Right now, in her condition, she could scarcely walk straight.

Head up, she carefully negotiated the stairs. Pausing at the top, she took a breath and mentally patted herself on the back. She'd made it.

Smiling at her accomplishment, she proceeded down the hall. Garrett's door drew her like a bee to honey. She stopped outside his door, leaning against it.

What was she going to do about him?

Chapter Twenty-One

Cat pressed her palm against Garrett's door, then laid her cheek against the wood. If only it were his body she was pressed close to. His chest that pillowed her cheek. His arms around her. . . .

However had everything gotten into such a mess?

Releasing a deep sigh that surely came from her heart, she pushed herself away from his door. She remained there a moment staring at the wood. Then she placed a kiss on her fingertips and brushed it against the door.

"Good night," she whispered.

Slipping into her own room next door, she crossed to the bed and flopped down onto the feather mattress, face first. She sighed deeply and proceeded to fall fast asleep. Fully clothed, bustle and all.

Hours later, Cat awoke to the sound of the loud pounding of a hundred little men in her head. She pulled the pillow over her head, trying to shut out the clamor.

It didn't work. The horrible noises were coming from within her head. And it ached.

A wagon rumbled by on the street outside, and it felt as if

it rattled every bone in her body. She groaned, covering her ears with her hands. She quickly fell silent. Even the sound of her own voice hurt her head.

Her stomach gave a roll, and she curled into a ball of misery. A sharp jab in her side startled her, and she almost sat up, but remembered her head barely in time and lay still.

What the—

She pulled at whatever was poking her in the side. Looking down she realized it was her bustle. Or what remained of her bustle.

Blinking, she looked a second time. She still had on her gown from when? Yesterday?

With sudden clarity she recalled Sarah's coffee. The woman should be charged with attempted murder, for Cat wasn't certain she'd live another minute. She could even still taste the lingering flavor of vanilla on her tongue. It had definitely tasted much better yesterday.

She'd only felt this bad one other time in her life. It had been the first, last, and only time she'd drank enough whiskey to get into a drunken state. The next morning she'd sworn never again.

Now look at her. And for what? For coffee!

A thundering started up outside her door, and without thinking, she yelled, "What!"

Then Cat grabbed her head in both hands. Right now she feared even a whisper might cause more pain.

"Cat? It's Sarah," came a weak voice from the hall.

Holding her head with one hand, Cat sat up. Gingerly she eased her feet to the floor and ever so slowly stood. The room stayed level, although she feared that she swayed a little bit from side to side as she shuffled her feet to the door.

With infinite care, she turned the lock, wincing at the click. She heard an answering moan from the other side of the door.

Pulling the door open, she saw that Sarah looked about as bad as she herself felt. Her friend gave her a wan smile, and Cat motioned her in with a finger to her lips.

Sarah walked slowly to the chair and sank into it with a sigh. "Morning," she whispered.

"Morning," Cat mumbled in return.

"Care for a cup of coffee?" Sarah giggled.

Cat threw her a look that would have stopped a gunfighter in his tracks. It had little or no effect on her friend.

Sarah reached into her pocket and withdrew the bottle of vanilla. Cat groaned in response.

"I never want to see that stuff again," Cat warned.

Sarah opened the bottle, took a swig straight from it, then handed it to Cat. "My husband always said, 'if a man's gonna drink, he'd better hit it again first thing in the morning or he's gonna think he's dying.' " She shuddered as the vanilla hit her stomach.

Cat stepped back.

Sarah reached out and put the bottle in her hand. "He always swore by it. Take it from me, he was right about that." She winked. "It's worked for me in the past."

At Cat's gasp, she added, "Granted, I haven't had to try his cure too many times."

Cat grimaced and raised the bottle to her lips. Shutting her eyes, she followed Sarah's lead. She resisted the impulse to hold her nose with her fingers. Her grimace turned into a shudder of revulsion. It tasted horrible.

Handing back the bottle, she walked to the bed and sat on the edge. "What did we do?"

Sarah gave a wan smile and raised her hands, palms up. "Drank a pot of coffee."

They looked at each other and grinned.

"You go on back to bed," Sarah ordered. "I'll come back and check on you in a couple of hours."

"Sounds wonderful."

As soon as Sarah left, Cat stripped down to her chemise and climbed back into bed. She pulled the coverlet over her head and fell fast asleep.

* * *

Garrett heard the sound of a door softly closing next door. He stood by his own door and listened.

Only one set of footsteps. It must be Sarah leaving. That meant Cat remained inside. He walked back across his room and sat on the edge of his bed.

He'd wait until he heard Cat moving about in the room, then he'd give her enough time to dress.

He couldn't very well go barging into her room when she likely as not wasn't decent, could he?

Although the idea did have its advantages.

The thought, however ungentlemanly it might be, brought a smile to his face as he pictured Cat in a state of undress. He felt his body begin to respond to the image, and he shifted uncomfortably on the bed.

What was taking her so long?

She wasn't escaping him again. They still had something to settle between them. And he wasn't about to let her slip away, not until they'd had a talk.

Not until she listened to what he had to ask her.

He tapped the toe of his boot in a nervous gesture he wasn't used to seeing in himself. Stopping, he listened carefully for any revealing noise from Cat's room, then rose and walked to the wall dividing them. He didn't hear any sound of movement from the room next door. Surely she hadn't fallen back asleep, had she?

Swearing that she'd chosen this particular time to sleep in, he turned on his heel and strode across his room. He picked up his hat and headed for the door. He was going for a ride. He needed to think. Away from the distraction of Cat Parker's delicious body.

Yet thoughts of Cat trailed along with him on his ride, no matter how hard he tried to clear her from his mind. What was he to do with her?

Love her?

The sudden suggestion nearly knocked him from his saddle. He couldn't be in love with her. No, that wasn't possible.

But he had proposed marriage to her.

He abruptly tightened his grip on the reins, and his horse drew to a halt. Easing up on the leather reins, he urged his mount on.

He'd only proposed marriage because Ty and Sarah had insisted, he assured himself.

And when had he ever done what anyone told him to do? his conscience prodded.

All right, so maybe he hadn't exactly been forced into proposing to Cat, he grudgingly admitted. He realized he hadn't done it solely out of a sense of guilt either. Or obligation.

In truth, he had to admit he'd proposed in part because he wanted her. In his bed and in his life.

However, the fact remained that he had nothing to offer a fine lady. Wouldn't a lady want a man who had a respectable job, regardless of how much money he had saved up? Some would consider his earnings through the years as blood money, although he'd never taken a dollar to kill anyone.

His thoughts came back to his current problem. What could he offer Miss Caitlan Parker?

Once again, he heard a repeat of Ty asking him to wear the badge of deputy full time. Garrett sat up straight in the saddle. It was finally time. He'd do it.

Turning his mount, he headed back to town. He had to see a man about a job. And to see a woman about a marriage.

Ty slapped Garrett on the back in congratulations. "It's about time you agreed to it."

Garrett raised his brows, but said nothing as he pinned the badge on. For good this time.

"Well, now that this is settled, what are you going to do about Miss Parker?" his friend asked.

Garrett dropped into the chair across from the desk and gave him a slow smile. "I'm going to propose." As Ty opened his mouth, Garrett added, "Properly this time."

"Good."

"What about you?" Garrett prodded.

"What about me?"

"When are you and Sarah—"

"Don't even think about it," Ty warned, tugging his hat low on his head.

Garrett held back his grin.

"Word is I'll be considered for that marshal job in a year or two more. If it happens, would you be interested in the sheriff's job here?"

Garrett let the grin free this time. It definitely looked like he had a future in Millwood. And a home, too.

"Sheriff?" Both Ruth and Judy came rushing into the office. Ruth stopped short of the desk, and Judy almost slammed into her. She peeked around Ruth's side, her head not quite reaching the taller woman's shoulder.

Garrett was the first one to his feet, followed by Ty. "Ladies—"

"We got trouble—" Ruth began speaking.

"They're tearing up our place—" Judy put in.

"You got to do something—" Ruth said.

"Yeah, right away," Judy ended.

Ty motioned to Garrett. "Looks like you got your first official duty. Trouble at the Long and Short Saloon."

Garrett followed the two women out, their chatter filling him in on the latest fight at the saloon. He settled his hat firmly in place and smiled.

Cat sat down to lunch with Sarah. They had decided on a special treat at Dena's Restaurant. Sarah claimed she wasn't about to cook after last night. Cat didn't blame her in the least.

Cat had scarcely taken a sip from her lemonade when Sarah leaned across the table and caught her other hand.

"You'll never guess what happened?" Sarah paused, letting the suspense mount.

Finally, Cat gave in and asked, "What?"

"Miss Simms ran off with that tenderfoot Louis Winston."

Cat knew her mouth had dropped open in surprise. "You mean they—"

"Eloped," Sarah announced, sitting back in her chair. "They left on today's train."

"The schoolteacher ran off with the Pinkerton detective?"

Sarah nodded emphatically. "It's the worst scandal to ever hit Millwood. I swear it's the talk of the town."

Cat smiled in return, but inwardly she cringed. If *this* was the worst scandal, they would have a heyday with the truth about who and what she was, not to mention why she'd come to town.

Sarah reached forward and grabbed both Cat's hands in her. "And the good news for you is that this means the town is short one teacher. Didn't Garrett say you came out here for a teaching position?"

Cat caught herself before she could deny it. She forced herself to nod mutely in agreement.

Liar, her conscience reprimanded her.

"Well, consider your search ended," Sarah announced with a flourish.

"What?" A decidedly uneasy feeling crept over Cat at the statement.

"I've suggested you to fill Miss Simms's job." Sarah grinned proudly. "Now you won't have to think about leaving Millwood."

Cat closed her eyes, recalling her rash statement to her friend over that darned coffee of hers.

She couldn't fill the position, no matter how much she might want it. The thought startled her—she did want the job of teacher in Millwood.

"Don't worry," Sarah assured her. "You've already got the job. It was finalized late this morning."

Dumbfounded at the news, Cat merely stared at her.

"Well, congratulations." Sarah squeezed her hands.

Congratulations, indeed. Now what was she supposed to do? Cat wondered.

She barely tasted their fine lunch, her mind in a turmoil. As they left, she invented an errand at the mercantile to give herself a few minutes alone to think.

In the mercantile, Cat made a show of purchasing a length of ribbon, some lace, and a new kerchief. She had to have something to carry back in case Sarah asked.

Deep in thought, Cat was no closer to an answer when she reached the boardinghouse. Maybe if she left things alone, it would work out. Dare she remain quiet about her true identity and take the teaching position?

She couldn't very well tell the truth and then hope to be offered the job. Shams.

She wanted the teaching job.

Not stopping to locate Sarah, Cat walked straight to her room. As she opened the door, a skitter of warning eased down along the full length of her spine.

Pausing, she stepped back and cautiously drew her derringer, wishing for something a lot larger and more powerful.

With a kick of her foot, she shoved the door open. What greeted her took her breath away.

Cat stepped into her room and scarcely bit back her scream of outrage. The bureau drawers hung open at odd angles, her gowns spilled from the armoire across the floor, and her carpetbag lay on its sides, its contents scattered.

Someone had ransacked her room. Thoroughly.

She slowly closed the door behind her as if operating out of a daze. Who would do such a thing? She didn't have anything worth stealing.

Remembering her cherished pearl-handled revolvers, she rushed across the room to her carpetbag. She found her guns lying beneath the bag.

She sat back on her heels with a frown. The revolvers were the only thing of any monetary value she owned. She'd purchased them herself with the money from the sale of the farm after Pa's death.

Why would someone ransack her room and yet leave her only valuable possession behind?

Something was wrong. Very wrong.

She carefully wrapped the guns back up and placed them in the bottom of her carpetbag. Spotting the old pink hair ribbon beside the letters, she grabbed them up and slipped them in the bag as well.

A shudder crept down her spine. Someone had read those old letters.

A tap on her door sent Cat jumping to her feet. She whirled around, pointing her derringer at the intruder.

Sarah screamed and fell back against the door.

Instantly contrite, Cat apologized, "I'm sorry. I had no idea it was you."

Sarah stepped gingerly into the room. "My, what happened?"

"I had an intruder." Cat followed her friend's gaze. The room was a disaster.

"Are you all right?"

Cat nodded and swallowed. "Thankfully, I wasn't here. I only now walked in on this." She spread out her hands and bit her lower lip. "I haven't had time to clean it up yet, but I—"

"No," Sarah ordered. "Ty needs to see this first."

Fear raced through Cat at the mere thought of a lawman checking her room. "No, it's fine. I'll just clean it up myself. It won't take—"

"Absolutely not. I'm going to get Ty," Sarah announced and swept from the room.

Cat groaned. There was no stopping that woman once she had her mind set on something.

One thing she did not need was a lawman in her room, snooping around and finding her Colts. Quickly she raced to the door and shut and locked it.

Next, she slipped the revolvers out of her carpetbag. She

slid one into the pocket of her blue gown, and the second into the pocket of a green gown. Smoothing the skirts she prayed the sheriff wouldn't think to check a lady's gowns.

She looked around her at the disarray. What more could go wrong?

Clapping a hand over her mouth, she wished she could call back the errant thought. It seemed every time, without fail, that she entertained that possibility it came true and something else happened.

Surely, this time . . .

"Cat?" A knock thundered at her closed door.

Shams, things had gotten worse.

She recognized Garrett's voice. What more—

She shut the thought off before it could be completed. Please let him go away, she wished, crossing her fingers.

"Cat?" he repeated. "Open the door."

Groaning to herself, she crossed the room and swung the door open. Garrett stepped inside, followed close on his heels by Sarah.

"I bet it was those troublemakers in the saloon," Sarah announced. "Good thing he ran those young guns out of town," she said with pride. She winked at Cat and motioned to Garrett's chest.

Cat followed her friend's gaze, and whatever she'd been thinking of saying left her mind completely. Garrett had a shiny deputy badge pinned to his shirt. Again.

"Garrett's agreed to take the job of deputy. Isn't that wonderful?" Sarah patted Cat's hands.

"I can speak for myself, Sarah," he said in a low, even voice.

"I know you can, Garrett."

He sighed and turned to Cat. "What happened?"

"I returned from an errand to find this." She spread out her hands.

"Anything missing?"

"I don't think so."

Cat bit her lower lip as he proceeded to check out her room.

She couldn't believe the news. Garrett was a lawman. Sarah's second bit of news struck her anew. He'd run the young guns out of town.

Shams. What would he do if he knew her true identity? Would he run her out of town, too?

She shivered, then determined to redouble her efforts at keeping up her lady's masquerade. At least a little longer.

She was thankful for Sarah's presence at the moment; it kept her from being alone with Garrett. She wasn't ready to face him yet. She had to rebuild her defenses.

Cat spent most of a sleepless night trying to accomplish just that. She tossed and turned, fretting over whatever she was going to do about Garrett.

Maybe if she tried avoiding him and allowed things between them to cool, then she could try again with him later. Much later.

Sometime near to midnight, Cat awoke with a start. She caught her breath and tried to lie perfectly still and listen. A slight rustle of sound alerted her.

Someone was in her room.

Fear lapped at her courage, threatening to cripple it. Her revolvers were clear across the room, still hidden in the pockets of her gowns in the armoire. She thought of her derringer, but it was safely tucked away in her reticule. On the table.

Did she have a chance of getting to a gun in time? She doubted it.

Since coming to Millwood, she had discontinued her habit of sleeping with a revolver under her pillow. Now she wished she had kept up the practice.

She couldn't move. Not even a muscle. Her limbs would not obey her commands.

Once again, she heard a noise, the slight scrape of a chair being moved. It gave her the impetus she needed. Sitting bolt upright, she opened her mouth and screamed. Then she screamed again, for good measure.

A door slammed down the hall, and she knew in her heart

it was Garrett. Gathering up her courage, she threw back the covers and ran for the door.

Cat turned the lock and threw the door open. A second later, Garrett burst into the room, gun drawn.

"What is it?"

"I thought I heard someone in my room." Cat hated the way her voice quivered, but she couldn't seem to stop it. She swallowed. "Maybe I was dreaming."

Garrett lit the lamp and held it up. Across the room, her carpetbag lay on the floor. He glanced from the bag to her.

Cat covered her mouth with both hands, unable to force out a word. Someone had been in her room.

"I wasn't dreaming," she whispered.

Garrett set the lamp down and walked across to the carpetbag. He set it upright, then bent down and picked up something from beside it.

When he turned to Cat he held out a white feather. She stared at it.

"What is that?"

"A feather," Garrett answered, rubbing the back of his neck.

Once again the hairs there were standing on end. He rolled the feather back and forth between his fingers. This one hadn't come off of one of the saloon girls' dresses as he'd supposed before.

Then where had it come from?

Garrett turn around, and the sight of Cat in the glow of the lamp held him in place. Her gown was nearly sheer backlighted by the lamplight. The thin material molded to her body and swirled about her legs. She took a step, and his breath rushed out in a ragged sound of pure need.

How he wanted her.

Cat took a step toward him, her eyes locked with his. He saw the faint trembling of her lower lip, and it was his undoing.

He crossed the distance separating them in three long strides. She didn't make a sound of protest.

He reached for her, drawing her to him. At that instant, she realized he hadn't taken the time to button his shirt. It hung open, and the bare skin of his chest brushed against her nightgown.

She could feel the heat of his body against her; it rushed through the thin fabric of her nightgown as if it weren't even there. He felt so warm, so strong, so wonderful.

Cat swallowed her wounded pride and slid her arms around his neck. When Garrett lowered his face to hers, she tilted her chin to receive his kiss. His mouth closed over hers. At the same time, he splayed his hand against her back and drew her so close that there wasn't space for a breath of air between them.

He deepened the kiss, slanting his lips firmly over hers. He clearly wasn't taking no for an answer. But she wasn't refusing.

Cat let her own hands trail along his neck and beneath the opened collar of his shirt. The strong muscles of his shoulder knotted under her fingers. She gently scraped her nails across the tops of his shoulders.

Garrett parted her lips and slid his tongue inside to the velvety softness within. He ran his tongue in and out, symbolizing the mating yet to come.

It brought forth a sigh of need from Cat that she was powerless to hold in. Garrett swallowed her sigh, taking her next breath with it. He ran his hands the length of her back, and Cat thought she would surely faint for real this time.

Her knees grew weak under his loving onslaught. She gripped his shoulders to remain upright. At this, he thrust his tongue deeper into her mouth, and she moaned in the faintest of sounds.

He swung her up into his arms and carried her to the bed. Pressing one knee onto the bed, he lowered her to the feather mattress, then followed her down.

One by one, he undid the tiny buttons fastening the front of her nightgown until, at last, she lay exposed to his eyes only. He braced his arms on either side of her and gazed down at her.

"Beautiful," he whispered. "So sweet."

Lowering his head, he brushed his tongue across the tip of

one rosy nipple. Cat couldn't hold back the gasp of surprise and pleasure. He returned his lips to hers in a long, slow kiss.

Easing onto his elbows, he cupped her breast with one hand. Murmuring softly, he trailed tender kisses along her lower lip, to her chin and along her jaw, then down her neck. He ended at her breasts.

Cat arched up against him, mindless of her movement. All she knew was that she needed to be closer. Closer to him.

Returning his lips once again to her mouth, he plundered hers, leaving her breathless. As he leaned away, she was powerless to resist.

"Cat?" he whispered her name in a question.

She stared up at him and knew she could give only one answer. "Love me?" she answered in a soft whisper almost too low to be heard.

"Yes."

Garrett took her lips again, this time with a passion that spoke of his need more clearly than any words could ever have done.

Raising his head slightly to give them both a breath, he placed a finger against her lips, then dropped another kiss, this one as soft as a butterfly, in their place.

Drawing away again, he stood to his feet, but his eyes never left hers. It was as if he were making love to her with his dark, intense gaze.

His hand dropped to the waist of his pants, and he unfastened them, lowering them and kicking them aside. He shrugged out of his unbuttoned shirt and returned to Cat.

This time his kiss seemed endless. He took her very breath away.

Cat clasped his broad, strong back, drawing him to her. She reveled in the strength of the muscles rippling beneath her palms. She felt so small, and protected, and cherished in his embrace.

He loved her breasts again, trailing kisses down to her flat stomach, then finally back to recapture her lips. When she thought she would surely die from the heat rising within her, he eased her legs apart and pressed into her.

Cat gasped as waves of sensation swept over her, taking her to the crest. Garrett filled her; then slipping his hands beneath her hips, he lifted her to him. She entwined her legs with his and followed where he led her.

Need spiraled up within, seeking release. Garrett held her tightly, drawing her to him, deeper ever deeper. Her lips clung to his as he carried them both up to the heavens.

Garrett called out her name at the instant of his release, and she followed him into paradise.

They lay entwined together for long, nearly breathless minutes. Garrett kissed her temple and drew her body close to his side, easing his weight from her.

Cat snuggled up in his arms. Heaven had never been closer than at this moment.

As a light breeze blew through the partially opened window, Garrett leaned up and drew the coverlet up in his hand. Glancing down at Cat, he took in her beauty. Lying there with her hair hanging free and spread out about her on the pillow, wearing only a sweet smile, she looked so very young, and innocent.

Something tugged at his mind. For a brief instant he could imagine her in faded calico instead of her silk gowns. Shock rolled over him in waves that stole his heartbeat.

So familiar.

The sight of the other, younger Cat brought back the three-year-old memory in a rush, and he stared at her, unable to move as the past caught up with him.

He *had* seen her in faded calico.

He'd made love to her with her wearing the old dress.

Except her name hadn't been Cat. It had been Laine.

Pain, more intense than a searing bullet, sliced through him, leaving him shaken.

Who the hell was she? And what game was she playing?

Chapter Twenty-Two

Garrett pushed himself away from her and got to his feet. Without a word he picked up his discarded pants and slipped them on. As he fastened them, his anger surged, nearly blinding him with its fury.

Grabbing up his shirt, he thrust his arms into it. Then, clenching his hand into a fist, he turned back to where she still lay in the bed.

"Cat?"

"Yes." She smiled at him.

"Or is it Laine?"

Her gasp told him his question had hit its mark.

Bitterness, pride, and regret tore at him. Beneath it all lay a pain too deep for words.

She'd certainly taken him for a fool. Yup, a prime fool.

Cat sat up in the bed, drawing the coverlet up over her nakedness. "You remembered?"

"I wish to hell I had forgotten you!" His voice was tight and harsh.

Without another word, he turned away as if the sight of her sickened him, and stormed out of the room.

The slam of the door behind him echoed and reechoed in her heart.

Cat dropped her head into her hands. As the shocked numbness wore off, the pain came and, with it, the tears that racked her body with silent sobs.

Garrett slammed his fist into the wall of the livery stable stall. His horse shied to the side at the unexpected sound.

Patting his horse to soothe him, he leaned against the stall. He was a prime fool if ever there was one.

Here he'd been worrying over how a fine lady like Caitlan Parker could ever accept him, a gunslinger. Meanwhile, she'd been laughing up her sleeve at him the whole time.

Hell, he'd even taken the job as deputy so he could have something respectable to offer her, to make a life for them together. He slammed one fist against the wood.

As the pain hit his knuckles, the past rolled over him in waves of misery. Cat was no fine lady from New York; she was a simple farm girl from Illinois, who had a penchant for jasmine.

He let the memories of one particular day flood him. Recalling it seemed to push out some of the pain. He'd been on his way to take his *Laine* the present of the scent bottle filled with jasmine. It had been the favorite scent of that nearly destitute farm girl. But he'd never made it to her pa's farm.

Some foolish hothead had charged him, nearly knocking him to the ground. When he'd staggered back away from the youth, he'd drawn out of force of ingrained habit. But he'd stopped just short of firing.

Not that it had made any difference. The young gunman had seen his chance to make a name for himself, and he'd issued the challenge. The kid had demanded a showdown in front of the townspeople.

Jesse Stewart. The name of the young gun sprang to his mind. He'd been nervous and shifty. Mighty edgy about something.

Garrett could even remember clearly what he'd been talking

about when the kid had knocked him down. The robbery, of course. It had been on all the men's tongues. The bank had been robbed in Springfield, a bank worker killed, and thousands of dollars stolen.

The young gun's challenge had effectively ended the conversation, then later the gunfight had cleared the robbery from the townspeople's minds.

Garrett closed his eyes against the memories, but they charged on, unwinding before him like the nightmare they had been. That one act had stolen his future from him. It had stolen his love away from him.

The town had been so outraged by the gunfight and young Jesse's death that they had even gotten together a lynching party. Forced to run for his life, he hadn't been able to return to his Laine like he'd promised. No, instead he'd abandoned her, leaving her behind where she'd be safe. However, he'd never gotten to tell her so. Never seen her again.

Until tonight.

He hadn't allowed himself the freedom to think about that day for a long time. He'd found the only way to shut out the pain of loss had been to shut out the memories along with the pain.

Back on that day, he hadn't been given any choice in the matter. No one in town was interested in hearing his side. He'd never been given the opportunity to tell his part in the gunfight. No, he'd had to make the decision to see Laine again and maybe endanger her as well, or leave and save his own life.

He'd had to face the shame of leaving her behind. Of knowing she believed he'd fled to save his own life. She'd never known the truth. He rubbed a hand over his eyes. It had been three years.

Three unbelievably long years in which he'd worked at burying that memory so deep that it would never resurface again.

He could see her clearly in her faded calico gown. Her golden hair blowing out behind her in a breeze, tumbling down her back in waves. Her eyes were the same shade as an emerald jewel.

A second picture merged with the first.

The same hair—one hanging down in waves, the other carefully pinned and curled atop her head.

The same honey-colored skin.

The same everything.

Laine and Cat Parker were one and the same woman.

Why hadn't he seen it sooner?

Sure, three years ago she'd been a young girl; now clothed in fancy gowns she was a woman. Of course, many people would never associate the two. But he should have known.

He should have known her.

Garrett felt as if someone had just gut punched him. The realization that Cat had been deceiving him hurt all the way to his soul.

He stood in place for a moment, fighting to drag air into his lungs. The past and present merged together for one pain-filled instant.

Cat had lied to him.

From the moment she'd stepped down off the train, she had lied.

Whatever game she'd been playing was over.

The lies had caught up with her. Cat raised her head and wiped away the traces of the tears.

Why did Garrett have to go and remember now of all times?

Her masquerade had cost her more than she'd ever dreamed. Why couldn't she have left the past alone? Why couldn't she have left her vow to Jesse unfulfilled?

Because it wasn't in her to do so. She now admitted that guilt over her last argument with Jesse had driven her to make amends to him after his death.

She closed her eyes, and that horrible day rose up before her like a specter. Jesse had been so edgy when he'd come to see her, telling her he had a gunfight and would make a name for himself. She'd told him their engagement was off. He'd been furious, swearing at her and telling her no it wasn't. He'd even given her a package to hold for them until after he returned from the gunfight.

But he'd never returned to her. She threw her head back, squeezing her eyes tight against the burning behind her lids, and drew in a deep breath. Jesse had died that day—by Jake Garrett's gun.

That gunfight had changed everything. Her life. Her future. Herself.

She wasn't Laine anymore. She'd become Cat in more than name only.

Laine had been an insecure young girl, needing someone to love her so desperately that she'd accepted the first young man that came along.

Cat deserved better.

She was stronger now. Not the type to let life run her. She'd choose her own future. And she wanted that future to include Jake Garrett.

As soon as it was daylight, she'd go find him. There had to be a way to make him understand. Pride be damned.

Dressed in the same green silk gown with emerald trim she'd worn the first time Garrett had kissed her in the mercantile, Cat dared to hope it would spark pleasant memories for Garrett.

If she ever found him, she thought in a rush of irritation.

She'd checked his room, but he hadn't been there. Sarah hadn't seen him, neither had Ty.

Tapping her foot, Cat looked up and down the dusty street. She'd checked about everywhere in town but the saloon.

Raising her chin in determination, she decided that was her next stop. Within minutes she stood below the sign proclaiming the Long and Short Saloon and boasting of the best liquor around. She'd heard that claim before.

She drew in a breath for courage and pushed the batwing doors open. And right into a man's face.

"Yeow. Blazes, watch where you're going," he swore at her.

Cat stared in openmouthed amazement at the sight behind the disgruntled man. A long, polished mahogany bar ran along the wall. But it was the painting behind the bar that held her rooted in place in utter amazement.

The painting was of a naked man!

Cat blinked and looked again. Sure enough, she'd seen it right the first time. Instead of the traditional painted picture of a naked lady reclining, this bar sported a man.

"Shams," she muttered.

"Are you insulting me?" The man she'd hit with the door grabbed her arm and yanked her into the saloon.

Cat nearly tripped over the flounce of her skirt. She waved one arm wildly to regain her balance. Her elbow almost caught his shoulder, but luckily he dodged it in time.

The short, stocky man stared at her. "I knows you. You did that on purpose, didn't ya?" He shifted his cigar with his tongue.

Cat was not in the mood for soothing a man's wounded dignity. She was tired, upset, and on the verge of more hated tears. She'd cried more since meeting Jake Garrett again than she'd cried in her entire life. And she didn't like it one bit.

"Leave me alone, you fool," she said, glaring back at the stranger.

"I'll teach a whore to talk to me like that." He spit out his cigar.

Before she comprehended his intention, he raised his arm and backhanded her. Cat reeled from the blow. Her jaw stung, and for an instant she could have sworn she'd seen twinkling stars.

"Shams." She shook her head to clear it.

As he raised his arm again, she yanked the derringer from her reticule and pointed it at the center of his forehead.

"Don't." Her single word held the authority of a shouted command.

Mouth gaping open, he stared at her.

As she saw his eyes narrow, she added, "Now leave me alone."

Stepping back, Cat kept her eyes focused on the man opposite her. She didn't trust him a whit.

A vague sense of familiarity nagged at her. Had she met him somewhere before?

"You'll pay for that," he vowed, spitting at her feet.

Cat swept her skirt away from him. At her movement, the man's beefy hand snaked out and yanked the derringer from her hand. He threw it out the door.

"Too good for the likes of me, are you now? Well, we'll see how good you are facing my guns."

Cat shook her head in refusal.

"Go get a gun and met me outside, or I swear I'll come find you. And maybe shoot up somebody else on my way."

"Cat?"

She stiffened at the sound of Garrett's deep drawl from over her shoulder.

"Cat, is there a problem?" he asked, stepping through the doors to stand beside her.

Not now, she wanted to scream at him. She'd been looking for him for untold time, and here he waltzed in at precisely the worst moment.

"No," she lied to him.

"Go away, lawman," the other man sneered. "This fight's between me and the whore."

"Not anymore it isn't."

Cat felt a chill go down her back at the coldness in Garrett's voice. It was also a tone that brooked no argument. But that didn't stop her from trying.

"Garrett, no. I—"

"Cat, go back to the boardinghouse. We'll talk later." Garrett nudged her toward the doors.

She planted her feet firmly and turned her back on Garrett. Instead she deliberately faced her challenger.

Swallowing all her pride, she met his hardened eyes. "I'm sorry if I offended you. Please accept my apology." It took all she had to extend her hand to the man.

He slapped her hand away. "No."

"Cat, go," Garrett ordered.

"No, I won't let you die for me."

"I won't be the one dying," he assured her.

She couldn't risk it.

"What's going on here?" Ty stepped into the saloon.

The sight of a lawman had never looked better to Cat, who had forgotten for the moment that Garrett now wore a badge. She whirled on the sheriff. "Stop them. They're going to fight."

"Garrett—"

"Leave it be, Ty." Garrett spoke in a calm voice. "I'm handling it."

"Sheriff? Ty?" Cat tugged on his arm.

Garrett nodded toward her. "Will you keep her out of this, so I *can* take care of it."

"Ma'am, you'll only make things worse," Ty said in a quiet voice.

She shoved his arm away. "Do something."

"I am." With this he caught her arm and pulled her out of the way of the men.

Cat had never felt more helpless or more furious in her life. Garrett stepped back and followed the challenger out into the street.

She kicked the sheriff in the shins. To his credit, he never lessened his grip on her arm.

"No, Miss Parker, one sound from you could get him killed."

She knew that fact. It caused her to sag against him at the warning words, then draw in a deep breath. No matter what, she wouldn't remain meekly standing by—doing nothing.

Cat wasn't the only one who refused to stand by the sidelines. Angel Tamera hovered directly in front of Garrett. She shivered at the prospect of taking the bullet meant for him.

A sudden thought gave her pause and sent every one of her feathers in a flurry. A gun had more than one bullet in it. What if the challenger fired a second shot after his first one hit her? That bullet might strike Garrett.

Oh, no it wouldn't.

Changing her plan, she flew straight for the challenger. Settling herself down beside him, she reached out a hand and waited. As he drew his gun, she stuck her finger into the barrel.

He pulled the trigger, and a muffled pop came from the gun, but no bullet. She'd caused it to misfire. The explosion sent the man to the ground, grabbing his wounded hand.

All about her, she could hear the voices of the crowd. But above it all came a very distinct shout.

"Tamera!"

Oh, feathers, she was in trouble again.

Sighing, she stuck her sore finger in her mouth. Then she flew for heaven, knowing what awaited her. Another lecture. Again.

At the sound of the gun firing, Cat yanked her arm from Ty's hold and shoved her way through the batwing doors. She didn't give a whit that the solid *thud* she heard was the doors hitting him. Ty staggered back, nearly falling to the floor.

Cat ran out into the street, searching for Garrett and taking in the scene before her. The man on the ground wasn't Garrett.

"Oh," she cried aloud, before she ran straight for Garrett.

She threw herself in his arms, nearly taking them both to the ground in her lunge. Only Garrett's natural balance and strength saved them from toppling over.

Before he could do more than catch his breath, she leaned up and kissed him hard on the mouth. It stole his breath clean away.

Garrett took one long, silent look into her face, then swept her up into his arms and strode away, heading for the boardinghouse. He couldn't for the life him think of anything else he'd rather do at that moment.

Cat gasped in surprise, her breath blowing softly against his ear. It heated his blood all the way to the soles of his boots.

He tightened his hold on her before she could utter a single word of protest. He had no intention of putting her down, no matter what she said right now.

Things were far from finished between them. And he intended to finish them. Now.

In response, Cat tightened her arms about his neck, as if holding on for her life. Did she actually think he might release her?

Not a chance, Garrett vowed. Not yet. They had some talking to do.

Talking was the farthest thing from Cat Parker's mind at that moment. She bit her lip to hold the shakes at bay. Just the thought that she could have lost him on that street today was enough to set every bone in her body to shaking horribly.

She shut her eyes against the very thought. Nothing could happen to him. She wouldn't let it.

She tightened her hold on Garrett and thought she heard a soft, "Oaf," come from above her ear.

Surely, she'd been hearing things.

She really should make him put her down, she thought in concern for his strength. He probably shouldn't carry her this far. She should . . .

At that moment, Garrett rubbed his hand over her back, and all thought of leaving his arms fled her mind for parts unknown.

Sarah met them at the door of the boardinghouse. She opened the front door and stepped aside.

"Is she all right?"

Garrett flashed her a wicked grin. "Quite all right."

"Oh," Sarah said, then fell silent.

"Sarah?" Garrett asked.

"Umm?"

"You might want to shut the door." His chuckle warmed Cat's ear, where she'd buried her face against his chest at the sight of their landlady and friend.

The door slammed with a thump.

"Thanks," he called over his shoulder.

Hefting Cat higher up into his arms, he strode up the stairs.

At the door to his room, he eased her to her feet. Reaching out, he snagged her one arm.

"You're not going anywhere."

Cat stared up at him mutely. Whatever had given him the idea that she had any intention of leaving right now? Or ever?

Garrett swung the door open and drew Cat inside with him. A small smile teased her lips as she heard him lock the door behind them.

She didn't exactly want any visitors. She had far different plans than entertaining company.

"We have to talk." He nudged her farther into the room.

Cat didn't need any encouragement. However, talking was the farthest thing from her mind at the moment. She'd nearly lost him, and she wanted to feel him. To know he was alive.

"Garrett," Cat interrupted in a soft voice. "Make love to me."

He stared at her for the space of a full heartbeat, and her courage almost wavered. Maybe he didn't want her. Maybe he—

"Oh, Cat. Darling Cat," he murmured the endearment.

As he stepped back a step, her breath froze in her chest. His hands lowered to his gun belt, and she breathed again. He unbuckled the gun belt and laid it across the chair. Next, he reached for the fastening of his pants.

Cat's throat went dry. She tried to swallow, but all she could do was stare at him.

This was much different than last night. It had been dark then, well nearly dark inside, and definitely dark outside.

And this was different from their time in the line shack. Then their world had been completely deserted except for the two of them. This time an entire town awaited outside.

She moistened her lips, unsure of what she should do or how she should act.

Suddenly shy, Cat lowered her gaze to the floor. She didn't know what she was supposed to do next. Was she to unbutton the pearl buttons that ran down the front of her dress? Or was he?

Garrett took the decision out of her hands with his soft command, ''Come here, Cat.''

She stepped willingly into his open arms. It felt like coming home to her.

Chapter Twenty-Three

Garrett pulled the light coverlet up to Cat's shoulder. She sighed and snuggled down into the feather mattress. Her eyes never opened.

He smiled in memory of precisely why she could be so tired.

Reluctantly, he turned away and tiptoed across to the door of his room. He liked the thought of Cat sleeping in his bed. What he wanted to do was climb back into that bed with her.

However, he had a job to attend to now. A smile still on his face, he slipped out the door. He took care that it didn't make a sound when he closed it. Let her sleep. She'd need her strength for tonight.

Humming under his breath, he took the stairs two at a time and closed the front door of the boardinghouse behind him. For the first time in his life he had someone to come home to. Tonight they would talk. First.

The day couldn't hurry past quick enough to suit him today.

* * *

Cat woke slowly, leisurely uncurling her legs and stretching. The sheet twisted around her legs. Opening her eyes, she looked, then blinked, then looked again.

She wasn't in her room. She . . .

Remembrance of the night before swept over her, and she hugged it to her, cherishing it. Cherishing him.

Garrett had been so wonderful. Tender, loving, passionate. She stretched her hands above her head and smiled.

She liked waking up in his bed. His bed.

She snuggled down deeper into the feather mattress, drawing the other pillow to her. She'd come so close to losing him yesterday. She didn't think she could ever go through that again. And it had all been because of her. And her past.

It was a past she wished she could forget. Cat desperately wished she could change it, but she couldn't, no matter how hard she might want to do so. And it wouldn't simply up and go away. She had to face it, and confess it to Garrett.

Would he understand?

He had to.

An hour later, Garrett wished the day had never started. He stood in Ty's office, facing the challenger from yesterday.

Healed sufficiently, the man now waited in a jail cell. His face had matched up to one of the wanted posters in Ty's possession. However, the gunman Hank Lorin wasn't any too happy about his quarters.

"You can bet Lazarus ain't gonna like you keeping me locked up here." Hank slammed his fist against the bars of his cell.

Garrett's head snapped up at the name. Where had he heard that peculiar name before?

Realization hit him. It had been the name of the man who had kicked him after he'd been shot. Garrett had felt the man's hatred reach out to him before he'd blacked out.

"Lazarus will tear this town apart to get back something he wants. You can believe that," the gunman threatened.

"We'll be ready for him," Garrett assured.

He turned away from the boastful prisoner. He'd taken two long strides when Hank started in again.

"Lazarus, he ain't got much use for lawmen, or jails, or that female gunfighter."

Garrett whirled around to face the man. He slowly walked back to the cell. The back of his neck prickled, giving a warning loud and clear.

"What female gunfighter?" he asked, with a distinct feeling he didn't want to hear the answer.

"Why, your lady friend yesterday."

Cat a gunfighter? No, it wasn't possible.

"You're lying," Garrett accused. His gut clenched, tightening into a solid knot.

"I ain't lying. Go ask her yourself."

At Garrett's hesitation, the man added, "You saw the way she drew that pea shooter at me. That ain't the way no lady handles a gun."

A part of him wanted to deny the truth. Another part of him knew it was true.

Something within Garrett crumbled. Trust.

Cat, a gunfighter?

No, the only reason other guns were traveling to Millwood was to challenge and kill him, to make a name for themselves.

Without realizing he did it, he shook his head.

"Still don't believe me?" Hank sneered. "Then you ask her 'bout that Franklin and Edwards range war a couple years back."

Garrett had missed that particular event. He'd been occupied elsewhere. But he'd heard tell of it. And there had been rumors of a female gunfighter in the midst of the range war. Word was she'd single-handedly run off a lynching party that had caught a man working for the warring side.

Garrett's chest felt like someone had headbutted him. Hard. *That female gunfighter had been Cat Parker.*

His Cat.

No, not his anymore. He didn't know the woman. All he

knew was the lies she'd put forth. The lies he'd so willingly believed.

Last night hadn't meant a thing to her except another step in her scheme to disarm him.

Once again she'd played him for the fool. And he'd fallen for it completely.

Damn, he'd fallen for her. So completely and totally that he'd never even suspected her of this type of treachery.

She'd come to town to challenge him. He knew it in his gut.

Fury exploded within him, blowing away all reason. Turning on his heel, he slammed out of the office.

Garrett stormed into his room only to find it empty and the bed he'd shared with Cat made up neatly. Outwardly there was no sign that last night had ever happened. Somehow that fact spurred his anger even more.

He was certain now that she'd seduced him as a ploy to avoid the upcoming confrontation and his demand for answers. Was there no end to her duplicity?

However, he was now aware of her deceptions, fully aware. Oh, he'd find her, and they would settle this once and for all.

If she wanted the gunfight challenge, then so be it.

In two strides he slammed out of his room. He didn't even pause to knock on the door next to his. He tried the knob and found it locked.

Using his shoulder, he rammed the wood. The lock hadn't been devised for strong protection, and it splintered at the impact. The sound of the wood splintering made him feel better.

''Cat?'' he called out, his voice as cold and hard as his heart.

He shoved his way into the room, then stopped dead still. He'd found her all right.

She sat in the enamel tub, up to her creamy shoulders in frothy bubbles. Just looking at her caused a burst of desire, but he squelched it heartlessly.

White hot anger replaced it. The beautiful woman sitting

there calmly bathing was as deceitful as they came. And she'd played him for the fool for the last and final time.

"You lying—" Garrett took a menacing step toward her.

Cat stared up at him, the expression on his face striking straight at her heart. Anger emanated from him in waves that she could almost see. And it was clearly directed right at her.

He knew.

She gasped.

Daring a look up into his eyes, she flinched at the fury and hatred she saw in their depths. Beneath the water, her hands trembled.

Yes, he knew it all.

She was absolutely certain of it.

"Garrett—"

He raised his hand to cut her off. "What, more sweet words for the fool?"

"No. It wasn't—"

"You're right about that. It wasn't anything. Was it?"

The pain she heard beneath the anger in his voice tore at her. She'd done this to him.

"What, Cat? No guns to greet my arrival?"

Her heart sank in near despair. She could tell there was no reasoning with him. He wouldn't be willing to listen to anything she could say.

"You know," she stated the fact in a flat voice.

"Oh, yes. I know *all* about you. And your guns." He glanced about the room, then returned his gaze to her. "Where are they?"

She couldn't lie to him. Something compelled her to tell him. "In the carpetbag."

"Oh, that's rich. So, I even carried them to the hotel for you." He gave a harsh laugh. "Did you intend to remind me of that fact when you challenged me?"

She shook her head mutely. For a minute she couldn't force a single word out.

"I wasn't—"

"Wasn't what, Cat? Wasn't deceiving me? Wasn't going to

challenge me? Wasn't going to kill me?'' He paused. ''Or at least attempt to.''

''I—''

''You can't deny it because it's true. Isn't it?''

Something in his voice begged her to do just that. To deny the charges he'd made. To prove otherwise to him.

Cat swallowed down the instant denial that sprang to her lips. She couldn't lie to him. Not now.

However, he was right. She couldn't deny it. Challenging him had been what she'd planned—at first. But not later.

Cat refused to give up, even in the face of his anger. She had to try to explain. She refused to simply let their love die.

If it wasn't dead already, a little voice of honesty whispered in the back of her mind.

She had to try to make him see. ''No, not after—''

''Like hell,'' he threw her words from before back in her face.

His eyes narrowed, and he stepped forward.

She wished she could be fighting this battle from a stronger point of defense than a tub of water, clothed only in a few foamy bubbles and scent.

''Will you listen to me.'' She slammed her hands down in the water, sending up a spray onto the floor and drawing his gaze to the disappearing line of bubbles.

Garrett cursed himself for the hot rush of desire that coursed through his body. He told himself he felt nothing for her— nothing whatsoever.

''Cat, there's nothing between us. Nothing at all.''

''Dammit, Garrett.'' Without thinking, she stood to her feet in desperation. ''Will you listen—''

''Don't degrade yourself further.'' The harsh coldness of his voice cut straight through her just as he'd intended.

Pain followed on its heels, and she reached out her hand to him.

He stepped away. ''Your attempt at seduction won't work a second time. I'm not interested.''

Turning away from her, he strode out the door. And out of her life.

With short, jerky movements, Cat caught up the towel and wrapped it about herself. She felt chilled clear to her bones. In fact, she doubted if she'd ever feel truly warm again.

Garrett's parting words had cut her to ribbons. She moved as if in a daze, a daze of pain so deep she couldn't face it. She pulled the first thing out of the armoire she touched, not even noticing the color of the gown.

Out of habit she dressed and slipped her feet into shoes. Then she shoved her carpetbag off the chair and sank onto the seat. She didn't know if she had the strength left to remain standing.

Pain so deep it nearly went beyond feeling coursed through her. She felt it seep even into her veins. This time it ran too deep for tears.

Minutes after the door slammed on Garrett's departure, a knock came at the door. Cat sighed. Had he thought of something else to accuse her of now?

Walking across the room, she threw the door open. Sarah stood in the hall. Her usual friendly smile was missing. It should have warned Cat, but her mind was too full of Garrett.

"Oh, Sarah," Cat swallowed, "Ah, this isn't a good time. I . . . I—"

"You lied to me. To Garrett. To the whole town," Sarah crossed her arms and accused. Her eyes glittered in anger.

Oh no, Cat thought, what else could go wrong today? Were the people standing in line to accuse her?

"Sarah, I—"

The other woman held up her hand. "I thought we were friends. Well, I guess I thought wrong."

"No!" Cat cried out in denial.

The woman standing in the hall had been her only friend. Her first true friend she'd ever had.

"Why did you do it?"

Cat winced at the pain in the woman's words.

"I trusted you." Sarah blinked several times as if blinking

away tears. "I got you the job as teacher." She rubbed her hands up and down her arms.

Cat reached out to her, but she stepped away.

"The town has asked me to tell you that your services are no longer needed to fill the teaching position. They figured since I recommended you, I could get rid of you. Leastwise that's what I was told."

Cat's breath caught in her throat with shock. She should have expected this, should have seen it coming, but fool that she was, she hadn't.

Of course a fine town like Millwood wouldn't want someone like her teaching their children. She knew they were right, but it still hurt.

Before she could say anything more, Sarah whirled around and raced down the stairs. Cat heard a door slamming downstairs.

She closed her own door quietly and leaned back against it. She slowly surveyed the room, as if saying goodbye. Then she realized that was what she was doing.

It was the only thing to do. She had to leave Millwood. And Garrett.

She couldn't stand to stay and see the repulsion in his dark eyes every time he looked at her. It was more than she could bear.

"I have to leave," she whispered to the room, as if saying her parting words to the place that had brought her so much joy and so much more pain.

"Please help me." The brief prayer came from her heart.

Swallowing down the lump growing in her throat, she crossed the room and opened her camelback trunk. She turned away and walked to the armoire. She wouldn't be needing the pretty gowns anymore. Her throat tightened. She'd kind of gotten used to wearing them.

Maybe she could make her living as a lady gambler now. It was certain she'd never be able to succeed as a teacher. Her past would always come along behind her and catch up with her. Like it had here.

As she ran her fingers over the ivory silk gown with its rich embroidery, the memories of Garrett nearly swamped her. Being held in his arms for a waltz. The kiss he stole at the dance. Sarah dumping the punch over him.

A smile tugged at her lips, but the sorrow was too strong for it to succeed.

Biting her lip, she turned away from the added pain of the pleasant memories and crossed to the bureau. She pulled open the top drawer, but it stuck almost the instant it began to open. She pushed at it, but it wouldn't budge. It was stuck so nearly closed that she couldn't get a single piece of underwear out of it.

"Shams," she said, using the substitute word out of habit.

She fought with the drawer for another five minutes before it finally gave. When it did, it sent her flying backward.

Cat landed with a *thud* on the floor on her backside.

She pushed herself to her feet and rubbed her derriere. Bending down she scooped up the underthings and dropped them into the bottom of the open trunk.

She turned back to the bureau, but once again, the ivory gown and its host of memories drew her. Instead, she walked back to the armoire. She slowly withdrew the gown from the armoire, then held it close a moment before she shoved the hopeless past aside and turned to walk to the trunk.

The lid of the trunk slammed closed, and she jumped back, clutching the gown to her. A second later, the shelf above the trunk collapsed. It landed atop her trunk, cracking the top.

She shifted the gown under her arm and attempted to lift the board off her trunk. It was too heavy for her to budge.

Cat stared at the shelf a moment in frustration. It didn't look near that heavy. She tried again, putting all her weight behind her effort. It didn't move even an inch. Shams, if she didn't know better, she'd think someone was sitting on top of the board.

Stepping back, she surveyed the situation. Her trunk was ruined, the bureau drawer lay top down on the floor, a scratch ran on the floor beside the bureau drawer.

She was obviously letting her distress affect her and getting careless in her rush. She had to calm herself or she'd never get the job of packing finished.

Cat stepped back, closed her eyes, and took several deep breaths. When she opened her eyes, she renewed her determination. She wanted to be packed and at the train station before Garrett returned to the boardinghouse.

It would be better for them both if she didn't see him again. If the entire town knew the truth about her, they might even extend part of that blame to Garrett. She couldn't risk it. He'd started a new life here.

She owed him a chance at that life. And the only way he could have it would be if she left town on the very next train.

Straightening her back in stiff determination, she crossed to the chair. She picked up her carpetbag, and promptly dropped it on her foot.

"Yeow," she yelped, hopping on one foot.

She rubbed her one hand. It stung. Darn if it hadn't felt as if the bag had been yanked from her grasp. She rubbed her fingers.

Something strange was going on. She knew that for a fact.

She reached for the bag again. The sharp, distinctive crack of gunfire jolted through Cat. She jerked upright, leaving the bag where it lay.

She cried out Garrett's name in horror.

Grabbing up her skirts, she ran for the door. This time, she took the stairs two at a time, not caring how much ankle she showed.

Nothing mattered except reaching Garrett.

Chapter Twenty-Four

Cat gripped her skirt tightly with her hands, yanking it out of her way, and ran straight for the center of town. She had to get to Garrett. She didn't care who saw her unladylike behavior.

It no longer mattered anyway.

Reaching the boardwalk, she skidded to a halt at the sight before her. Garrett stood outside the Long and Short Saloon— safe and sound. She resisted the almost overwhelming impulse to run across the street to him and throw her arms around him.

She saw that there had been trouble, only of the minor kind. In one hand Garrett held a rifle, and with the other he supported a very inebriated Mr. Bates, the piano player.

Cat sighed in relief. Nothing more than a drunk getting a little too rowdy at the saloon. She felt like a fool thinking of the way she'd panicked and run through town. As if Garrett would have welcomed her concern.

Not likely.

Garrett chose that moment to glance in her direction, and their gazes locked. Deliberately he turned his head and led the drunk away.

He had ignored her.

She couldn't believe it. He must truly hate her to snub her that hurtful way in front of the entire town. She could feel the curious stares. It made her decision to leave easier.

She *would* be on the train today.

Head held high in an outward show of pride that she was far from feeling, Cat returned to the boardinghouse. And her packing. She didn't even bother to change into her traveling suit; instead she remained dressed in her lavender silk gown with its fine bustle and double ruffled flounce edging the hem.

She set to packing with renewed determination. Nothing would stop her this time.

It didn't. This time the fallen shelf lifted easily from her trunk. In practically no time, she packed her clothes within and closed the damaged lid as best she could. She'd worry about getting it repaired at the next place she stopped.

She didn't care where that happened to be—so long as it was far away from Millwood, Texas. And Jake Garrett.

It was no trouble hiring someone to take her trunk to the train station. She was certain the good citizens couldn't rid themselves of her fast enough.

Standing on the train platform, she heard the sound of gunfire again. This time, she stayed put. Likely it was more trouble at the saloon. She forced herself to study the horizon for the approach of the train, and shut out everything around her. It was the only way she could bear the pain of leaving.

Garrett kept one hand resting lightly on the butt of his revolver. This time the trouble was real. And deadly. He faced the armed riders. The outlaw gang had caught them unawares.

He spared a quick glance, expecting to see Cat standing on the boardwalk with the other townspeople. But she wasn't there.

Good, it meant he didn't have to worry about her running right into the middle of the volatile situation.

He needed all his concentration to handle the problem, facing him. Even then it might not be enough.

He could feel Ty's tension from where he stood beside him. And he could well understand it.

They were outgunned. Two to eight.

He didn't like the odds. Not one bit.

He could draw and get off a couple of shots before he took a bullet. Maybe Ty could accomplish the same. However, the handful of townspeople on the boardwalks likely wouldn't be so lucky. Any move from him could cost someone else their life.

"We've come for Hank Lorin," a man yelled out from the back of the group.

The man on the lead horse held up his hand, and the speaker fell silent, then said in a low voice, "Sorry, Lazarus."

Garrett stiffened imperceptibly at the name. So this was Lazarus. He took in the man's appearance with a quick, assessing gaze. He recognized that the lead man was trouble from his boots up.

The outlaw leader sat uneasy in the saddle, and his pale blue eyes had a wild look to them. Something about the man bothered Garrett, but he couldn't quite put his finger on it. It continued to nag at him, threatening to distract his attention.

"Hear you got something that belongs to me," the leader finally spoke.

Garrett couldn't stop his own reaction. His head jerked in a giveaway gesture. He knew that voice.

His mind traveled back for a brief moment to when he'd been lying on the ground with a bullet in his back. Even now he could almost feel the sharp jab of pain in his side from the outlaw's boot. The man had taunted him then. Now that same voice came from the pale-eyed man facing him from the back of a horse.

He recognized that same voice from a different time, too. Only the name hadn't been Lazarus. Garrett searched his memory for the answer.

Past and present merged together in his mind for one moment. He stared at the face of the man he'd killed three years ago.

Jesse Stewart. The man who had come back from the dead.

As the sound of the commotion continued from town, Cat pulled her focus away from watching for the train.

Whatever was going on?

She glanced about, and felt rather than saw trouble. It weighed heavy in the air all about her. And it had her sixth sense reacting in spades. Every hair on the back of her neck tingled.

She'd had the feeling enough times in the past to respect it. And to act on it.

This time she walked toward the center of town with calm, deliberately quiet steps. Anyone seeing her stride would recognize it as a gunfighter's. Slow, even paces with a tense alertness to each move.

She reached the street and spotted the group of riders. Easing up to where the small crowd of townspeople stood, she purposefully stayed in the background, using the crowd to conceal her presence.

She stared at the group of men facing Garrett down, and fear stole her breath away. The outlaw gang was armed and looked to her practiced eye as if they meant business.

Easing backward, she remained at the very back of the small crowd. She knew it could endanger Garrett further by distracting him at the wrong time. She could even get him a bullet. She shuddered at the thought.

She recognized two of the riders' horses as the same ones who had attempted to ride into town before. Only this time she counted eight riders.

She swallowed down the rising fear. It seemed to root her to the spot. She forced herself to take a breath and take a tentative step.

Perhaps she could slip away unnoticed and retrieve her own revolvers from the carpetbag.

She'd take it one slow, easy step at a time so as not to draw any attention to herself. Then she would . . .

The leader spoke, his voice clear and cold. She couldn't move a muscle and stared transfixed at the man. It couldn't be.

"Jesse?" she mouthed, but not a sound came from her lips.

Without even realizing it, she shook her head in denial. Then Cat fainted for the first time in her life, crumpling to the ground.

"Well, fast gun, it's time we have ourselves a second try at seeing who's the best," Jesse ordered. "Meet me outside town now. Oh, and bring the female gunfighter with you."

"No." Garrett's denial rang out loud and clear.

The harsh laugh from Jesse chilled him.

"This ain't no choice. You do as I say or we start shooting up your fine town." He gestured with his gun.

"And I'll kill you," Garrett stated matter-of-factly.

"But not before a lot of these fine, upstanding, innocent people die. Is that what you want?" Jesse challenged, leaning forward in the saddle. "I'm already dead, remember? Next time, you should shoot to kill."

He intended to. Garrett clenched his jaw until it hurt.

"I hear you're a man of your word." Jesse gave another harsh laugh. "So, give me your word you'll meet me, and my boys and me will leave peaceful like. And your fine people can go back to their businesses. Alive."

"Garrett—" Ty stepped forward.

"One more word, Sheriff, and I'll drop you where you stand. This here is personal."

"Leave him be." Garrett's voice cut through the air like a whip. "I'll meet you."

He'd do as Jesse wanted. He'd give his word; he just wouldn't include Cat in it.

He faced the realization that he loved her more than life itself. If they wanted him—fine. But he'd die defending her.

Three years before he'd faced a choice. That time he'd chosen his life over Cat's heart.

This time he wouldn't let Cat down.

He chose her. He'd keep her out of this. And alive.

"Alone," Jesse added.

"Alone," Garrett agreed.

"What about Hank?" one of the men asked.

Jesse waved an arm to silence him. "Leave the fool. He got caught, didn't he?"

Then Jesse pulled on the reins, backing his horse up. He turned to Garrett. "Don't forget the female gunfighter."

"I'm not." Garrett wasn't forgetting her for one minute. But he wasn't bringing her either.

"Oh," Jesse added as if it were an afterthought, "one of my boys will stick around here to see that you do keep your word." He gestured to the church.

Garrett risked moving his gaze from the outlaw for an instant. He spotted the reflection of sunlight off a rifle barrel out the second-floor window of the church. He clenched one hand. The outlaw had thought of everything in advance.

"Fast gun," Jesse called out. "You don't know how many others of my men I left hiding away in your town, do you?" he taunted.

Wheeling his horse around, he charged down the street. The riders followed.

"Ty, you take care of the town. I—"

"You can't—" his friend argued.

"I have to. I gave my word." Garrett faced him. "And I won't let him have Cat." He squeezed his eyes shut, then added in a low voice, "I love her."

"I'm coming with you."

"No. You heard what he said. And I spotted a gunman in the church."

"So did I. As soon as I take care of him, I'll be right behind you with a posse."

Garrett knew it was useless to argue. Ty had his mind made up. Now, he only hoped the posse would get there in time to be of help. He had a bad feeling about all this.

Settling his hat firmly, he turned away and headed for where he'd left his horse tied in front of the saloon.

* * *

Angel Tamera plopped both her hands on her hips. Just what did Jake Garrett think he was doing risking his life this way?

She absolutely refused to allow it.

He wasn't going anywhere without her. She would not fail in her assignment to protect Garrett. She charged after him, catching her toe in the hem of her gown. Stumbling, she fell, sprawled on the ground.

Oh, feathers.

She stood up, brushed off her gown, and straightened her halo. She had a job to do.

Closing her eyes, she concentrated as hard as she possibly could. When she opened her eyes, she glanced down, and a wide smile creased her face. She'd done it!

There she stood in the form of a little girl, innocent-looking enough to fool anyone. She couldn't have been more than six.

Closing her hands together to hide her secret, she ran after Garrett, her pigtails flying out behind her.

"Mister?" she called out, her voice small and childlike.

Garrett stopped a moment and turned around.

It was all she needed.

Tamera threw herself at him, catching him about the knees. She hugged him close, whispered a silent prayer, then smiled up at him.

"Be careful," she told him.

She pushed away, sliding the little derringer into his boot with her movement. Spinning away, she ran as fast as her chubby little legs could carry her and dashed around the corner. Then she disappeared.

Garrett stared after the child, touched by her concern. He took a step toward his horse and felt the object in his boot. Waiting until he slipped his foot into the stirrup, he glanced down. A shiny derringer gleamed back up at him.

He stared at it, completely at a loss for words. Then he whispered his own prayer of thanksgiving and swung up into the saddle.

* * *

Jesse was waiting for him a short ride outside of town. Garrett recognized the true cowardice that had been eating away at the man. He could sense the other man's need to kill him in an attempt to rid himself of the self-contempt.

Behind Jesse waited the remainder of his gang. Garrett tensed. He didn't stand a chance, but he'd anticipated the same. It was as good a day as any to die. And he'd do it again to save Cat's life.

He kept his gaze fixed on the challenger, watching Jesse's eyes gleaming with enmity.

"Where is she?" Jesse called out.

"She's coming," Garrett lied to save her. "Let's get on with this." Slowly, he dismounted from his horse.

"Unbuckle your gun belt." Jesse leveled his gun right at Garrett's chest. "And do it real slow. Then let it drop."

He'd expected a double-cross like this. The uncomfortable knot of the derringer in his boot felt better and better. Still, Ty had better arrive with that posse soon or he didn't stand a snowball's chance in a hot oven. A very hot oven. He slowly unbuckled the belt with one hand and dropped it gently to the ground.

"Now step away from it."

Garrett took a measured step away, stalling for all the time he could manage to get.

"I lost three years of my life because of you," Jesse snapped in accusation. "Do you know what it's like watching yourself be buried? Losing everything because of one man? You owe me."

"It was your decision." Garrett shifted his stance, making himself less of a target and keeping his attention on the other man's eyes. They now flickered with a hint of madness.

Jesse grinned and aimed the gun at Garrett's chest. He paused to savor this moment. He took too long.

Garrett heard the pounding of hoofbeats. From the corner of his eye he spotted Cat. He stiffened at the sight.

Stay away, he ordered her silently.

As usual she ignored his wishes.

Cat reined in her mount and slid down from the saddle.

"Stay back, Cat," Garrett ordered her, not letting his attention waver from the gun facing him. "You belong in town."

"Sarah said the same thing. I grabbed the closest horse and rode out."

"Cat—"

"It's too late to argue with me now. I'm here."

"Ah, my unfaithful fiancée at last arrives," Jesse cut in, his voice unsteady. "I owe you, too."

Cat watched as he began to tighten his finger on the trigger. She did the only thing she could. She grabbed her skirts, pulling them up out of her way, and ran straight between the two men.

She skidded to a halt directly between Garrett and Jesse, with her back to Garrett.

"Caitlan," Jesse said with a touch of disdain. "Get out of my way."

She could feel the hatred coming off him in waves. She couldn't be certain if it was directed at Garrett or herself. It didn't matter. She intended to stop him. No matter what.

"Jesse, you'll have to kill me first before you get to him."

"How touching," he sneered.

"I mean it."

"Get out of the way," he ordered.

"No." She stood steadfast.

"Cat."

She nearly turned at the sound of Garrett's deep voice, but she stopped herself just in time.

"Cat, get out of here," Garrett demanded.

His fingers brushed her arm, missing her, and she stepped forward out of his reach, still remaining between him and the gun.

"I'm not moving, Jesse."

If she could delay them long enough for the sheriff to get here, they had a chance of surviving. Either way, she wouldn't let anything happen to Garrett.

He wouldn't die for her. Not if she could help it.

When she'd come to with the aid of Sarah's distasteful smelling salts, she'd nearly fainted again when she learned Garrett had ridden out to meet Jesse alone. Did he have a death wish?

She'd grabbed a horse and raced off after them. There was absolutely no way she was going to allow Garrett, the man she loved, to fight her battle for her.

Now she only hoped Ty and the posse were close behind.

"Don't fight about it." Jesse laughed, but it was a harsh, grating sound. "You'll get to die together. But he goes first."

"No!" Cat screamed.

"You both cost me too much to live. Now move, Caitlan."

Cat suddenly recalled the package he'd left in her care and took a chance on its importance. At least she hoped she was right.

"You shoot him and you'll never learn where your package is."

Jesse jerked his head to glare at her with unsuppressed greed.

"That's what you were hoping to find when you had my room ransacked, isn't it?" she dared to taunt. "But you didn't find it."

It worked. Jesse turned his full wrath and the aim of his gun on her.

"Where is it?"

Cat gave him a slow smile, stalling for time.

"How much of it have you already spent?" he demanded, giving a scathing glance to her fancy dress.

Cat's smile wavered. So, all those years ago, he'd given her money to hold.

She realized that the man she'd thought she loved three years ago had merely been using her to hold the proceeds from a robbery for him. He hadn't loved her any more than she'd truly loved him. She now knew what true love was, thanks to Garrett.

"You used me, didn't you?" She raised her chin and faced Jesse.

"You had your uses," he sneered at her.

She had to resist the urge to reach out and slap that sneer

from his face. He'd faked his death, caused her guilt and pain, and for what? For money. Her vendetta, her vow, and three years of her life—for nothing. For this, she'd lost her chance at happiness with Garrett, the man she loved. But Jesse wouldn't win this time.

Too late she felt Garrett's hand brush her elbow and latch on to her. He pulled her to the side out of Jesse's line of fire.

"You were the one who robbed that bank in Springfield, weren't you?" Garrett spoke up, drawing his attention away from Cat.

"Don't act like you didn't already know that," Jesse shouted. "That's why you suddenly got so friendly with her. To get my money."

Garrett knew his mouth dropped from shock. "You couldn't be more wrong."

"So, you thought the two of you would run off with *my* money. Well, I put a stop to it."

Garrett stared at the other man, waiting for the slightest sign of an opening.

Jesse glared back at him, hatred in his very stance. "You knew it was me. You and those men were gonna have me jailed. You were talking about me when I shut you up—"

"Damn," Garrett swore.

All that had happened three years ago had been a misunderstanding. The paranoid young fool had assumed the men's talk of the robbery concerned him, and he'd challenged Garrett to keep his wrongdoing secret.

"Wrong, Jesse. I didn't know who robbed that bank. We were merely talking when you plowed into me."

"No."

Garrett gave a wry smile that didn't reach his eyes. "See, it was all for nothing. You were wrong."

He hoped to anger him, maybe goad the other man into acting rashly. It was the only chance he had of saving Cat's life.

Cat stood still, letting the men talk. She could feel the time left to them slipping away. But every minute longer they took was one minute closer to the posse. Where was the posse?

Jesse once again aimed the gun at Garrett. "Tell me what you did with the money or I pull the trigger."

"I buried it next to your pine box. In your grave," Cat blurted out, taking a step toward Jesse.

Garrett saw his chance. Shoving Cat aside, he pulled the derringer from his boot. He fired as he knocked her to the ground. She hit the dirt with a thud and a yelp.

"Roll, Cat. Roll!" Garrett commanded.

She obeyed instinctively, and Jesse's bullet thudded into her bustle. The force of the impact and the shock left her breathless. She lay unmoving for a moment, the wind knocked out of her.

"Cat!"

She heard Garrett yell for her.

The sharp crack of a gun firing again brought terror to her heart.

Chapter Twenty-Five

Cat raised her head up in time to see Garrett and Ty both fire simultaneously.

Jesse jerked backward, then crumpled to the ground. Most certainly dead this time.

She lowered her cheek back to the ground and sucked a breath into her air-starved lungs.

It was finally over.

"Cat?" Garrett cried out her name in agony.

He was at her side in three long strides. Reaching out, he gently rolled her over, afraid of what he'd find.

Cat raised up and threw her arms around him, holding on so tight he could barely breathe.

"Where did you get hit? How bad is it?" he asked her.

She drew back, and when her eyes met his, he noticed a tinge of embarrassment in her emerald depths, but no sign of pain. "What is it?" he asked.

"He shot my bustle," she whispered.

Garrett leaned back and stared at her. "Your what?"

"My bustle," Cat said louder and pointed at her backside.

In amazement, Garrett stared at the singed cloth now resting at a crooked angle above her derriere. "Well, I'll be damned."

He heard Ty's choked cough from behind them.

"Is Jesse . . ."

"Yes," Garrett answered her softly.

"I'm glad. It's probably wrong to feel that way, but he would have killed you." She couldn't hold back the shudder that shook her shoulders.

"It's all right," he assured her.

"I have to tell you. He lied, I'm not his fiancée. I broke the engagement with him after I met you. But he wouldn't listen. He—"

"It doesn't matter anymore."

"It does to me," she whispered, searching his face for any sign that there was a shred of love left remaining for her.

What she saw in his eyes gave her hope. She raised a hand and tentatively laid it against his cheek.

"Do you hate me?" Her question came out on a soft breath tinged with hope and yet heavy with despair.

"I could never hate the woman I love enough to die for." His voice was low with feeling too deep for mere words.

With a gunfighter's speed, Garrett pulled Cat to her feet and into his embrace. Lowering his head, his lips took hers in a kiss to heal all hurts.

Cat wrapped her arms around his neck and clung to him. She never wanted to let him go. "Never," she whispered.

Garrett pulled back and gazed down into her face. Pain etched his dear features. "Never?" he asked. "Won't you even give me another chance?"

Speechless, Cat stared up at him. Another chance?

She shook her head, and placed her fingertips over his dear lips. They were warm beneath her touch.

"I meant I never want to let you go," she explained.

Garrett blinked, taken aback.

"Jake Garrett, I love you terribly, and if you ever propose again, I'll—"

"Cat." He kissed her fingertips. "If you'll be still long enough, that's what I plan to do."

She gasped, then promptly shut her mouth.

Garrett smiled, and then in that low, seductive drawl she loved, he asked, "Cat Parker, love of my life, will you marry me?"

In answer, she raised up on tiptoe and kissed him with everything she had in her.

Around them the townspeople broke into applause.

Cat drew back, and Garrett looked up to see almost every member of the town in a half circle around him and Cat. He couldn't believe it. The entire town had followed him to back him.

Most sported a weapon of some kind. The remaining outlaws had dismounted and surrendered. Millwood's jail would be full today.

"To the deputy and our new schoolteacher," someone shouted out. Another round of applause followed.

Angel Tamera stood beside Garrett, adjusted her halo, and smiled. This time she didn't even flinch when she heard St. Peter call her. She stayed long enough to blow a goodbye kiss to Cat and Garrett. This time, quite pleased with her actions, she didn't lose a single feather.

As Garrett drew Cat back into his arms, the applause increased.

"Shall we go home and celebrate in private?" he whispered against her ear.

"I thought you'd never ask," she whispered back. "Love me, Garrett?"

"Forever and ever, my darling Cat."

"Yes." She could spend an eternity looking into his love-filled eyes.

Garrett lowered his head and met her lips with a kiss that promised an eternity of love.

Epilogue

Millwood, Texas, 1881

The church organ wheezed out the notes of "Here Comes the Bride" through the small church. Cat winced at the sour note. Miss Ellen, her teaching replacement, still hadn't mastered the persnickety organ.

Cat turned in her seat in the front pew and craned her neck to get her first glimpse of the bride. It seemed the entire town had turned out for the wedding and to christen the new church and school, both built with the reward from the return of the buried robbery proceeds.

Little Amanda led the way down the aisle, grinning from ear to ear. She held a small basket of flower petals close to her chest.

Sarah had finally agreed to Ty's persistent proposals of marriage. Cat smiled to herself and rested one hand on her protruding stomach. It had only taken once for her to accept Garrett's proposal.

Their baby kicked as if in protest. A wide grin replaced her smile. Make that two times, she amended, recalling his first poorly managed attempt. However, when he'd asked her out of love, she hadn't hesitated.

A hush fell over the congregation as Sarah stepped into sight, looking beautiful and nervous. However, it was the man escorting her down the aisle who took Cat's breath away.

Garrett. Her husband.

She rubbed her hand across her stomach, thinking of their baby waiting impatiently to be born. Just then, the baby kicked again, this time much harder.

"Just a little longer, darling," she whispered, rubbing the low pain in her back.

She wasn't letting anything stop this wedding.

Nearly holding her breath against the oncoming pains, she watched Sarah walk to the front of the church where Ty stood waiting.

Garrett placed Sarah's hand in Ty's, gave his friend a wink, and made his way to Cat's side. Sliding into the pew with her, he clasped her hand in his and kissed her palm.

A flare of heat rushed up her arm, and she gasped. He could still heat her with just a touch or a look. She curled her fingers around his hand. And held on.

"Remember?" Garrett leaned over and whispered in her ear.

His breath stirred the hair at her temple, and she closed her eyes with a sigh. "Umm." She snuggled closer against him, biting her lower lip as another labor pain came.

Garrett brushed a soft kiss against her temple and nuzzled her cheek. Cat thought she heard someone clear their throat from somewhere above her, but that was impossible. Wasn't it?

As the ceremony proceeded, Cat prayed she could hold out. A sharp pain caught her unawares, and she gasped.

"Are you all right?" Garrett asked.

Before she could answer, another pain hit her.

"You may kiss the bride," the preacher announced.

Cat let out a loud sigh of relief.

Garrett tightened his hold on her hand. "Cat? Is everything all right?"

"Yes," she gasped, clutching his hand. "I'm just having our baby."

"The baby?" Garrett's shout disrupted the entire congregation.

"Shh," Cat said in a low voice. "It will take a little longer."

Sarah rushed to her side. "How long have you been in labor?"

Cat gave her friend a wan smile. "About half an hour. Or so."

Garrett jumped to his feet. "Why didn't you say so sooner?"

"Nothing was making me miss this wedding," Cat declared.

Garrett scooped her up into his arms. "Well, they're married now. I'm taking you home."

"But—"

"Ty," Garrett called out, "bring the doc. And Sarah, too."

Turning on his heel, he carried Cat down the aisle and out of the church. The congregation's applause followed them.

At the sound of a scream from Cat, both men headed for the decanter of whiskey on the sideboard.

"I don't know how much more of this pain I can take," Garrett set the glass of bourbon down untouched and headed for the stairs.

"You're not going up there, are you?" Near horror tinged Ty's voice.

"Yup. Come with me."

His friend's face paled. "I'm not going up there. Not even when it's Sarah's time."

Garrett left him standing alone in his rush to reach Cat. As his boot heel hit the top step, he heard the cry of a baby.

"It's here. Ty, it's here."

"What is it?"

"A baby."

Garrett turned and barged his way into the room and rushed to Cat's side. She smiled at him, and he kissed her lips tenderly.

When he drew back, she caught his hand. "Look, your son." She held the baby in one arm, her world complete.

"A son," he whispered, reaching out with a finger and touching the baby's cheek.

He turned to Cat. "Thank you."

She gave him a wicked wink. "The pleasure was all mine."

"Not entirely." He winked back at her, causing her to blush.

Unexpectedly their son cooed and waved a tiny fist. Cat lovingly touched his small hand.

Angel Tamera leaned back from kissing the baby and smiled serenely. Her fondest wish had been granted. She was to be their son's guardian angel. She tilted her head. She could've sworn she heard someone say, "Heaven help us."

"I've heard that's a sign they've been kissed by an angel," Cat whispered in awe at her son.

"And his mother?" Garrett asked in that drawl she so loved to hear.

She grinned. "I've been kissed by the best in all Texas."

Garrett leaned closer and took Cat's lips in a kiss of his own, a promise of love for eternity.

BOOK YOUR PLACE ON OUR WEBSITE AND MAKE THE READING CONNECTION!

We've created a customized website just for our very special readers, where you can get the inside scoop on everything that's going on with Zebra, Pinnacle and Kensington books.

When you come online, you'll have the exciting opportunity to:

- View covers of upcoming books
- Read sample chapters
- Learn about our future publishing schedule (listed by publication month *and author*)
- Find out when your favorite authors will be visiting a city near you
- Search for and order backlist books from our online catalog
- Check out author bios and background information
- Send e-mail to your favorite authors
- Meet the Kensington staff online
- Join us in weekly chats with authors, readers and other guests
- Get writing guidelines
- AND MUCH MORE!

**Visit our website at
http://www.zebrabooks.com**

ROMANCE FROM JO BEVERLY

DANGEROUS JOY   (0-8217-5129-8, $5.99)

FORBIDDEN   (0-8217-4488-7, $4.99)

THE SHATTERED ROSE   (0-8217-5310-X, $5.99)

TEMPTING FORTUNE   (0-8217-4858-0, $4.99)